Yanked out of he

Grace glanced up at Neil and followed his gaze to a man who stood about six feet tall with wavy light brown hair. She blinked, realizing the flyer did not do him justice.

In person, he was dressed in a pair of Timberland boots, Levi's jeans, and a blue and white flannel shirt under a rugged Sandstone jacket. His shoulders were broad and masculine, as if they could withstand a hefty stack of 2x4s with little effort.

He stepped forward, pausing only to rip the flyer off the post on his way by. She pressed her back against the leather cushion, finding his expression unreadable, his gait purposeful.

He stopped a few inches from where she sat. "I'm afraid you're wasting your time, Miss…"

"Evans. Grace," she said, surprised by his slight Irish accent and unfriendly tone. She wondered what Neil had said to him to cause such a reaction. Then again, maybe the flyer had something to do with his curt introduction.

Well, she didn't care. Too much depended on her staying in Mistletoe, with or without Ayden McCabe rendering a smile or a pleasant hello. Too late for polite conversation, she stood. "You could at least hear me out," she said, straightening to appear taller, although she barely cleared the bottom of his chin.

His face softened, but not enough for her to relax. Then the corners of his mouth lifted, and her pulse sputtered. "Look, I'm flattered, but I'm not interested."

In Mistletoe

by

Tammy L. Bailey

In Mistletoe

Cover Art by *Diana Carlile*

The Wild Rose Press, Inc.
PO Box 708
Adams Basin, NY 14410-0708
Visit us at www.thewildrosepress.com

Publishing History
First Champagne Rose Edition, 2016
Print ISBN 978-1-5092-1110-4
Digital ISBN 978-1-5092-1111-1

Published in the United States of America

Dedication

To Zak and Ben.
You are my sunshine.

Chapter One

"I'm never about meddling into anyone's business, mind you," Jolene Watson, the small town's train attendant said, "but what brings you to Mistletoe?"

Grace Evans leaned in closer to the rumbling heater of the older woman's vintage Jeep Wagoneer, still trying to get warm and sort out the last twelve hours. "I'm…I'm looking for someone." Grace turned to glance out the passenger side window. It had begun to snow since they left the train station, the hurtling flakes a contrast to the darkening sky and mountainous backdrop. She felt thousands of miles away from San Francisco instead of just eight hundred.

"Well, if you're looking for a man, I might have to warn you, there aren't many here." Jolene paused to give Grace a gentle jab with her bony elbow. "Of course, as pretty as you are, I wouldn't be surprised to see you caught under a mistletoe or two before you leave."

Grace sent the woman a nervous smile, having enough man problems with her current boomerang ex-boyfriend to avoid standing under the poisonous plant for the rest of her life. For now, Grace needed to undo the emotional cataclysm caused by her younger sister's selfish need to find herself. *Who decides to disappear four weeks before their wedding?*

"I do appreciate you driving me to O'Shannon's,"

Grace said, changing the subject. "When I looked for hotels in the area, it was the only place I could find." There was one more on the outskirts of town, but it was booked for another week and way out of her price range. The woman nodded, leaving Grace to wish she had planned this trip a little better. For one, she should have paid the money for an airline ticket instead of trusting her car to make the trip. Sometimes being frugal did not pay off at all. Now, she believed her carelessness had cost the down payment on the shop she was hoping to purchase.

"Of course, there's always Hearth's Gate Bed and Breakfast."

Pulled out of her depressing thoughts, Grace repeated the name aloud. "Hearth's Gate?"

Jolene's heavy silver bracelets clanked as she rotated the steering wheel. "Yes, although, it hasn't been open since Ida and Connor McCabe passed away. Their son lives at Hearth's Gate now. You'll like Ayden. He's very handsome and such a gentleman."

Grace opened her mouth and then smashed it shut, believing she'd zoned out too long to ask any questions at this point.

"He was in the military, you know, but he doesn't talk much about it. He built me a deck before winter set in, no charge, and always makes the most delicious breads for the charity auction. Oh, he's such a fine young man, and handsome, too," Jolene repeated.

Grace stifled a nervous giggle, wondering if this Ayden guy also leaped tall buildings in a single bound. "He sounds…perfect."

"Perfect and single," said the gray-haired woman. "At thirty, he just hasn't met the right woman. He likes them tall, blonde, beautiful, and empty. Now, how are you going to settle down with someone like that?"

Grace shook her head and sighed. The last thing she needed in her life was drama, especially someone else's. Of course, she did sometimes dream of some billionaire stealing her away or having a gorgeous man kiss her in an elevator.

"See, he needs to meet someone like you. You're grounded, and you can't be more than twenty-three, right?"

Despite the bizarre exchange so far, Grace almost choked on the woman's latest admonishment. "Twenty-five, but I don't—"

"You're not really his type, mind you."

Grace didn't know if she was being insulted or complimented. When she thought Jolene wasn't looking, she glanced down at her petite form and smoothed her straight mocha-colored hair. She'd planned on getting some highlights, until her best friend Betsy talked her out of the appointment. *"Are you crazy? Your dark hair brings out the green in your eyes."*

"And that is the place where we hold the annual Mistletoe Christmas Eve *Eve* Dance."

Grace blinked into the thickening snow toward the brick building decorated in red and white holiday lights.

Beyond lay a snow-capped village with sharp slanted roofs and cross-timbered buildings. On salted sidewalks, groups of people gathered, the cold not stopping their merry conversations or shopping excursions. As Jolene drove by at a snail's pace, a few of them waved, the woman quick to offer a cheerful exchange.

"Here we are." Jolene put the old wagon in Park before the carryout sign.

Grace ignored the unexpected butterflies and clutched the door handle as the car jolted underneath them. Gripping her light jacket, she braced against the blustery wind and met Jolene in the rear of the vehicle.

"You're not much of a planner, are you?" Jolene glanced over Grace's San Francisco attire.

Grace blew out a wintry breath and reached for her suitcase, believing she should have done a better job of researching Mistletoe, Washington, before throwing a few clothes together, jumping in her car, and racing up here without a plan in place. "I have my moments," she commented and smiled, prompting Jolene to send her an animated wink.

With her luggage in tow, Grace followed the woman under a green and brown sign into O'Shannon's.

Dark cherry wood, along with the heat from a hulky gray stone fireplace, pulled Grace further inside. Around her, the polite and gregarious crowd lowered their conversations to a hum.

"I'll go ask Ewan if he has any rooms available," Jolene said, leaving Grace by herself.

To avoid the curious faces, Grace twisted to a wall that held pictures of the local sports teams and a few famous visitors. After a few moments in the lulling time, a colorful flyer stapled to one of the rounded wooden posts near the bar caught her attention. She stepped closer, intrigued by the sexy man on the front. He wore a skin-tight black T-shirt that hugged his muscular torso. His short brown hair lay damp against his smooth forehead. As her midsection gave an unexpected flip, her gaze slid to the caption below his tapered waist. *Date needed for Mistletoe's Christmas Eve Eve dance. Call Ayden McCabe at 555-1212 if interested.*

"He has nothing to offer you," Jolene said, rattling Grace from her mesmerized stupor.

"What?"

"O'Shannon's. Ewan said he's all booked up."

Grace's shoulders dropped, and she fell against the wood post, defeated. What was she supposed to do now? She couldn't afford a bed and breakfast, and since she'd left her car in Vancouver, Washington, she didn't even have one to sleep in at the moment.

"Let's go see if Ayden has room for you at Hearth's Gate."

Grace opened her mouth to protest, but Jolene was already heading toward a lanky man in a gray Stetson. Relenting, for the moment, Grace followed, watching the woman draw up behind a skinny cowboy and tap him on his bony back. *This is Ayden McCabe?* Grace glanced back at the flyer, believing both Jolene and the advertisement had grossly exaggerated the man's attributes.

"Neil O'Shannon, meet Grace Evans. She's come all the way from San Francisco, and she's looking for Ayden."

Grace stifled an embarrassing wince as the cowboy turned and lifted the bill of his hat with the end of his freckled index finger. "Well, who ain't?" He tipped his head back further, revealing a set of ruby red eyebrows. "You're pretty."

"See. I told you," Jolene said with a wink, a good luck, and a then a loud goodbye.

Left dizzy from the last few moments, Grace sliced her gaze back to Neil to find him leaned against the glossy bar, his elbows propped up, his hands interlaced across his narrow belly. "But you're not really his type."

Tired and frustrated, she forced a cordial smile, not caring about Mr. Adyen McCabe's damn type. She just needed a place to stay for a few nights that didn't cost the rest of her life's savings. To be honest, she had no idea what B&Bs cost these days.

"Look, Neil, I'm a little desperate at the moment, so if you could tell Mr. McCabe that I'd be willing to offer one hundred dollars a night, he might be willing to—"

The cowboy's lips curled into a humor-filled smirk. "In that case, I'll give him a call."

To Grace's complete mortification, the man did, his conversation bouncing off the high beamed timbers and wooden column posts. She didn't think it would ever end until Neil pulled the phone from his ear and grinned. "He'll be here in five."

Her stomach somersaulted at the announcement, her feet shuffling behind Neil's moseying gait until a bombshell of a waitress with flashy red nails tried to stop him.

"Have you talked to Ayden?"

"Yep," the cowboy replied and continued walking.

Grace trailed behind Neil wondering if her sister had been so afraid to face her fears that she'd taken out a map and thrown a dart toward the north, the point stabbing this remote Christmas town in the middle of nowhere.

"He's here."

Yanked out of her reflection, Grace glanced up at Neil and followed his gaze to a man who stood about six feet tall with wavy light brown hair. She blinked, realizing the flyer did not do him justice.

In person, he was dressed in a pair of Timberland boots, Levi's jeans, and a blue and white flannel shirt under a rugged Sandstone jacket. His shoulders were broad and masculine, as if they could withstand a hefty stack of 2x4s with little effort.

He stepped forward, pausing only to rip the flyer off the post on his way by. She pressed her back against the leather cushion, finding his expression unreadable, his gait purposeful.

He stopped a few inches from where she sat. "I'm afraid you're wasting your time, Miss…"

"Evans. Grace," she said, surprised by his slight Irish accent and unfriendly tone. She wondered what Neil had said to him to cause such a reaction. Then again, maybe the flyer had something to do with his curt introduction.

Well, she didn't care. Too much depended on her staying in Mistletoe, with or without Ayden McCabe rendering a smile or a pleasant hello. Too late for polite conversation, she stood. "You could at least hear me out," she said, straightening to appear taller, although she barely cleared the bottom of his chin.

His face softened, but not enough for her to relax. Then the corners of his mouth lifted, and her pulse sputtered. "Look, I'm flattered, but I'm not interested."

She opened and closed her mouth but was unable to say a coherent word through an entire verse of "Jingle Bell Rock." When he began to saunter away, she panicked. "Okay, I can pay you three hundred dollars for three nights." She really couldn't, but she had nowhere else to go.

He swayed back toward her, his dark brown eyebrows raised, one higher than the other. "Three nights?" he repeated, his gaze sweeping over her like a sweltering Mediterranean wind. He grinned, a curious and secretive expression that sent a hot tendril down her spine. Although they had barely enough daylight between them, he managed a step closer.

"Don't you think you're being just a little pretentious…Miss Evans?" He lifted his hand, his thumb and index finger pressed close together for visual effect.

Pretentious? Grace hoped beyond all reasonable expectations, she didn't need more than four days to run into Danielle or find someone who knew of her whereabouts. Their mother's frail sanity depended on Grace bringing Danielle home. First, though, Grace needed a place to stay that didn't require taking out a small bank loan to get her home.

"All right, two nights, but for that price, I do expect breakfast," Grace said, hands on her hips and believing if she needed more time to find her sister and drag her back to San Francisco, she'd figure out a way to convince him then. "A full-sized bed is fine, and I can be very quiet. You won't even know I'm there."

He canted his head, amusement dancing in his arresting blue eyes. After a moment of disconcerting silence, he finally whispered in her direction, "If I'm making you breakfast afterward, I better damn well know you're there."

"Hi, Ayden."

Grace jerked her head in the direction of the

waitress Neil spoke to earlier. Like the last time, the woman noticed no one except the person with whom she spoke.

"I'm really surprised you made that flyer," she said, her lips protruding in an exaggerated pout. "Why didn't you just ask me?"

As if invisible, Grace stood trying to lower her gaze but finding herself drawn to Ayden who stood so close she thought if he turned his head and she moved hers a sliver, her lips might brush his neck.

"My damn sister made that flyer, Rachel, and the last time we spoke, you were—oh, let me see if I can remember it correctly—moving on."

She puffed up, her bountiful breasts lifting to graze against his shoulder. "I said that because I wanted you to beg me to stay."

"Hmm," he commented with a shrug, causing the woman to draw back and slap him across his beautiful face. The cracking sound caused more than a few heads to twist in their direction. As Rachel stomped off, Ayden massaged the red handprint on his cheek.

"You're very popular, aren't you?" Grace said, unable to stop the words from tumbling from her lips.

He worked his jaw and sent her a sideways grin. "I can be."

Affected by his easy flirting, Grace slid back into the booth, her thoughts swinging to the last time she'd spoken to her ex, Rick. She wondered what he might have done if *she'd* had the nerve to slap him with such frustration? It seemed every time they broke up, the very next day, he was dating someone, always with a three-syllable name. Monica. Sabrina. Tiffany. Then, like every other time, he'd call and want to get together…to talk.

"Why?"

Grace had somehow forgotten she wasn't alone and raised her head up to find Ayden seated across from her, no worse for wear over his and Rachel's heated confrontation.

"Why what?"

He inhaled, his eyes narrowing over his Romanesque nose. "You're a pretty girl, Grace—"

"I swear, if I hear one more person tell me that again today—" She stopped short of a threat, finding Ayden's fully curved lips lifted in a lopsided smirk and his eyebrows arched in avid curiosity.

"You don't think you're pretty?"

Grace shook her head. "It's…not that. I'm just not used to being told a lot, that's all."

He didn't say anything, his penetrating gaze causing a ripple of unexpected excitement and a wave of nerve-tingling caution.

"You know," he finally said, "for the life of me, I don't get why you think you need to *pay* me to have sex with you."

Chapter Two

"What!" Grace leaped from her seat, Ayden following, his features contorted in a harrowing pose. He reached out, and she yanked away, humiliated and embarrassed he'd thought such a thing.

She wanted to yell at him, set the moment straight, but she couldn't catch her breath.

"It appears, I might have jumped to the wrong conclusion—"

"M-might have? Don't you think you're being just a little...pretentious?" she said, still annoyed that he'd thought her so desperate for a man she had to pay a guy to sleep with her.

"Perhaps you should sit down and explain exactly why you're here and why you want to pay for a room at Hearth's Gate." He pointed back toward the booth.

Warning bells told her to run...very fast, away from Ayden McCabe. "I think I'd rather see if there isn't another place around here for me to stay." She sent him a tired headshake and reached for her suitcase when his large hands wrapped firm around her small wrist. Wondrous, exciting heat pulsed against her skin.

"I'm sure I wounded a little bit of your pride, Miss Evans, but trust me when I say you're not going to find another place for miles."

With two dozen people watching them, she relented on a long exhale and slipped back behind the table, much of the bar beginning to pay more attention to them than to the multiple screens above their heads.

When she didn't start the conversation, he did. "My name is Ayden McCabe. I own a construction company, and I've lived in Mistletoe…most of my life," he said, stretching his hand toward her. She hesitated long enough to prompt a humor-filled laugh, deep and jaunty. "I don't bite." He kept his arm locked before her.

It wasn't his *bite* she was worried about. Despite the internal warning, she lifted her hand and slipped it into his, the warmth of his palm caressing, the strength of his grip enthralling. He smelled nice, too. Not like department store cologne. It was more like warmth, nature, and sensuality rolled into one.

"Grace Evans. I…uh, don't own anything, although I'd like to one day. I work in a bakery, and I've lived in San Francisco *all* my life."

He nodded. "All right, now tell me why you're here."

She grabbed for her purse, rummaging through the cluttered compartments to pull out the item that had started this entire misadventure. She hesitated before handing him the holiday postcard, front side up.

"About twenty-four hours ago, my mom found this slipped inside the mailbox. It's from my sister Danielle who's supposed to get married on Christmas Eve *Eve*."

Ayden glanced over the mailer depicting the picturesque Christmas town of Mistletoe, Washington. He flipped the card over and read her sister's neat handwriting. Since Grace had recited the words over a hundred times on the train, she knew what it said by heart: *I needed some time to think. Don't tell Trevor. I don't want to hurt him. Love you, Danielle.*

When Ayden finished skimming the back a few times, he lifted his gaze to Grace and rested his elbow on the long table. She tried not to stare as he raked his thumb over the sensual curve of his mouth, his strokes hypnotic and causing a slow heat to spread through every cell in her body.

"So, are you here to steal her away?"

Grace deliberated on her answer, unsure if he was being serious or sarcastic. "She's supposed to get married. I've been sent to keep her from making the biggest mistake of her life."

Ayden glanced around before his gazed sliced back to her. "Sent by whom?"

She stared at him until her fidgety movements lifted the corners of his sensual mouth.

"Look, I don't need to explain everything to you. So, if you don't have room for me, I'd appreciate it if you'd not waste any more of my time." She was tired and angry that this trip to make things right, to fix things in her small, broken family again, had set her back so far with Rick and opening her own place. Once, just once, she wished she knew how to speak up for herself and say the word no.

While she waited for Ayden to answer, she blew out a shaky breath and squeezed her eyes closed until his masculine voice breached her consciousness.

"What are you thinking?

She only needed a second to reflect on his question. "That I'm going to wake up soon and realize you, this moment, and this place are just a grand figment of my imagination."

Despite the busy jukebox and the humming of the

bar crowd, Grace heard nothing, not even a slight stirring coming from his side of the booth. Forced to flip her eyelids open, she found him still there, anything but a creation of her tired mind.

Above, a tear-shaped lamp illuminated his attractive mouth, incisive eyes, and clean-cut jaw. When she tried to make her mind think about Rick, she couldn't even remember the shape of his face.

"Excuse me." Grace popped up, believing if she spent one more second sitting across from Ayden McCabe, she'd risk the chance of falling face-first into a romantic crush doomed for a heartbreaking end.

She stepped at a rapid pace across the planked floor, aware of every prying eye on her. Inside the lady's room, she plopped her purse onto the marble sink before lifting her face toward the mirror. How anyone thought her pretty, she didn't know. Her disheveled hair surrounded a face so pale it almost appeared to glisten.

Damn near exhausted, she bent over to splash a handful of cold water onto her pallid features. If she decided to take the rest of her money and go back to California, what was the worst that could happen? *Did insane asylums even exist in California any more?*

"So, are you Ayden's choice?"

Through moistened bangs, Grace peered into the wall-length mirror to find the woman who'd slapped him; her tall form leaned against one of the bathroom stalls. Her stance defiant, her expression unsmiling, the woman tapped her long fingertips against crisscrossed arms.

Grace inhaled, the warm scent of cinnamon and potpourri filling her nostrils and burning her throat. She turned and braced herself before the perfectly featured woman. She had not one corn-silken hair out of place and her eyes were as large and brilliant as two fluorescent moons.

"I've known Ayden all my life," the woman said. "I've been in love with him since grade school, along with a lot of the women in Mistletoe."

Grace intended to reassure Rachel of her unromantic intentions toward the town's hero. All Grace wanted was to find Danielle, return home, and figure out what to do next with Rick and the rest of her life. She understood she might have to start planning things and sticking to them, instead of always flying by the seat of her pants.

Yes, things had to change, not only with her life, but with Rick. She just didn't know if she had enough nerve to make it happen. One phone call was all it took, but Rick refused to answer his phone. Worse, she refused to leave the message.

"You probably don't want any of my advice, but I'm going to give it to you anyway," the woman said in a cool and sultry voice. "Ayden is an old spirit, born with more pride and chivalry than three of Jane Austen's characters put together. Once you lose him, he's lost forever."

With those incisive and literary words, the woman slinked out the door, leaving Grace to decide if she needed to reread *Emma, Persuasion,* or *Pride and Prejudice* all over again.

****

Ayden downed the rest of his beer, unsure whether what he was about to do was a brilliant idea or one drastic and tragic mistake. He knew nothing about Grace Evans except that she was uncommonly pretty with perhaps more freckles on her small nose than most women he knew. She also appeared a bit unorganized and seemed to carry the weight of the world on her small shoulders. He had no doubt most of that world didn't even belong to her.

However, she was nice and didn't seem to want anything from him except a room. As he planned his next move, she exited the bathroom behind Rachel, her fine features perplexed and pinched into careful deliberation. At least she didn't head straight for the exit; she ambled toward their booth.

When she sat down, she tucked a wisp of dark shoulder-length hair behind an ear, a nervous habit he found innocent and sensual at the same time. Not that he liked to memorize a woman's attributes; he did find her deep hazel eyes intriguing, especially when she narrowed them in serious thought.

"I guess I was wrong about you. You *are* very popular around here," she said, peeking up from her timidity.

He chuckled and sank against the cushioned seat, believing Grace Evans presented him with more problems than he was ready to handle. Yet, he knew she awarded him a solution to at least one of them.

On a gamble, he shifted forward and drew out the flyer he'd ripped off the wooden post a few feet from them. On the table before her, he flattened out the edge and tapped the center where his face lay wrinkled and distorted.

"Not that I agree one should try and find someone who has voluntarily disappeared, but I want to propose a scheme of sorts. I can help you find your sister, but I need something from you in exchange."

She glanced up, her glittering eyes narrowing to distrusting slits in the muted lamp light. He thought about recanting his thoughts, convinced no one would ever believe she'd caught his attention, for he preferred them taller, a little vain, and more liberated. This girl, on the other hand, barely cleared his chin, possessed not one conceited bone in her small body, and appeared, at present, as cautious and jittery as a baby rabbit ready to bolt.

He waited for the displeasure of such a woman to sink into his gut, causing him to change his mind. When, after a few moments of glancing at her wondrous brown-hazel eyes, his body reacted more with temptation than reluctance.

"You need me, Grace. I can see it. I can feel it. And I can help you."

She shook her head, making him wonder how often she accepted help from anyone. Too stubborn to give up on her, he settled in and presented his case. "My sister—her name's Maggie—has it in her romantic head that if I find a woman to settle down with, I won't sell Hearth's Gate. Nothing could be further from the truth."

Grace's pretty gaze narrowed. "Okay…but I don't understand how I can help."

He smiled at her naïveté. "All I'm asking you to do between us locating your sister, is stay close to me, pose as my girlfriend, and in the end, crush and leave me a dejected mess. Maybe then Maggie will stop interfering in my personal life."

Grace blinked long lashes at him. "Girlfriend? But…I-I don't think I could…be your girlfriend or even do something so heartless."

He had to laugh at her innocent response. "Grace, I

have no intention of losing myself in the charade. I'm just asking you to help teach *my* sister a lesson."

The sooner the better, he thought. He needed to sell Hearth's Gate in order to pay for the low bid his construction company made on the county contract. With Maggie breathing down his back about keeping it, this was no different from what their mother did to their father. Although he'd loved his mother, she was a woman who spent so much time planning everyone else's life, she didn't even stop to consider what his father or anyone else wanted. Now, they were both gone. Losing someone, Ayden realized, made one reevaluate their life and the burden of loving another human being.

"So, all I have to do is to pretend to be in love with you?"

He shook himself from his thoughts and narrowed his gaze, afraid to say the wrong thing lest she run screaming from O'Shannon's, or worse, get lost in the sham and declare them engaged by the Christmas Eve *Eve* Dance. This was a thin rope he had to cross. A very thin rope.

"Love is an awfully strong word, Miss Evans. Besides, it will only be for a week, just long enough to convince Maggie she can stop trying to find me a wife."

Grace chewed on her bottom lip and blinked her hypnotic eyes. "Will your sister believe you've met someone and fallen in love in such a short amount of time?"

Valid question. "Ah, you don't know Maggie. She's a hopeless romantic...love at first sight, that sort of nonsense. But just in case, we'll try and avoid her at all cost, until we know enough about each other to pull this off."

He grinned, enjoying waiting for Grace's answer. In the meantime, he waved to the nearest waitress his sister had yet to fix him up with, signaling her to bring them another round.

"I-I think you should know," Grace said, her voice apologetic. "I'm not very good at pretending. Danielle says I have the tendency to wear my heart on my sleeve, which at times, can get pretty messy." She sent him a quick smile as if she'd confessed to some silly secret she'd held onto most of her life. "Your sister would see right through me."

He nodded his understanding. "My sister sees what she wants to see."

"But—"

"And I'm willing to take that chance."

Grace dropped her gaze to the flyer, using her index finger to pull it closer to where she sat. He studied her reaction and her delightful facial features, staring long enough to make her wiggle in her seat. He supposed he should have waited for her to drink another mug of beer before popping the question. The one she was nursing was still three-fourths full.

"How many women answered her ad?" Grace finally asked, her eyes still diverted to the picture of him this summer during an impromptu rugby game in the field behind O'Shannons.

He drew out his phone. Ten more responses lit up both his text message and missed calls. "At least twenty-five."

His phone dinged again, and he glanced down, finding a new text message from his nephew's pre-school teacher. "Twenty-six."

Grace tilted her head. "Don't you think it's strange, after receiving so many offers, that you wouldn't consider one of them?"

Yes. However, he wanted Grace. For, unlike the women of Mistletoe, she had somewhere else to go when this was all over. He kept this resolution to himself, waiting for her to make a decision. When she said nothing, he played one last card. "I won't demand anything from you, not even a penny of the money you offered earlier."

This information brought her closer to him, yet she remained quiet. His gaze lowered to her lips, her concentrated nibbling causing them to plump up into a delectable ruby shade.

"I don't know, Mr. McCabe."

"Ayden."

She sent him a nervous smile. "Ayden."

He liked the way she said his name. Shy with a touch of silkiness. "You have nothing to lose here. And I promise—nothing emotional."

This time, she made a face. "Nothing emotional? What does that even mean?"

Her brown-hazel eyes changed in both shade and mood. Before she managed to add a disapproving comment, he suggested, "We might have to work on your assertiveness, though. I may be able to convince people I prefer brunettes over blondes, but you need to loosen up a little more."

She recoiled. "I'm certainly loose enough."

He disagreed behind a fresh mug of dark beer, drinking a generous amount before resuming his thoughts aloud. "You sit there, and sometimes, I swear you stop breathing."

She didn't hesitate to retaliate. "Yeah, well, you're not my type either."

Her jealous comment caused the corners of his mouth to lift. He was curious now and a little eager to discover more of what motivated her.

"Let me guess, he's five-eight, black hair, green eyes, and drives a Hybrid.

She shifted toward him, defiance showing in her stiff pose and coiled hands. "Five-ten, dark-brown hair, topaz eyes, and drives a Volvo."

His humor faded the second she revealed there was, in fact, someone else in her life. He squashed the sudden disappointment, telling himself he'd much prefer her attached. He only wanted her to play a part, not act upon it. "And is he wondering what you're doing right now?"

Ayden waited as she rummaged through her purse to retrieve her phone. Her short-nailed index finger pressed a few buttons until she found the message she sought. "He says he misses me, and can't wait to see me." For effect, she imposed an embellished smile, disclosing the tiniest dimples on each of her cheeks

"You're right." Ayden regretted having asked the question in the first place. "You're not a very good liar."

Grace closed her eyes, appearing to fight back a flood of unkind words. In a matter of moments, his views changed regarding her relationship status. *Did he really want her to be single?* He wrestled with himself on why he cared either way, a twinge of guilt at what he'd proposed forcing him to pause.

Until now, every woman he'd dated in the last eight years crumbled before him on their first date, unloading what seemed like a decade of personal overstuffed baggage upon him like an avalanche. He expected Grace to be no different from the rest and waited for her burdens to tumble forth. To his surprise, she fluttered her long lashes and then released a heavy exhale. It occurred to him: this woman would rather die than show a crack of weakness.

"All right." She said the words both labored and uncertain. "You will help me find Danielle, I can stay at Hearth's Gate, no charge, there will be no emotional intimacy, and at the end, I leave you a dejected mess."

He nodded without smiling. "Exactly."

She shook her head and blinked, a sign of a heavy thinker. "This is insane."

"Grace." He reached out his hand to fold over hers. They were small, warm, and soft. "I can give you what you want, and you can give me what I want." He hesitated, dropping his gaze to her lips.

On a reluctant nod, she gave the answer he wanted. "Fine."

His head tilted, and his eyes narrowed. "Great. Should we kiss to seal the deal?"

Chapter Three

Before Ayden, Grace's round cheeks lit up like she'd just eaten a firecracker. He liked the color on her, and he liked that she didn't grasp at the first opportunity to make their relationship physical right away.

"I-I think we should shake hands for now."

His lips curled into a wry smile. "Of course." Still, he drew closer over the table, so close he could feel her soft breath caress his cheeks. "Just so you know, once the deal is sealed…with a handshake, it can't be broken, no matter what."

She glared down at his extended hand. Maybe he had pushed her too far. "Grace." Now, he didn't want her to think too long on what he'd proposed.

"Oh, all right," she huffed out and thrust her small hand into his. As they sealed their fate, he wondered who stood the most to gain and who the most to lose. Unsure how deep he wanted to dive into that answer, he folded his palm around hers, roused by the tender heat radiating from such a small part of her petite body.

"Ayden?"

He glanced up to find his sister standing above them, her blue eyes as big as Mistletoe's moon before Christmas. When he felt Grace's hand begin to pull away, he tightened his grip, slicing a gentle warning in her direction.

"Hi, Maggie." He brought his other hand to cup

Grace's thumb. In smooth and erotic rhythm, he caressed her velvety skin, a diminutive whimper escaping deep in her throat. "Maggie, this is Grace Evans. Grace, my sister, Maggie McCrery."

Grace presented her free hand and offered a timid wave. "I've heard a lot about you."

Maggie didn't even bat a purple dusted eyelash. "Oh, that's amazing since I've never heard one thing about you."

An awkward silence followed as Maggie lifted her cheeks into an overly friendly smile in his direction.

"I'm Ayden's…girlfriend," Grace said after a nervous inhale, her obvious inability to tell a lie showing like fireworks on the 4th of July.

"Maggie, how's Kyle? Is the Army letting him come home for the holidays?" Neil stole up from out of nowhere, placing an affectionate arm around her and adding, "Oh, I see you've met Grace. Ain't she pretty?"

Maggie bobbled her head in baffled agreement. Desire to take control of the situation forced Ayden to stand and bring Grace with him, their hands still very much intertwined.

"Sorry, Maggie, but I'm late dropping off some blueprints."

His sister scooted to the side, her mouth open and her voice seemingly stuck on what she wanted to say. "But…but…you're still coming to dinner tomorrow, right?" she called. Grace stumbled behind him, her suitcase in tow and the entire bar as quiet as a room full of marble statues.

"Damn," he muttered, forgetting all about the infamous Christmas tree dinner at the McCrery House. It meant more to Maggie this year than any other since her husband's National Guard unit had shipped out to some undisclosed location for a twelve-month deployment. They weren't even due back until February.

"Dinner?" Grace echoed low, her quiet voice trembling.

Ayden shifted back to reassure her. "Don't worry. There will be too much festive mayhem for Maggie to pay too much attention to us." At least, he hoped so.

****

Between the booth, the bar and the door, Grace panicked. She didn't remember drinking any beer, but her mind remained foggy and her judgment too impulsive to believe she hadn't taken a sip of something potent.

Oh, what had she done? Not only would Ayden McCabe's plan not work, she would humiliate herself in the process. Not that this didn't happen once a month with Rick. In addition, she knew nothing about Ayden. Well, except he was the town's favorite bachelor, a superhero, and a combination of two, perhaps three, of Jane Austen's most portrayed characters.

She waited for a pang of apprehension, something to tell her he was not to be trusted. However, nothing, not even a tiny voice to warn of some impending doom, rose to caution her.

Still, he escorted her into the night, believing it too late to change her mind. She didn't halt until a blast of frigid air and wet snow hit her face.

"Grace?"

She sniffed, the glacial air freezing her nostrils together for a strange and scary moment. He appeared not to notice as they stood together, their fingers interlocked, his smooth and sensual palm stroking against hers.

Despite his impeccable, though impenetrable reputation, she wondered if she was putting too much faith in a man she'd only just met. What woman threw herself at the mercy of a stranger, a striking and intriguing stranger, but a stranger all the same?

Her hesitation to go any further prompted him to turn away, his expression stern and distant. When she thought he might dive into a tantrum over her sudden change of heart, he instead twisted back around and pulled her close to him.

His hands captured both sides of her arms, forcing a puff of icy air from her lips.

"Give me one day, Grace. If you change your mind, I'll drive you to the nearest vacant hotel, fifty or so miles away and pay for your stay, no questions asked."

Lost in his nearness, she murmured her thoughts. "But, Maggie—"

He crooked his index finger under her chin, forcing her lips closer to his. "One day," he whispered. Then he stepped back, his sudden abandonment causing a visible and lingering shiver. She tightened the light jacket around her body until Ayden shrugged out of his coat and placed the masculine-scented covering across her shoulders.

Entranced, she lingered until he lifted her suitcase and placed it in the back of his truck, covering it with a sapphire blue tarp. She managed a few unsteady steps to the passenger side, surprised when he followed and proceeded to open the door and help her inside.

"I have to drop off something at work. Do you

mind?"

So unused to being asked her opinion or permission, she sent him an awkward headshake, finding it more and more difficult to deny him anything.

He closed the door and waved to an older couple before joining her in the driver's seat.

"What is a Christmas tree dinner?" she asked.

He glanced out the back window, smudged gray from salt and grime. He didn't answer until he backed out and shifted the truck into Drive, his gaze steady on the road ahead. "Every Saturday after Thanksgiving, Maggie invites a few of us over for soda bread, stew, and potato cakes. In exchange, we help decorate the Christmas tree. With her husband overseas, there was no way I could say no."

"Oh." Grace fell silent, the quiet, she supposed, too much for him to take.

"It really isn't all that bad."

"No." Grace regretted how she'd sent him the wrong impression. "It's just been a long time since…" She trailed off, not even sure how much she wanted him to know about her.

"Since what?" The genuine concern and interest in his deep tone caused Grace to glance into the lapsing landscape. On her side, before a dark purple sky, architect-designed gingerbread houses sat adorable and inviting. They complemented the town and brought an alluring draw to its already cheerful atmosphere.

"It's been a long time since I've celebrated Christmas." She paused, fighting the urge to reveal more of her past. She'd never had anyone ask so many questions about her personal life before.

"Oh, a non-believer?" he said.

She turned to see his features stretched into what seemed like disappointing lines. Why she cared what he thought of her, she didn't know.

"No," she corrected, afraid she'd have to expose a part of her past not even Rick cared to know. She thought about remaining silent, changing the subject, or pulling the door handle and jumping from the cab, anything to avoid talking about her dysfunctional life.

"So, then are you a female Ebenezer Scrooge?"

She scoffed. "So, then are you always this nosy?"

He bent toward her and chuckled. "I can be." His sideways smirk, a trifling gesture if there ever was one, sent her heart lurching. Something about his calming openness prompted her to bare more.

"It's just that I don't have many enjoyable moments about the holiday. That's all."

She thought he'd let it go. Most men did, or at least, most men she knew, one of them in particular. With Rick, whenever she braved a serious topic, the direction of their relationship for example, he'd downshift into blissful ignorance or retreat.

"What, did Danielle get more presents than you?"

Grace jerked her head in Ayden's direction, unsure if he was joking or being serious. Fine, if he was this curious, she'd tell him. It served him right for prying into her past. "No. My dad left my mom on Christmas day. From that point forward, I relate the *merry* holiday to one of the worst days of my life."

She brought in a shaky breath, realizing she'd unleashed fourteen years of anger and hurt down on a man who, less than an hour ago, thought she wanted to pay him to have sex with her. Mortified by her words and by the shocked look on his face, she angled her head toward passenger side window.

Grateful he didn't try to comfort her or say something stupid, she sat in contented silence as he maneuvered the truck up a narrow driveway, the bumpy lane riddled with muddy holes and slushy snow.

"What's this?" She rotated in his direction, hoping he'd forgotten the last few moments of their conversation.

He blinked at her with narrowed eyes before nodding. "Well, if all goes well, my next project. The county wants to build a tourist lodge to bring in more money. McCabe Builders is bidding for the job, and I wanted to show the blueprints to a few of the men to see what they think. They have a stake in this, too."

A little familiar with the bidding process, Grace wanted to know more. "So, do you have a good chance of getting the job?"

Ayden tossed her a quick glance, surprised she cared to ask him any more questions.

"I don't know. A larger company from Bellevue is also offering, and they have much more capital, enough to come in lower, much lower."

"Why don't you come in lower then?"

"If someone offered to buy the B&B, I would."

"Oh." Grace noticed the disappointment and firmness in Ayden's stern tone.

"Sometimes it's substance over means; matter over money." He shifted his truck into Park and lifted his arm to wrap around the back of her seat. Grace froze, her pulse jumping into an erratic rhythm. He was going to kiss her and she was going to let him.

Chapter Four

The few seconds of anticipation proved to be a grand disappointment as Ayden reached back to pull out something behind the seat, bypassing her lips for a rolled-up tube with black lettering: *Blueprints*. Her cheeks burned with embarrassment, and she ducked her head to keep him from noticing.

"I won't be long." He left the truck running and the heat cranked all the way to the right.

While she sat alone, she glanced around, amused to find a *My Favorite Uncle* coffee mug jammed in the cup holder near the cassette radio.

From the mirror dangled a set of metal dog tags. It was too dark to make out anyone's information. Still, her fingers skimmed over the raised typeset until the door jerked open.

Ashamed at her nosiness, she fell back against the seat, afraid she'd intruded too far into his private life. Seemingly clueless to her snooping, he dropped in beside her, adjusted the dog tags, and circled the truck back the way they came.

"You were in the military?" she asked, wondering if he'd shut down and change the subject.

Ayden smiled. "I was, but I'm sure you already knew that, right?"

She dipped her head. "Yes, Jolene Watson is probably one of your biggest fans. She has you perched upon a pretty high pedestal."

In the diminished light, Grace noticed how his jaw clenched and his features turned a shade darker.

Up a slight hill and on a curved horseshoe driveway, he remained aloof and reflective, easing the truck to a stop before two post lights at a two-story, gray-stoned house. The large wraparound porch stood as the house's most welcoming feature.

Beside the stone house stood another, half the size but exquisitely charming and quaint. With no lights shining from the windows, she wondered if it remained shuttered for any particular reason. She returned her attention to the main house ahead.

"Is this—"

"Hearth's Gate? It is now," he said, before bumping his shoulder against the door and jumping out to retrieve her suitcase. She fumbled for the handle, her mind sobering at the bizarre circumstances surrounding their agreement.

She must have dallied too long, glancing up to find him already opening her door. He extended his hand, her acceptance of his offer as natural as blinking.

Still, she stood unused to this kind of attention or care. Most of her life, her sister and mother had depended on her to open the doors, take their hand, and guide them where they needed to go. She had been their rock for more years than she cared to count. She believed Rick saw her the same way. No matter what he did or how he acted, she'd remain his rock and his lighthouse, always steady and waiting for him whenever he became lost. Sometimes she wished she had her own lighthouse built upon a steady rock, and anchored with a love she only read about in romance novels.

"I stay in the main house. The one beside is nothing more than a workshop now," he said.

Grace peered back to the one and half story stone structure. She remembered the shop she'd been thinking about turning into her own café and bakery. Of course, gazing upon this quaint house made the place in San Francisco appear plain and unappealing now.

"I'll show you to your room before Maggie flounces over, lobbing more questions at us than we have answers."

Grace agreed, allowing him to lead her into an inviting foyer, soft skylights illuminating the solid oak flooring and a curving oak staircase.

"I always keep a room ready for Maggie and the kids. Since Kyle's deployment, she likes having a place to stay when things get a little overwhelming."

"You have a beautiful place," Grace said in awe of the antique furnishings and traditional paintings hanging on the Tuscan-painted walls.

He glanced around before returning his attention. "Thank you." He said nothing else as Grace sensed his unwillingness to get too close or reveal much of his parents' legacy.

He stepped onto the staircase, her suitcase still in his hand. Near the arched window halfway up, he paused, glancing back to make sure she followed.

A crystal chandelier dangled above them, swathing a soft light over his strong jaw and intent gaze, causing her heart to flutter like a captured sparrow.

"Grace?"

She needed a distraction. "Tell me you can find Danielle."

He didn't hesitate. "I can find Danielle."

Satisfied with his answer, though flustered over her constant reaction of him, she lifted her foot to take the first step, realizing it sealed their fate.

Like the downstairs, the upper level opened up into quiet splendor and coziness. In the hall, warm colors of tan and burgundy enhanced a marble table placed between two closed doors.

"This is my room." He pointed to the right. "That will be yours." He paused as if to give her time to change her mind. When she said nothing, he continued. "The linen closet is at the end of the hall, and the bathroom is behind us."

"Does that mean we have to share a shower?" The idea was too intimate to contemplate.

"Only if you want to," he responded, misconstruing her question with a flirtatious suggestion.

A reply froze on her lips. He sent her a smirk before stretching in front of her to open the door, his mouth drawing a few inches from hers. Grace held her breath and the urge to lean forward.

"It can get a little chilly in this room at night, so I'll make a fire and bring out some extra blankets before you go to bed."

She stood before him, motionless, lost in his thoughtful nature and sensual scent. Crisp air, soap, and radiating heat oozed from his body, drawing her ever closer. Now, she understood everything Jolene bragged about him. If he did own a cape, Grace wondered where he stored it.

Too easy, Grace thought, for her to become attracted to a man who treated emotional relationships like kryptonite. Maybe that's why so many women answered his sister's ad: he was a challenge to be won or conquered. Grace knew, however, that men like Ayden McCabe set the rules of engagement and never detoured. He was as determined to remain alone as women like Rachel and the twenty or so others on his voicemail were determined to claim him.

Resolute to remind herself of this every time he drew within a breath of her, she stepped into the room. Reminiscing over her mother's hysteria and her sister's foolish behavior kept Grace focused on her mission and her future, wherever that lay.

"Where do you want it?"

She twisted back to Ayden, her head shaking from his question. She believed he'd somehow read her mind until he raised her suitcase, his eyebrows quirked and waiting for her answer. Embarrassed at her whimsical thoughts, she pointed toward the white metal brass bed, a snowy-white down comforter spread across the mattress, a wine-red throw folded at the foot. On each side hung two double-hung windows, matching curtains draped over one single vintage wooden rod.

Near the foot of the bed sat a white brick fireplace, a set of five-arm candelabras and an oval mirror resting on a mahogany mantelpiece.

He placed her suitcase upon the bouncy mattress, clapped his hands together, and turned to face her. "I don't know about you, but I'm starved. I have some leftover stew, and we can make some sandwiches."

"That sounds heavenly," she said, realizing she'd been too upset to eat much of anything between San Francisco and Mistletoe.

"Then I'll meet you downstairs?"

****

Ayden observed Grace's cautious smile. Innocent and brave, uncertain and demure, he knew it wouldn't be long before she forgot their pact and started asking questions about a future together.

Of course, he anticipated some physical contact between them. He recognized the interest and curiosity in her eyes right away.

However, determined he'd made the right decision regarding their agreement, he left the room and pivoted left at the bottom of the steps, twisting in the direction of his updated kitchen. For six months, he'd labored, installing tall French doors leading onto a twenty-foot deck, polished oak cabinets, and black marble countertops that helped pull the spectacular mountainous view inside.

With Grace on his mind, he opened the fridge and carted out last night's dinner, all the while vowing to remain unaffected by her nearness.

As she lingered longer upstairs, he checked his phone, deleting seven new messages and dialing an old friend who had recently left the military to start his own investigative company outside Seattle.

"Fitzy, it's McCabe."

"Well, how the hell are ya, Lieutenant? Me and Hogan were just talking about you…wondering if you were ready to move to Seattle and become part of our team. Hey, Hoge, it's the lieutenant." There was a pause. "Hogan sends a salute."

Ayden grinned. "I hope it's a respectable one."

Fitzy chuckled. "Always, sir. What's new?"

Ayden was still unsure of all the pieces and parts to Grace's sister's sudden escape. "How are you at locating someone who may or may not want to be found?"

"Well, if you remember, we specialized in the latter." Fitzgerald took a loud sip of whatever he held his hand, followed by an exaggerated, *Aaah*.

"How old are they?"

"Old enough to get married." Ayden dumped the congealed stew into a large steel pot.

Fitz howled as Charlie Hogan, Fitz's wingman since their tour in Afghanistan, spewed a string of curse words for scaring the hell out of him.

With the speaker muffled from Fitzy's hand, Ayden thought the man did a horrible job of explaining the situation. "I think the lieutenant's planning to get married if we can find the woman."

"No, Fitzy," Ayden corrected him. "She's a sister of a friend, not anyone I know personally."

"Oh, of course." A momentary pause followed. "You can count on us. As soon as you can, email me a picture of the woman along with any other information, a cell phone number, address, things like that. I'll have her found before you can say I do."

Ayden started to correct his platoon sergeant again, but the man was fully engaged in answering the deluge of questions from Hogan yelling across the room. "What? Is the lieutenant getting married? You owe me fifty bucks!"

"No," Fitzy called back, "I don't owe you any money. I told you once, and I'll tell you again, Lt. McCabe will settle down when camels fly."

Then the phone call ended, leaving Ayden to reflect over Fitzy's words.

"Oh, the stew smells wonderful. Do you want me to make the sandwiches?"

Ayden glanced up to find Grace shuffling into the room, hair pulled away from her face in a haphazard ponytail. He thought she looked more at home here than anyone he'd ever invited in the door. "Yes, you'll find everything you need in the fridge and on the counter over there." He pointed to a green vintage breadbox his mother brought over from Ireland.

His gaze followed Grace's easy gait to the box first, unable to take his gaze away as she pulled out some Irish sweet bread. From his mother's recipe, he'd made a few extra batches to give to the charity auction for Thanksgiving.

"I spoke to a friend of mine in Seattle who has an investigation service company. He needs all the information you can give me on Danielle."

Grace froze midway back to where he stood. "I thought you'd…that *we'd* try and find her. She said she was staying in Mistletoe. Surely, it won't take long to ask around, show her picture, find someone who's seen her."

Ayden stopped what he was doing, taken aback by Grace's frantic response. He rounded the counter and met her in the open space between them. "I hate to be the one to break this to you, but your sister hasn't set one foot in Mistletoe. She's either lying or leading you on a wild goose chase. I tend to believe the latter, for some reason."

Grace's delicate eyebrows drew together. "But…but that doesn't make any sense. God, none of this makes any sense. She'd never do this to Trevor."

The concern in her face forced Ayden to soften his tone. Before him existed a woman left by her father at such a young age and forced to grow up fast and, apparently, become the *fixer* in the family. Whether she knew it or not, she stood like concrete, set to crumble at any moment.

"So, does Trevor know he no longer has a willing fiancée?" Ayden asked.

Grace's shoulders stiffened. "Danielle is not unwilling. I…I know she's not." She paused, her pretty face lined with uncertainty. "It's complicated."

"Aren't all relationships?" Ayden asked, his voice low and steady. He wondered on a consistent basis if his mother had taken advantage of his father's willingness to stay here. While resentment of her began to nag at him, guilt burned a slow hole in his stomach. If only his father had had a backbone and his mother had listened, they might still be alive today, maybe living back in Ireland. And his friend and comrade might have—

"You don't know them," Grace mumbled, more to herself than to him. Under hooded lashes, he watched her throw a few things, literally, between slices of the bread he'd made. In silence, she brought the plate over and placed it on the island countertop.

They ate, he unable to take his gaze from her for more than a few seconds at a time. At last, her spoon scraped the bottom of her bowl, and she sat back, her eyes filled with satisfaction. "That was the best meal I believe I've ever had." She placed her small hand against her flat stomach.

"Well, I'm glad you liked it. It was my mom's recipe."

Her lips parted, and her gaze lifted at a slow rate to his face. He knew then, she'd been told about his past. He'd learned long ago, nothing was sacred here, not even to a mere passerby. "I'm very sorry about your parents," she said, her voice quiet and cautious.

He nodded and narrowed his eyes. "Let me guess. Jolene again? And what else did our busy train station attendant say about what happens in Mistletoe?"

He leaned forward, resting his elbows and forearm on the table. He only hoped Grace knew nothing of the legend surrounding the Christmas Eve *Eve* Dance. The last thing he needed was her getting some romantic notion about them staying together after this.

Chapter Five

Grace considered her first words. She wanted to know more about the man she was supposed to pretend to be in love with, the man who made her heart jump every time his gaze lowered to her mouth. She cleared her throat and shook into an indifferent demeanor, knowing he could see right through her if he wanted. "She said your parents ran Hearth's Gate before they died and that you'd come back here to take care of your sister."

"I see."

"How long were you over there?"

He hesitated, making her wish she hadn't asked the question. After several moments, he sent a quick smile. "Not long. I was a very young officer, and I was on patrol when I received the news of my parents' deaths. After that, I put in for a hardship discharge, left my men and a good friend behind, and never looked back."

Grace didn't know what to say to a man who'd fought a war and lost his parents at the same time, so she didn't say anything. They sat in stillness for a moment, she picturing him in charge of a group of men willing to die for their country. He appeared so brave and fearless on the outside, but on the inside, she wondered how much alike they really were.

"What are you thinking, Miss Evans?"

Surprised by her thoughts and his questions, she

jumped and then dipped her chin to her chest.

"Oh, come on. I see a hundred questions swimming around in that pretty…fine head of yours."

She giggled, remembering the warning of anyone calling her pretty again. Instead of revealing her thoughts, she threw a question at him that was unexpected, for both of them. "So, are you planning on taking anyone to the Christmas Eve *Eve* dance?"

The corners of his mouth turned downward, and he pulled back, making her wonder if she'd crossed some unknown boundary. Instead of retreating, she sat waiting for his answer. She also sat staring at his mouth for a few wild heartbeats before he leaned forward, his fingers coming so close to touching hers.

"You're going to be home soon, I'm sure, too busy to think of who I may or may not be planning to take anywhere."

Grace tried not to imagine his body flattened against Rachel's at the legendary dance, his lips pressed against her temple and words of endearment on his tongue.

His smile returned. "Look, Grace. I promised I'd find your sister, so don't get any bright ideas of staying any longer than a few days. We have an agreement, and I expect you to uphold your end of it."

Offended that he had to remind her of their emotionless pact, she tilted her chin higher. "I hate to blow a hole in your ego, Mr. McCabe, but I'm looking forward to returning to San Francisco and my—"

****

Ayden didn't know why, but believing she was going to say *boyfriend* sent him over the edge of calm. He reached her, bracing his arms on each side of her and pushing her gently against the counter. Her peppery breath fanned across his face, her small breasts rising fast to press firm against his chest. Blood rushed through his veins and to the more masculine parts of him. He locked gazes with her, his jaw tense and his tone warning. "From this moment forward, the only boyfriend you have is me, are we understood, Miss Evans?"

She swallowed loud, her mesmerizing brown-hazel eyes blinking, her tongue darting out to wet her lips. *Damn, he wanted to kiss her. Hard.* But what signal would that send her? He had no doubt she'd believe she had a future here like the others. "You could not be more wrong in your assumption, Mr. McCabe. I was about to say, my life. And we both know I don't have a man waiting for me, or at least, I haven't had one for three weeks and five days," she said in tantalizing whisper.

He pushed away, angry with himself for not staying in control of his thoughts and emotions. She lured him, with her pretty eyes and a tantalizing mouth. He fisted his hands and willed himself to place more distance between them. When he'd separated them by a few feet, she cleared her throat and changed the subject.

"It was very noble, what you did," she said after a long silence between them.

He shook his head, unsure of what she'd meant.

"Leaving your career behind to take care of your little sister."

He never thought it was noble. Not even once. "It was a long time ago." He grabbed Grace's empty bowl and placed it in his to put into the sink. He wanted to end it there, believing he had when she asked him the question he thought he'd never have to answer again.

"Why did your parents call this place Hearth's Gate?"

He opened and closed his mouth, struggling with an explanation without actually having to show her. After all, what good came from unlocking that door again? When Grace continued to sit, blinking at him, innocent and curious, he walked around to stand before her. In a casual gesture, he presented her his hand.

"Come with me." Like the several times before, she surrendered her palm against his, the contact growing more comforting and natural, more self-indulgent and pleasing.

Through a set of solid French doors, he guided her, the room swathed in darkness and stale air. Since he'd refused to replace the chandelier bulbs that had blown out, one at a time, nine years before, he let go of her hand to search for a dusty candle and match. He found both on the timbered mantel above the shadowed hearth.

Scents of sulfur and wax filled the room as he lit the blackened wick and turned the flickering light to the grand stone fireplace. He wasn't surprised by Grace's reaction, her eyes wide, glittering, and full of admiration for the place his parents cherished.

"It's…breathtaking." She left him to glance around the room and to glide a hand over a long double pedestal dining table. He was sure, if he closed his eyes, he could still hear the many guests who would gather for breakfast in the mornings. With the memories came the numerous times he'd fought with his father about stepping onto the frozen porch to retrieve the logs for the fire.

"Aye, son, but our guests will be waking soon," the man would say in his heavy Irish lilt.

Ayden believed Hearth's Gate never saw a day unoccupied. With its dining room always bursting with laughter, his mother always smiling, he thought it would last forever. Well, until he returned to find the room filled with black-clad mourners, their wrenching sobs replacing the once delightful gaiety.

"Ayden?" Grace's quiet and angelic voice at his right arm caused him to choke back a treasure trove of raw emotions.

"You should have seen this place before—"

Unprepared to share more than he already had, he blew out the candle, grasped Grace's steady hand and led her back toward the kitchen, shutting the door on the room and the memories.

She respected him enough not to ask any more from him. After cleaning the kitchen, they sat at the breakfast table as she showed him the picture of Danielle, pretty like Grace but with longer, lighter hair, sparkling green eyes, and a carefree smile.

"She looks like you," he said.

Grace's nose wrinkled. "No, Danielle is gorgeous and has left a trail of broken hearts down every street in San Francisco since she was sixteen. She was lucky to have met Trevor. After one date, he vowed he was going to marry her—" Grace stopped short, and sighed. "She's so spoiled; she doesn't know how lucky she is to find someone like him. He's perfect and loves her so much."

"Perfect?" Ayden interrupted.

"I didn't say he was perfect."

Ayden nodded, suppressing an obnoxious grin.

"Yes, you did."

Her features changed, her teeth drawing her bottom lip in to nibble for a few moments. "I mean…I meant perfect for her. Danielle needs someone to coddle and bend to her every whim, and Trevor does so without her ever having to ask."

Ayden slid close enough to pick up the subtle smell of Grace's vanilla- and sugar-scented skin. "So, is that what you're looking for? Do you want to find someone to take care of you and bend to your every whim?"

Her gaze shifted away from him, and he knew she was either getting ready to hand him an excuse or a lie.

"Since I'm not currently looking, I'm not sure how to answer your question."

His attention dropped to her mouth, wet and red from trying to avoid answering him. From what he knew about her so far, she put everyone else first, unsure or unwilling to transfer any responsibility. Even if she did find someone who was willing to live for her and only for her, Ayden wondered how fast she'd walk away. Maybe run was a better word.

He decided he had plenty of time to figure out Ms. Evans in the next few days and so changed the subject. "If you want to go get settled in, I'll gather some firewood from outside."

"Okay," she agreed. He drifted toward the sliding glass doors when she called him back around. "Do you mind if I take a shower?"

His mouth opened, but he just stared at her. Was she asking or inviting him? Of course, this wasn't the first time he'd been asked, but the question was usually followed by a come-hither look and a tantalizing exit in order to get him to follow. Instead, Grace stood there, her black lashes blinking in half-second intervals. He realized soon enough he'd dated too many women with only one thing in mind.

"It's all right if I don't," she said after he didn't answer her right away.

He nodded to shake out of his thoughts. "Oh, yes, of course. Have at it."

She sent him a curious smile and rotated toward the hallway. By the time he'd gathered enough wood for the fireplace and traipsed upstairs to her room, the water in the main bathroom was already running. Left alone, he tried to focus on not burning his fingers on the match as he heard the scrape of the shower curtain and the squeak of the nozzle.

"Get it together, McCabe," he mumbled to himself, forcing his mind to block out the image and sounds of trickling water over bare skin. *Grace's bare skin.* Damn. She might not have wanted him to think of her in such a way, however, it didn't prevent his mind from calling up the image over and over again.

An agonizing fifteen minutes later, she stumbled into the room, her eyes wide, her arms crossing over a form-fitting blue T-shirt and a matching pair of boxer pajamas that barely cleared her upper thighs. At her navel, the thin fabric clung to her damp skin.

In one exhale, the blood drained from his head and straight into his groin. Like any blue-blooded male, his gaze drifted at a slow pace toward her glowing face. She blinked at him, reminding him of an innocent angel caught between two worlds. Unfortunately, her appearance spurred him into a devil of a mood.

"Did you stop to think that what you're wearing might be a tad inappropriate?" he said, his tone gruff and husky.

Her arms dropped to her sides, her small hands fisted and ready to battle. In her bare feet, she padded across the oak floor and stopped less than a foot away. By her heavy breathing, he knew he'd just swatted at a hornet.

"Not that I'm an expert on fires, but I didn't think it would take more than five minutes to start one. To be honest, I didn't think you'd still be here," she said, her voice shaking. He thought she was done until she brought in a few more deep breaths.

"Besides, if I'd not been in such a hurry to leave San Francisco, where it's probably sixty degrees at the moment, I would have spent more time searching for my mother's full length nightgown with the frilly ruffles instead of grabbing this."

Ah, there it was. She'd found her voice and spirit, unleashing God knows how many hours of travel and anxiety in one fell swoop. Of course, she'd not worn the skimpy attire to coerce him into making love to her. Damn, he'd been dating way too long.

"I'm sorry," he said, beginning to unbutton his blue and white flannel. When she jumped back, grabbed the blanket off the bed and covered herself, he froze at her insinuation and the fact that his motion caused her to retreat clear across the room.

"I'm not going to seduce you, Grace. I'm just giving you something else to wear. It's much warmer than what you're clad in at the moment. Like I said, it can get cold in here at night."

He yanked the ends of his shirt out of his jeans, adjusted his black T-shirt and stalked the rest of the way over to hand her the button-down. She hesitated before dropping the blanket and plastering his offering against her damp body.

"Oh," she said, hurriedly jamming her arms into the sleeves and crossing the front like a shield. Not once did he think to glance away. The hem of the shirt skimmed across a pair of silken thighs, their curves more than inviting in the firelight.

"I want that shirt back before you leave," he said, trying to keep his voice level. "Don't think I won't find a way to get it back if you have a mind to take it with you."

She sent him a curt, wordless nod before reaching up to tuck a dark lock behind her ear. He stood in her presence, not moving and not wanting to leave. He had too much he wanted to know about her, and not just how her skin tasted or how her lips felt pressed against his.

"Well…I'm up at six every morning," he said, jerking himself from his dangerous thoughts. "Whenever you're ready, we can start searching for some clues to your sister's…disappearance."

He turned before Grace said a word, content to block out the sweet smell of warmed sugar and vanilla lotion drifting to him from her glistening skin.

In desperate need of a cold shower, he left the room and let the icy water flow over him before retiring for the rest of the night. His mind swirling with the events of the day, he lay upon his bed, shirtless, his body craving a small sampling of the woman who occupied the next room. After counting beer, boards, and nails for over an hour, he thought he'd succeeded in drifting into an agitated doze when the sound of shattered glass and a woman's scream split the night.

He bolted upright, jammed into some jeans, and tore into the hall, fumbling for the knob to Grace's room. With his heart pounding and his stomach tied into a sickening knot, he yanked the door open, his name on her lips.

"Ayden?"

"Grace?" he echoed into the muted firelight.

At his voice, she rushed forward and straight into his arms. He still didn't know what caused the crashing until he caught site of the window, an angry icy wind fluttering one sheer curtain, the other struggling to free itself of the saw-toothed windowpane.

"What happened?" he murmured.

Grace mumbled an incoherent answer, her hot breath playing like fire against his bare skin. As her hands wrapped around his waist, he searched anxiously for what caused such a hellacious crash.

On the floor about four feet in front of him, lay a rock about the size of his fist.

He made a low growl in his throat, the sound causing Grace's trembling body to pull back.

Still wearing his flannel, she glanced up. He cupped his hands to her face and lowered his body to gaze straight into her frightened eyes. "Are you all right?"

Before she could answer, a whizzing sound pierced the air. Another rock, this time larger, whirled into the room and skidded to a stop one foot away. Grace let out another scream and threw herself against him, wrapping her small arms around his waist. Her body trembled and her heart thumped so hard he could feel it batter against his bare skin.

"God," he exhaled, realizing how dependent she

was on him to keep her safe. It was empowering and damn frightening at the same time. "Grace," he said again, trying to separate her enough to see her face. When she agitated her head and clung tighter to him, her small palms branding his flesh, he thought for such a little thing, she possessed an enormous amount of strength. "Grace, I want you to go to my room and shut the door. All right?"

Her rapid exhales fanned across his chest, and he lifted his head to draw in a controlling breath. The intoxicating smell of her sweet skin wrapped around his senses, igniting his blood and the pulsating points in his body. He realized, for the first time, he hadn't thought much of this agreement through. Where he liked a pair of sashaying hips and a woman who knew what to do with them, he'd found Grace. Only, he wasn't supposed to find her appealing or sensual, and yet, as he stood there, in the middle of whatever the hell was going on outside his window, all he wanted was to lower his mouth and discover the taste of her tongue as it intertwined with his.

"Go to my room, now," he ground out, causing Grace to jump slightly away from him. He lifted his hands and wrapped them around her upper arms, pulling her away. She blinked her long lashes, her hazel eyes large and staring at him with surprise and confusion. "I'll be back in a few minutes," he assured her with a softer tone.

Her gaze darted to the open door and then back to him before she nodded and walked away. He watched her go, *her* hips swaying with a soft glide that was all her own. He stood unmoving, waiting for the sharp and lusting arousal to subside. Then he stomped downstairs to gather his winter garb. With both his mind and body in turmoil with one another, he seized the doorknob and turned the cold metal with a mighty vengeance.

The night air smacked him in the face, the lamp from his porch, spotlighting the trespasser and possible vandal.

"Eloise Riley?" he called as the familiar silhouette of his ex-girlfriend, thrice removed, scurried into view.

"Ayden, I'm so sorry about your window," she said, her breath spilling out in puffy white clouds. "I merely wanted to get your attention."

He only had to take one look down the length of her long lavender trench coat to know she wasn't wearing anything underneath. "Someone could have gotten hurt," he scolded her.

She drew back, and he knew he'd wounded her by his blistering response. "Well, you weren't waking up fast enough," she said, her teeth starting to chatter.

"You targeted the wrong room, El!"

Her lips protruded in a pout. Despite his anger, he felt sorry for her. "Come on. I'll make some coffee to warm you up, but then you'll have to go."

A smile returned to her captivating and painted face. The ruby red lipstick and fake lashes irritated him. He had to admit, however, she was one of the most beautiful women he'd ever dated. With sleek blonde hair and brown eyes, he wondered why she never pursued a career in modeling. Instead, she became an elementary schoolteacher, moving to Mistletoe with the intent of becoming a full-time writer during summer break. Then her long legs and willowy form had intrigued him right away. However, after two dates she talked of marriage and moving in, and not necessarily in that order.

He'd tried to slow things down but became restless after three months, calling it quits in the middle of O'Shannon's.

To keep both of them from getting pneumonia, he grasped her hand, noting how different her palm felt against his as compared with Grace. El had longer fingers and she gripped hard as if she was afraid he might let go sooner than she wanted.

On purpose, he guided her into the house with his left hand so he could let go to switch on the kitchen light. "Have a seat," he said, in a less than inviting tone.

El slinked away, doing a poor job of keeping the coat clasped shut. As predicted, she wore nothing underneath except a black lace bra and a pair of matching panties. At any other time, he might allow his gaze to linger on her slender form. Tonight, he just wanted to go check on Grace.

"Why are you so angry?"

Ayden pressed the button on the coffeepot to heat the water before rotating back around. El had come for one reason and one reason only. The blasted flyer his sister had posted. As much as he loved Maggie, he wanted to strangle her at this very moment. After all he'd done, everything he'd given up for her, this was her thanks to him.

The coffeepot began to hum, so he popped a dark roast in the machine, not even sure what kind of coffee El preferred. Either he didn't remember or he'd never asked. He brushed away the reasons and placed a medium-sized mug on the drip tray and punched the middle button. The less he gave her to drink, the sooner he could check on Grace. *Grace*. Ever since she'd wrapped her small arms around his waist, he thought of little else but ways to have her do it again.

Then the air changed behind him, and he whipped around to find El, her coat lying in a puddle at her long bare feet. Like any warm-blooded male, his gaze fell and locked on her full breasts. In a seductive motion, she raised a lengthy, mauve-painted fingernail to push the strap down around her upper arm. He realized he hadn't been with a woman in a few months and believed if Grace hadn't stirred his blood already, his body wouldn't be jumping to attention with such arousing force.

"I miss you, Ayden." El motioned closer, her hands reaching out to spread open the coat he'd put on before traipsing outside. He wished he'd thought to put a shirt on underneath it. With his chest bare, her cold fingertips slithered up to cup the back of his head. He grabbed her wrists before she could stake her claim on his lips, shoving her away with a gentle push.

"There's someone else, El," he said, intent to announce Grace's name before things went any further.

El's response was to send him a coy smile and bite down on her lower lip. For whatever reason, she always went overboard, trying too hard when it came to them. She also always wore a little too much perfume, nothing subtle or intoxicating, like vanilla and sugar.

"Yes, Ayden, there's always someone else with you, but you're never serious. I think…I think we had something special, and if you give me another chance, I promise I won't mention having babies or getting married."

"Babies?" Now, that was a new one.

Eloise stretched her long neck forward and kissed

him firm on the lips. The sharp intake of breath from the doorway caused both of them to push away from each other.

Ayden lifted his head to find Grace standing a few feet away still wearing his shirt, her dark lashes fluttering with curiosity…and uncertainty.

El was the first to talk, not even attempting to hide herself from Grace's shocked gaze. "Oh, well, I didn't realize you had company, Ayden."

He opened his mouth to say…something when Grace pulled herself from her stupor and padded over to where El stood. Grace lowered her gaze to the woman's feet and then back up to rest on her face. "I don't think we've been formally introduced. My name is Grace Evans, and I'm Ayden's girlfriend."

Ayden sliced a glance at El who stood, her mouth open, her eyes narrowed at Grace. "I don't believe that for a second," she said, her head tilted at a haughty angle.

"It's because I'm pretty, isn't it?"

Grace lifted one dark eyebrow, waiting for El to answer her question.

El huffed out a sigh. "As a matter of fact, you're not Ayden's—"

"Type." Grace nodded. "I know."

The two women stared at each other until El let out an unfeminine growl, scooped up her coat and dashed out of the room. When the door slammed in the foyer, Ayden turned to Grace and smirked.

"That was interesting."

She agreed with a bob of her head. God, she was a sight to see. Her dark hair lay frizzy on one side and the sleeve of his oversized shirt hung off her left shoulder.

"Do you always have half-naked women come to your door in the middle of the night?"

He had to think about this one. "Define *always*?"

"Geez." She rolled her eyes and walked away, disappearing into the foyer, her footsteps light on the stairway.

For a long time, he leaned against the sink, the aroma of rich coffee and Grace Evans keeping him in place. At half past two, he finally ambled back up the dark staircase and stepped into his room. He was about to shed his jeans when he realized his bed lay occupied.

He ambled closer to where Grace slept, a demure hand resting at her face and the other tucked under her chin.

A sliver of moonlight danced upon her cheeks as a wisp of breath sounded through her closed lips. A primitive curiosity urged him forward; however, a gallant disposition made him lift the quilted blankets to sweep them over her shapely hips.

Wide-awake, he sauntered back to her room and began the task of cleaning up. After covering the open window with an old bedspread and refilling the fireplace with enough wood to last through the night, Ayden plopped onto the springy mattress and prayed for sleep, his mind resting long before his roused body.

Chapter Six

A dust of the sun's first rays crept across Grace's closed eyelids, stirring her awake. She stretched and yawned, the stimulating scent of spice and crisp cologne forcing her to remember where she was, and why.

In a flash, her mind whipped to Danielle, and then Mistletoe, and then Ayden McCabe. Of course, this led her to remember the half-naked woman standing in his kitchen, their lips locked together in a steamy interlude. Her stomach gave a strange revolting twist. *No.* She would not feel jealousy for a man who didn't know how to remain faithful, even if they were in a fake relationship.

"Humph," she grunted, remembering how angry he became when he thought she was about to mention *her* ex.

Even though she hadn't heard from Rick in two weeks, she was expecting his call. He always reached out to her when he thought she had moved on without him. Unfortunately, Grace had yet to learn those baby steps, choosing to stand still or even stand up for herself. *Ah, until then.*

For now, she needed her phone. She had to see if her mother had called with any news about Danielle. Of course, she was also curious if Rick had called, *damn him.* Only her phone was in the other room where she was sure Ayden slept.

On a sigh, she closed her eyes and relived the night before and the feel of Ayden's arms wrapped around her and her cheek pressed against his bare chest. Not that Rick wasn't muscular, but he wasn't as tall and he always smelled of whatever cologne he'd sampled at the closest pharmacy on the way to her place. She didn't know if this made him too undependable or just plain cheap. Either way, she loved Ayden's scent. His cologne was subtle but masculine and mingled well with the smoky Mistletoe air.

Still unsettled by what she had seen in the kitchen, she peeled back the covers and crept across the hall. She hesitated at the doorway, until, on tiptoes, she infringed upon the cloaked room.

She held back a shiver as cold air poured in from behind a patchwork quilt hung in a haphazard manner across the broken window. Though beautiful and well crafted, it did little to cut the arctic air, not that the magnificent figure sprawled across the dainty bed seemed to mind.

He lay half-bared, the heavy blankets pulled to his waist, exposing the taut contours of his washboard stomach and the smoothed hardness of his chest. Her insides fluttered with cautious awe, her rebellious mind able to imagine a night wrapped in his powerful embrace.

Heel to toe she treaded forward until her bare knees grazed the bed and her feet rested atop a white and maroon Ziegler rug. Her mistake was not in her approach, but the long exhaled sigh of whimsical wonder.

As quick as a blink, he reached up and hauled her

down, her heart pounding in erratic cadence as his powerful body crushed her against the coil mattress.

"Never sneak up on a man when he's sleeping," Ayden rasped.

Grace stared up into the harsh lines of his handsome face, his eyes closed and his jaw jumping with irritation. She knew she'd surprised him. Still, knowing this was her fault, did little to lessen the fact she lay underneath him, her pulse throbbing, a tremor of heat rippling along her stretched spine.

No longer chilled, her mind clamored for a reason to push him away. At last, his eyelids opened, his deep blue eyes glittering with an emotion she'd never seen before. His jaw chiseled, his mouth slightly open, she waited for him to say something, do something.

In the frosty silence, an overwhelming urge to lift her head and touch her lips to his, began to weave uncharted thoughts through her mind. She believed he had the same thought, when the familiar ring tone of Eminem and Rihanna's duet of "I Love the Way You Lie" resonated through the room.

"Rick!" she cried, using her arms to shove at Ayden's chest.

"It's Ayden, sweetheart." He rolled to one side to set her free.

This was the call she'd been waiting for…since yesterday…before meeting Ayden McCabe. Weak kneed and frantic, she scurried away and across the bed on all fours, falling flat on her stomach to retrieve her large knockoff handbag from the floor. As the song played, she righted herself and flipped the guilt-laden present from Rick upside down, spilling the contents a few inches from Ayden's elbow.

In her haste, she'd forgotten about the romance novel she'd bought before getting on the train, a book with a muscular kilted man on the front, holding a bodice-popping woman with fiery red hair. Before she could stuff the guilty indulgence back inside her purse, Ayden plucked it from her unsteady hands.

"Give it back."

He ignored her and turned to the earmarked page, his gaze skimming over the passage she'd last read. Fire lit into Grace's face, remembering, with lascivious clarity, the lovemaking scene between the two characters. All the while, her phone continued to ring. Impatient and embarrassed, she held her hand out, waiting for Ayden to give her back the book. Only, he didn't, his gaze lowered to the descriptive and bold words. Desperate, she lunged at him, missing horribly, and landing halfway off the bed, her head dangling close to the floor. After she'd righted herself, she realized the room had grown silent. Her phone stopped ringing.

Dammit!

"Her quivering breasts—"

Mortified, Grace attempted to snatch the book back, only to have him pull it away. She was about to go after it when the familiar ring echoed in the cold room.

Her mind raced, her pulse fluttered, though the origins she'd yet to distinguish. She planned her thoughts and practiced her words. *Not this time, Rick. You're a bastard. Leave me alone. I hate you. Yes, I guess we could work it out.* They all came to mind at the same time.

Unsure what she'd say once she heard his voice

again, however, she swiped at the smudges under her eyes and smoothed down her hair.

"You do realize he can't see you?" Ayden whispered.

She sent him an annoyed glare before clearing her voice and answering in her best seductive voice. "Hello."

"Grace, where the hell are you?"

She cringed at Rick's brusque question, her gaze lifting to Ayden as he shifted closer. "Charming," he mouthed with a smirk.

She narrowed her gaze before showing him her back.

"Grace, darling. Why don't you come back to bed? I'm getting cold." Ayden spoke loud, seductive and clear.

"Who said that?"

Ironic, she thought, the conversation reversed from the last time her and Rick talked. Shaking off the memory of him with Tiffany, or was it Monica, she answered him with the first thing that popped into her brain.

"Uhhh…an actor on *Days of Our Lives*…I think?" She didn't know why she lied.

Then she made the mistake of glancing back to Ayden who was now lounged against the headboard, hands behind his head, biceps flexed in a striking, calendar-like pose.

"A soap opera, at seven thirty in the morning?" Rick asked.

Grace closed her eyes, picturing him walking to his job as an information security analyst, impeccably dressed with not one wrinkle on his tailored Armani suit. It was one of the reasons she'd fallen in love with him. She liked order and neatness, although he caused the exact opposite in her life.

Several long moments passed before she heard him sigh. "It doesn't matter, that's not why I called."

"Why did you call?"

"I just stopped by the bakery where you work and guess what?"

"I…I wasn't there?

"No, Grace. You weren't there. Betsy, your weirdo friend, said you took two weeks off to go to some place called Mistletoe, Washington. What the hell's in Mistletoe, Washington?"

Unprepared for the onslaught of questions, she debated whether to tell him about Danielle or not. She opened her mouth and then closed it. "Rick, this really isn't a good time, but I think we need to talk. Can I call you back?"

"What?" The shock in his voice threw Grace into a montage of speechless answers, causing her to wonder if she'd, in the three years of knowing him, ever posed the question.

"I'm taking a shower," Ayden blurted into the discomforted lapse of conversation, the bed groaning and squeaking under his muscular weight and his legs swinging to the cold floor.

"Who's taking a shower, Grace? That voice isn't from some damn soap opera. Who are you with?"

Grace let her forehead fall into her hand before withdrawing the phone from her ear and tapping the end call button with a hesitant thumb.

Ayden continued his journey toward the door, she resisting the urge to hurl her iPhone at the back of his head. He'd messed everything up between her and Rick. Of course, she realized, it was easier to blame Ayden for the missed opportunity to tell Rick to go to hell, than herself. Still, she was angry, confused, and disappointed, hopping off the bed and scurrying to block Ayden from exiting the room.

Before his beautiful presence, Grace raised a shaky finger, hoping to scold him with a few choice words. Only those words stuck in her throat as he edged closer, his chest grazing her unbound breasts. The charge at his nearness sent a thousand delicious prickles through her body.

His hands grasped both her shoulders, encapsulating and sturdy. In a mesmerizing voice, he spoke near her right ear. "I'll bet you Hearth's Gate, Rick's packing his bags right now and mapping out directions to get to you as fast as he can."

Ayden then drew her closer, his warm breath a thrilling tickle against her exposed neck. "If he means that much to you, instead of wanting to throw that phone at my head, in a few days, you might want to thank me." He paused, his gaze lowering to her lips. She swallowed hard, feeling his warm and delicious exhale. "Of course, I do expect a grateful kiss when he comes to whisk you away."

Before she could say anything, Ayden let go and sauntered out of the room.

The air from the open window caused goose bumps to erupt all over Grace's skin. At least, she blamed the frigid air. They could well have been from the wonder of how much she wanted to *thank* Ayden McCabe right now.

In a state of peculiar bewilderment, Grace floated

to her suitcase and rummaged for a few warm clothes. More particular than yesterday, she searched for her brown and tan button-down hooded cardigan knock-off and dark brown pants. She'd finished applying some light makeup when the phone rang again. This time it was Betsy, her friend and confidant since starting their jobs at Neece's Bakery six years before.

"I thought you'd be up," she said in a chirpy mood. "So, how's it going?"

"Well, aside from dodging hurtling rocks through a bedroom window and telling a man I'd play his girlfriend to teach his sister a lesson, just great."

"Geez, Grace. You should have left San Francisco years ago."

Grace had to disagree. "It's not as romantic as it sounds."

"If you take Rick out of your life's equation, anything's romantic. So, what's this boyfriend's name?"

Grace shrugged away the wary sensation and sighed. "Not that you'd know him, but his name is Ayden McCabe, and he owns a bed and breakfast here."

"Is he nice?" Betsy asked, her question said in a whimsical manner.

Grace felt the warmth of a slow blush creep into her face. "He's nice."

"Cute?"

"No."

"You don't think he's cute?" Betsy's voice raised an octave higher before she paused to clear her throat. "I mean…with…a name like Ayden—"

"He's sexy as hell, Bets," Grace whispered. "If that's what you're getting at with all your questions."

"I'll change the subject."

"Good idea," Grace said.

"Have you found Danielle, yet?"

Grace moaned. She didn't like *that* subject either. "We're working on it."

"We? Who, you and…Ayden? I think I smell a good love story. "

Grace leaned over to see if he might be lurking somewhere in the hallway. She hadn't heard the shower running for one full minute now. "No. It's strictly a business deal," she said, leaving out the just physical, no emotion part. "He helps me find Danielle, and I pretend to be in love with him, until he's ready for me to break his heart."

There was a long pause before Betsy spoke. "And you think my schemes of getting you to dump that loser, Rick, are insane. Oh, speaking of the loser, he popped by looking for you."

Grace dropped her head into her hands. "I know. He called."

A heartbeat later, Grace heard Mr. Neece's voice yelling for Betsy to get off the phone and get back to work.

"Useless psychology degree," Betsy mumbled. "I'll talk to you later, babe. Text me with any news. Love ya. Bye." Her friend blew a quick kiss through the phone.

Grace hung up and finished getting ready. She'd taken one last look in the antique mirror when she turned to find Ayden in the doorway, tall, imposing and ruggedly handsome. *No. Definitely not cute.*

"We can grab a cup of coffee and some breakfast at Rosie's Café on the corner," he said, leaning his shoulder against the doorframe, sporting a denim work shirt, a pair of dark jeans, and an irresistible grin.

She inhaled, his crisp and spicy fragrance infusing the cold air with a haunting scent. She forced herself to look away from him to start putting the pile of items she'd dumped earlier back into her purse.

"And then we'll find out some information about Danielle?" she asked, checking to make sure her phone was set to its highest volume. One day soon, she needed to change Rick's ringtone to something less insulting or humiliating.

"There are a couple places we can visit before we show up at Maggie's dinner."

Grace stifled a groan, the reality of the promise she'd made with Ayden setting her nerves on edge. *Girlfriend,* she sighed to herself. After three long years with Rick, she wasn't even sure she knew what being someone's girlfriend involved.

On a whim, she halted halfway between the door and bed. "Are you sure you have the right woman for this? It's been well established that I'm not your type, and my experience in relationships is somewhat limited."

She'd blurted out the last part wishing she hadn't given him the impression that she knew nothing when it came to men. By Ayden's raised eyebrows and crooked grin, she knew he'd drawn the right conclusion of her dismal, if not nonexistent, personal life.

"Not one word." She brushed past him toward the stairs. She wasn't a virgin, but she couldn't remember the last time she shared a night with a man who didn't grab his cellphone a few minutes later to check his texts.

Wanting nothing more than to think of something else, she glanced down the other end of the hallway, the corridor dark and a tad eerie, as if shut off from the rest of the house. She believed four more bedrooms lay just beyond the staircase, maybe once with their own romantic theme or cultural motif.

"I closed them up eight years ago," Ayden offered and nothing else, placing a gentle palm against the middle of her back to urge her toward the stairway.

She respected his privacy enough not to ask any more questions, descending the stairs and reacquainting herself with the beautiful and inspiring first floor. At an antique hall tree he paused to secure their coats, Grace taking a moment to glance into the beveled mirror and its stained glass sides.

"Here, you're going to need something warmer to wear."

Behind her, he placed a wool jacket around her shoulders. Before she thought to ask if it belonged to the woman in the kitchen, he bent close to her ear, saying simply, "It's Maggie's."

The sleeves hung longer than her arms, but she was grateful for his attention, and it kept out the draft much better than the jacket she'd brought from California. "Thank you."

He nodded, his gaze drifting over her face to settle on her lips. She wondered if he thought about kissing her as much as she thought about kissing him. Well, if he did, he let the moment pass without even attempting to lean forward.

Too eager to take her mind off his mouth, Grace swung around toward the door, their fingers clashing as they grabbed for the doorknob at the same time.

"I've got this," he instructed, reaching behind her.

"Are you always this chivalrous?"

"I can be," he said with a lopsided grin. Outside, the wind whipped at her cheeks. Above, the sky was gray and thick, a teasing of snow beginning to fall onto her nose.

She didn't realize she was lingering too long until Ayden grasped her hand and pulled her along at an easy gait to his truck. Like the times before, he opened her door, continuing his gentlemanly ways.

Grace liked having her hand in his. In the few times she and Rick had ever held hands, it was so loose she had to make an effort to keep them locked. With Ayden, their palms always touched, the heat from his skin and the sturdiness in his strength awakening a new want inside her. It also gave way to great disappointment whenever he dropped it away.

Inside the truck, she waited for him to join her. Unused to the glacial air, she sat bunched in a ball on the frozen leather seat, longing for the moment when the heater would defrost her nose and toes.

Several icy breaths later, Ayden slid in beside her, the engine roaring awake with the turn of the key. "I should have thought to warm up the truck for you," he said, his face serious and remorseful. "I'm not used to having company."

"I'm not that fragile," she teased, settling back and admiring the snow-capped mountains ahead of her and Ayden steering the wheel with one capable hand. She thought he wanted to say something, several times, but stared straight ahead, instead.

After a few minutes, he maneuvered the front wheels into a square parking lot, half-filled with cars and weatherworn SUVs. He parked the truck but kept it running and the heater blowing toward them. She assumed he'd been trying to figure out what he wanted to say all the way from Hearth's Gate.

"My sister's flyer is still out there, and after last night's events, I don't know what to expect anymore."

Reminded of the window, Grace touched his sleeve. "What did happen last night?"

He gazed at her for a few perplexing moments before propping his knee up and rotating around, his long arm coming over to settle behind her. "What you saw"—he paused to shake his head—"was nothing. She came thinking, believing, I wanted to rekindle something that never got started in the first place."

"But—"

"Look, I've had a lot of women in my life, Grace, and I don't regret any of them. Sometimes it was my fault, sometimes theirs, but once it was over, I didn't look back and I didn't think twice about the decision. I move on. It's my way."

Grace exhaled, bothered by his bizarre creed and sudden confession. She realized Ayden had more ex-lovers than she had excuses. Though he continued to *move on,* he remained as alone as she did, a woman who refused to budge even one inch forward when it came to Rick.

"Then I hope to God I don't fall in love with you," she laughed, half joking.

Only, a challenge flashed in his dusk blue eyes. For a moment, they didn't move and they didn't blink. She realized and accepted she wanted him to kiss her, not a peck, not a tease, but a kiss that would cause a systemic blip on the magnetic grid.

Chapter Seven

Frozen in place, Grace believed this was the moment that would test their physical, not emotional, agreement. Only, a breath later, he lowered his head, switched off the truck and opened his door with a sudden jerk. She sat baffled and confused as he hastened to her side, his strides determined and wide.

An awkwardness passed between them until he bustled her inside the cafe, tipping his head to the old, the young, and the in between while bypassing a sign that read Seat Yourself.

Heads turned and whispers heightened until she and Ayden settled into a secluded booth next to the rear exit door.

Unsure of what to say, she grabbed up a menu and shielded her face from his sight. It stung her pride that he didn't even attempt to take advantage of the moment between them. Maybe being *pretty* was not enough to lure Ayden McCabe over to her side of the truck.

Embarrassed that she'd let herself believe there was a mutual attraction, she hid behind the menu, reading the breakfast items for the fourth time. Then his finger appeared between the creased pages and pulled the crayon-marked, coffee-warped, list of options down toward the table.

"You're angry?" he simply asked.

His recognition of her sulky change in mood

humiliated her further. God, if he attempted to apologize for not being attracted to her, she might resort to stabbing him with a fork.

"I'm not angry with you," she admitted grudgingly. "I…"

"Wanted me to kiss you."

Grace's mouth dropped open, stunned by his blatant comment, though true. Still, mortified, she swung her head around to see if anyone could hear them. He, of course, glanced around, as well, mocking her paranoid behavior.

"It's okay, Grace." This was all he said, his head dipping to survey the menu, his light brown eyebrows drawing together in perplexed thought.

Left dangling by his comment, she hissed toward him. "What's okay?"

He didn't even attempt to gaze up, his long and dark lashes lowered to shade his aqua blue eyes. While skimming the multiple breakfast choices, he answered her, nonchalant. "I wanted to kiss you, too."

She prepared herself for a response, just not that one. If they both wanted to kiss each other, how in the world didn't it happen?

At last, she found her voice, though high and embarrassingly squeaky. "Okay…but why…didn't you?"

He leaned across the table toward her, coming inches from doing the exact thing they were discussing. "Because, we should keep anything physical between us where there are enough people to talk about it. Gossip spreads fast in Mistletoe, and we need Maggie to believe everything everyone sees. Besides, I'm the one who ends up with a broken heart, not you."

Now that was very arrogant. Grace drew away from him, believing if they shared a moment, a touch, a kiss, a night, did he conclude he'd step away an unscathed man, incapable of…well, looking back?

She harrumphed aloud, drawing his attention and a narrowing gaze.

"Hey there," said a bouncy auburn-haired girl with green eyes. She propped a writing tablet onto her rounded belly, her face aglow with the expectancy of motherhood. On the left side of her uniform rested her lopsided nametag, her name imbedded in the black rectangular frame. Sarah.

Grace braced herself for another one of Ayden's admirers, afraid to wonder if he'd somehow left this woman with more than what both of them expected.

"You must be Grace," the woman said in a gleeful tone. "Neil told me all about you last night. Said you swept poor Ayden here off his feet, and sure enough you did."

Left astonished, Grace opened her mouth to dispel the outlandish fabrication when Sarah rotated to Ayden, swinging her pen like a sword in her manicured hands.

"The usual?"

Ayden nodded.

"And how about you? The French toast is fabulous, and Henry back there squeezes the oranges fresh every morning."

Since Grace was too distracted earlier to pay any attention to the menu, she agreed to the suggestion.

"French toast and the usual, coming right up."

Sarah stuffed the pad in her apron, thrust the pen into her red ponytail, and waddled away. Unable to resist, Grace followed her form, surprised to see Neil slip into view from the entranceway. Wearing his cowboy hat, he accosted the young pregnant waitress, laying a long and hard kiss upon her ruby lips.

The crowd cheered him with vivacious claps. When the public display of affection ended, Neil tipped his hat and swaggered toward their table.

"Well, good morning. Glad to see you two worked everything out," he said, making himself comfortable at Grace's hip. She gawked as he withdrew his hat and, with an intimate stretch, placed it on the other side of her lap.

"Much obliged if you keep that safe for me," he said, with a devilish wink.

"Neil, don't you have a few projects to attend to this morning?"

Neil slapped the table as if the question reminded him of something. "Yes, I do. Maggie asked me to go pick out a Christmas tree for her and the wee ones. I don't suppose you'll want to come along?"

Ayden shook his head. "I have some business in town, and Kyle bequeathed the Christmas tree duty to you, remember?"

"Yes, boss, and being that it's the weekend, I thought I'd recruit some help." He whipped around to Grace. "How about you? I'll even let you use the axe."

Grace sat in bewildered contemplation. "Well…I don't think…"

"She's part of the business, Neil," Ayden interjected. "Besides, Grace prefers chainsaws."

Neil, in all his redheaded glory, turned with goggled eyes in her direction. "Well, I'll be." He rested his fingers on the table to drum them along with the holiday music playing in the background.

Then, as fast as a hawk, he scooped up his hat, placed it on his head, and tapped the top with a swift hand. "I'll see you two tonight, then." Like a scene from a John Wayne movie, he strutted away, the door's bell jingling a happy tune with his departure.

"I think he likes you," Ayden said, surprising Grace by his soft and thoughtful tone.

Grace dipped her head to hide the blush creeping into her cheeks. "He's cute."

"Yes, and he thinks he is. There lies the problem."

Still miffed over Ayden's comment regarding her weak heart, she lashed out. "You know, the only difference between the two of you is Neil doesn't hide the fact that he believes he's God's gift."

The food arrived a second later, Sarah placing a heaping pile of French toast, and a steaming platter of scrambled eggs, sausage links, and smothered biscuits between them.

Ayden waited with flaring nostrils for the girl to leave while Grace searched for the closest restroom. *Coward.* As an awkward silence passed between them, he scooted forward.

"That's such an insightful assessment for knowing me less than twenty-four hours, Miss Evans."

She flinched from the truth in his words rather than his tone. She supposed he'd never let her get to know him. It was his flight vest, his suit of armor. Keep everyone out so no one gets hurt—well, almost no one.

"Yes, I suppose you're right." She thought if she knew him one hundred years, she'd never be able to draw any conclusions about him. He was too locked up to reveal anything about himself. As usual, he remained guarded and quiet until she set her fork down and leaned back, stuffed.

"Shall we get started?" he asked, scooting his plate away, not one crumb left behind. The crooked grin he liked to send her had long disappeared, his mood bleak and heavy.

Despite their small spat, he grabbed her hand, dropped some cash on the table, and led her to his truck, the snow falling around them.

He opened her door and helped her onto the cold seat. "Where are we going?" She was afraid they were headed to Maggie's already without a plan, without knowing each other well at all.

He didn't answer until he'd shut himself inside the cab beside her. "Hawthorne's Drug Emporium."

For the entire ride through the peaceful town, he didn't say a word.

****

Ayden didn't know what to think. He'd never met a woman like Grace Evans, a woman who glanced upon him and saw more than his hardened exterior. It frightened and exhilarated him at the same time. He vowed, however, to keep his distance. Women like her were dangerous. They feigned innocence, all the while plotting how to get him to change his life to suit their dreams.

Still, he knew it was only a matter of time before she incited him enough to want to cross the line between make-believe and reality. By then, he hoped Rick would be there to take her home.

Rick, Ayden brooded, his mind unable to forget the expression of excitement and shock when her phone rang this morning. A second before it did and in a momentary lapse of reason, he'd bent his head with every intention of kissing her.

Her scent sweet, her body firm, he ached to hold her against him again, to sample, for a tiny moment, her reserved willingness. Yes, although she'd startled him, he'd recovered enough to reach out and grab her, taking advantage of the situation to pull her underneath him. After a few minutes of internal restraint, he realized she invoked in him an unfamiliar weakness. She also unleashed unfamiliar jealousy, the thought of her with someone else putting a hole in the pit of his stomach. Dammit, he didn't need to see her as anyone but a means to an end.

"So, how long have you and Rick been together?"

From his peripheral vision, he saw her head turn toward the opposite window. He waited patiently as she gathered her thoughts to tell him what he needed to know.

"My favorite color is lavender, my favorite sport is football, my favorite movie is *Beauty and the Beast*, and my favorite—"

"Your favorite movie is a cartoon?"

"Yes. What's wrong with that?"

He honestly didn't know, although he thought it strange. Instead of voicing his thoughts, he kept his mouth shut. Her gaze left his face to blink straight ahead, her arms placed in a defensive pose across her firm breasts.

"I hate shopping," she continued. "I love cold sheets, and I always skim to the end of a book to make sure I know how it ends before committing to reading it."

She let out a rush of breath, as if the task left her exhausted. He supposed she waited for him to bare his own soul, and he struggled on where to start.

"I don't have a favorite color or movie, real-life or otherwise. I detest flavored coffee and artificial sweeteners, and I prefer a warm body lying underneath me over a pair of cold lonely sheets any day."

She clicked her tongue and pivoted again in his direction. He pretended to pay more attention to the road than her surprised reaction. He hadn't meant to incite her. Most women he knew, or at least dated, saw his comment as an opportunity. Grace, he knew, saw it as an insult.

"Cold sheets might be lonely, Mr. McCabe, but *I'd* prefer to lie on them for the right reasons than to have someone warming them for the wrong ones."

At last her words called him out, but he refused to reveal anything about what he did regarding women and why. All Grace needed to know was what lay on the surface of their relationship. Everything else was off limits.

Still, as he steered the truck to the drug store, he tried not to imagine her in the illusionary bed they'd made over the last few minutes. She belonged to someone else, even if she was as confused about the relationship as he was now. After he helped her find Danielle, after she shredded his heart in front of Maggie, she'd leave and never think of him again. The thought put him in an even darker mood.

"May I see the picture and the postcard again?" he asked, attempting to take his mind off his struggles.

As quiet as the sunrise, Grace withdrew the items from her purse and handed them to him. A split second later, she glanced down to check her phone. He had no doubt about the number or message she hoped to see. It riled him, and he shook his head, visible enough for her to notice.

"What?" she asked, her tone soft, her question calm and searching.

He maneuvered the truck into a narrow parking space before professing the truth. "Your goddamn ringtone is about a broken and abusive couple, it being tied to a man who yells at you for not being at his beck and call. Yet, you sit there, pining for him to throw you a line. I don't get it."

She opened her pretty mouth to answer him, but closed it and turned away. He didn't move, believing she had an answer for him. He just needed to wait.

"My friend Betsy snuck the ringtone on my phone. I just keep forgetting to change it."

"So, now that you are…reminded, this might be a good time, don't you think?"

Her little nose flared with indignation. "Why do you care?"

Yes, her boyfriend, ex or otherwise, wasn't Ayden's business, but it didn't stop him from placing his hand out, palm up. "Let me see your phone."

She sat, unmoving, until she realized he wasn't pulling his arm back until he had her device in his hand. She scoffed before mumbling something but gave in without too much more protest.

Her phone was easy to access, too easy, and it only took him a few minutes, to change the song and hand the iPhone back to her. For whatever reason, she didn't bother to investigate which song he'd chosen, preferring to stuff the device back into her pocket and let the conversation go.

Believing he'd been triumphant in at least one

argument for the day, he escorted Grace into the store. With its original planked floor, oak shelving, and potbelly stove in the corner, it seemed torn straight out of an episode of *The Waltons*. As with every year, the couple covered the place in holiday decorations of every nostalgic era. From snow globes to rotating trees, the place was a wonderland of fantastical Christmas indulgence.

"Ayden, my boy."

"Mr. Hawthorne." Ayden stretched out his hand for a gentle, but firm handshake.

The man smiled, his sky-blue eyes twinkling behind a set of thick glasses. In the background, Bing Crosby's "White Christmas" popped and crackled on a vintage turntable. The man pointed with his thumb toward the back. "Wilhelmina has some rum cake wrapped and ready for ya."

"As always, it is much appreciated," Ayden said, grateful for Mrs. Hawthorne's generous amount of rum in her old recipe, especially as of late.

Mr. Hawthorne nodded before glancing at Grace, hesitating to return his gaze to Ayden right away. Ayden knew the word *pretty* hung on the tip of the man's tongue.

"This is Grace Evans. We were hoping you could help us with something." Ayden curled his hand around Grace's side to haul her closer. The sweet smell of her enticed him, and without thinking, he reached up to stroke the nape of her neck.

She stiffened, resisting his daring behavior at first. Then, as if remembering their pact, she relaxed against his hip, her hand lifting to spread against his chest.

Like an electric charge, unexpected and swift, his

heart catapulted into an erratic beat. Afraid she might read too much into his physical reaction, he slid her fingers closer to his ribcage. He hoped it presented a good enough barrier.

He could not, however, place a strong enough wall between them as her hourglass figure stroked against his lower hip. For a distraction, he let her go and pulled the items from his coat pocket, setting it down on the glass counter.

"You're the only place that sells this postcard. It's a long shot, but do you remember the person who purchased this, possibly in the last few weeks?"

Mr. Hawthorne picked up the postcard and angled his head to better decipher what he held in his hand. He then wrinkled his eyes and slanted his head in the other direction. "I don't remember who bought this. Maybe the missus will know. I'll be right back."

This left Ayden alone with Grace, she remaining as quiet as the falling snow. Drawn in by her subtle presence, he turned her toward him.

"If we find Danielle today, we still have a deal, remember?"

Grace's hazel eyes flickered, always brilliant, forever searching. Then she smiled, and his breath caught. He only had a moment to wonder at the unexpected reaction when Wilhelmina shuffled in from the back.

"Ayden, dear." She came around the counter to give him a hug. "How is Maggie?"

"Meddlesome."

The woman giggled and handed him the cellophane-wrapped cake, his mouth already watering to taste a sample. She turned toward the woman standing beside him. "And you must be Grace Evans?" she said, beaming.

The spirited attention caused a peach-colored blush to rise in Grace's cheeks. "Yes." She leaned into him. *God, she felt good.* For more reasons than one, Ayden had not one bit of faith either of them would leave the drugstore with their false relationship unscathed.

"Delightful," Wilhelmina finally said, her gaze jumping from him to Grace like a child in an ice cream shop.

"Ayden asked if we might remember who bought this postcard from us recently," Hawthorne spoke up. "Perhaps your memory is better than mine."

Ayden glanced down at Grace, her gaze intent on the examining couple. Since they'd walked in, she'd barely said a word. Hell, if not for the occasional sigh, he might think she'd stopped breathing again.

Reluctant to take his gaze away from her, he sliced a quick glance at the older woman. She lifted the glasses from around her neck and peered down.

"Is it possible the person in the photo was the one who purchased the postcard from you?" Ayden said, hoping his hunch was right.

Wilhelmina's head agitated with an animated shake. "The person who purchased this postcard wasn't her."

For the first time, Grace stepped forward and said more than two words. "Are you sure?"

Ayden tried to ignore the panic in her voice. He understood the urgency to find Danielle. He just didn't want to think Grace stood too desperate to leave Mistletoe or the plans he'd put in place.

Wilhelmina, oblivious to his concern, beamed

brightly. "I remember that day well. It was a few weeks before Thanksgiving, and I'd just received a box of Christmas postcards I'd ordered. I don't like to put them out too early, you see. Anyway, a young man approached me and asked if he could purchase one."

"A young man," he and Grace said in unison.

Chapter Eight

Wilhelmina Hawthorne nodded. "Yes, peculiar fellow. He was covered from head to toe in winter clothing, the tags still dangling from his plaid toboggan hat and orange puffy vest." The woman paused to chuckle behind her hand. "He was such a sight to see."

"Was he alone?" Grace asked.

"Yes, though someone might have been waiting for him outside. Though, if you ask my opinion, he wasn't from Mistletoe, or Washington, for that matter."

Ayden grasped Grace's shoulders and gently guided her around to face him. "Do you have any idea who it could have been? Who may have been with her?"

"No." Grace's features fell into a somber pose, and he wanted to give her a little hope of what happened to Danielle.

"And he purchased *this* card?" Ayden lifted his gaze back to Wilhelmina, knowing quite well the answer.

The woman nodded once. "This very one. He was adamant about buying the card, although, upon further inspection, the printing company misspelled Washington. See here." She pointed to the word nestled above the infamous picture of the town's annual Christmas lighting ceremonies.

"I allowed him to keep it for free since I planned to

ship the box back and have them re-do the cards."

Grace returned her attention to the Hawthornes. "Could you tell the color of his eyes or…or the length of his hair?"

Wilhelmina dropped back on her heels and inhaled. "I'm sorry. For whatever reason, he didn't want to be recognized."

Grace's shoulders slumped under Ayden's palm.

Ready to leave, he extended his hand to Mr. Hawthorne and nodded a farewell to his wife. "Thank you for your time."

Ayden dropped his hand, finding Grace's small fingers and folding them in his. They were halfway out the door when Wilhelmina yelled, "Wait!" across the store.

Believing she'd suddenly remembered something about the man, he and Grace turned.

"Look. You're standing underneath the mistletoe."

Grace lifted her face to his and then toward the dangling plant. She held her attention there, surprise and then comprehension staining her round cheeks.

"You have to kiss," Mr. Hawthorne said.

Ayden shrugged, unable to hide the fact that he did want to kiss her, and had wanted to ever since he saw her sitting in O'Shannon's. However, he also didn't want to break his own rules of engagement when it came to women. He always waited for them to kiss him first.

Of course, Grace's eyebrows furrowed, her attention pulled from him to the Hawthorne's and back again. The longer she made him wait, the faster the blood rushed through his veins.

After she nibbled on her lip, enticing him more, she

stepped closer and lifted on her tiptoes. At the very moment when her lips would have touched his, her pocket book shook with the tune he changed on her phone.

"Foolish," by Ashanti, blared on its highest volume, sending Grace fumbling to answer it. She also sent him an annoyed expression before shuffling away, attempting to find a place where her voice didn't echo. Unfortunately, or fortunately, depending on the recipient, she chose the least resonant corner, the tall nostalgic Santas doing everything to block his view of her and Rick's conversation or her reaction to what he said. With her back to Ayden, all he could see was her hand gently caressing a majestic snow globe.

In the meantime, the Hawthornes had planted themselves behind the counter, refusing to move or assist Francis Tisdale who'd come in to fill her numerous prescriptions. After three long minutes of waiting, Ayden had had enough. He strode toward Grace, his temper tittering on furious.

"I will. I love you, too," he heard Grace say, forcing him to stop short on his approach. She turned and smiled, innocent and breathtaking. How in the hell did anyone think she was simply pretty?

Spurred into a devil of a mood, Ayden rotated in the direction of the door, irritated he cared so much about who she loved or didn't. He tried to escape, for both their sakes, before Wilhelmina caught them again. Unfortunately, between Grace's forgetfulness and his brooding, they met under the damn mistletoe, again, at the very same time.

"There's no way around it this time." The elderly woman beamed from behind the counter.

****

Grace tried to calm her clamoring heart, wishing she had waited until Ayden left before making her way to the exit. Now, here she stood, staring up at him, his eyebrows narrowed and his lips stretched into a thin line.

"Go on, my boy," Hawthorne cheered. "As pretty as she is, you might lose her to the next fellow who walks in the door."

A muscle jumped in Ayden's jaw before he stepped a whisper closer and cupped her face. She held the air inside her lungs as he brought his lips down to meet hers. A wave of tender heat sent her heart fluttering in all directions.

Now she understood why women broke windows in the middle of the night for him. Undemanding, his mouth shifted, drawing a whimper from deep in her throat. He parted her lips and dipped his tongue inside her mouth, teasing her with soft and unhurried strokes. Dizzy and weak, Grace wanted to melt against him, to forget they were only doing this to satisfy an older couple's nostalgic influence. Then he pulled away, leaving her breathless.

"That was lovely," Wilhelmina said, breaking the fleeting and bewildering moment. Grace shook herself and glanced up at Ayden, neither a smirk nor a smile showing her what he thought of their mistletoe moment. Without at word, he escorted her outside, the frigid air cooling her heated skin and reeling senses.

"Now that that's over with…" Ayden said in a tone that was both casual and unaffected.

The cloud nine Grace had been floating on for the last few moments, suddenly opened up, sending her spiraling back down to earth. Despite sounding impassive to what had just taken place, he yanked at her door and helped her inside before stalking around to join her. As she glanced at his stoic profile, he jerked the truck in gear with short, aggressive movements. She wondered if his stormy mood might have to do with them having to kiss so soon.

"Look, I'm sorry we didn't find anything else out about Danielle," he said after a long, brooding moment.

Grace knew he didn't mean what he said. She still needed to convince his sister his heart was vulnerable enough to break. "You know, you could have just told them you don't like public displays of affection," Grace blurted out, still stung by his casual reaction to their first kiss. Not that she expected him to drop to his knees and declare some sort of unbridled passion for her. *Damn*. A half-cocked grin of approval would have sufficed.

"You know, I hate to be the one to break this to you Grace, but I have no problem with public displays of affection, and just about everyone in Mistletoe knows it."

Grace had to clench her teeth to keep her jaw from dropping open. He had no sense of subtleness when it came to reminding her how many girlfriends he had and what he'd done with them. She tried to think of something to say, but he beat her to it.

"Which brings me to this point, I think we need to spend some time…kissing, before we show up at Maggie's and start fumbling for each other's lips like a couple of thirteen-year-olds."

"Well," she said, trying to keep up with him. "I've never fumbled for anyone's lips, ever, and we already *did* kiss!"

"That"—he lifted his index finger into the air to make his point—"was not a kiss."

She sat blinking at him and then glancing around, wondering if she should take his comment as an insult. "Then, what would you call it?"

He didn't answer her, choosing to swing the truck into a horseshoe parkway between town and Hearth's Gate. The majestic view of the snow-covered mountains against the now-azure sky astounded her. So did the seriousness in his gaze when she finally twisted around to confront him.

"What…are we doing?" She pinned her back to the passenger side door.

"I'm going to give you a lesson."

She gawked at him, managing to squeak out an eventual reply. "A lesson in what?"

A cunning grin touched his lips, the same grin she knew turned women's knees to liquid. She glanced away for a moment, trying to soothe the revving of her pulse and the sting of the insult. She never thought herself as a bad kisser, and it was mortifying to believe he'd reached that conclusion after only one short, though significant incident between them.

Still trying to pluck the stinger out of her pride, she lobbed an insult back at him. "Well, if I could use some lessons on kissing, then you could use some lessons on manners."

"Manners? To whom are you comparing me? Rick?"

Grace drew back, astonished and speechless. If she thought it at all possible, she might believe Ayden McCabe was jealous. Then, it hit her like an avalanche.

She'd left him under the mistletoe after her phone rang and then ended the call with the most endearing words in the English language. *I love you*.

"Just so you know, I was talking to—"

"I know exactly who you were talking to, Grace, and like you've said, it really isn't any of my business. However, for the sake of our agreement, I do need you to stay in character. You're not supposed to break my heart until *after* you've made some effort to claim it."

As the truck idled, they battled with Grace reaching back for some much-needed ammunition. "I understand full well the extent of my agreement, and by the time this debacle is over, you will get exactly what you deserve."

He drew a few inches from her mouth. "In that case, be careful of where you stand in this town, Miss Evans. A phone call might not be able to save you next time."

He lowered his gaze to her lips, the gesture stealing a heartbeat and raising the heat inside the cabin to sweltering. All of a sudden, she remembered the ring tone he'd changed for Rick's incoming call.

" 'Foolish'? Really?"

He shrugged, and she understood exactly why Rachel had smacked him yesterday. Ayden McCabe loved women. He also loved to keep them at an arm's distance, probably to keep their slaps from causing too much damage to his face. Regarding Grace, however, he only cared about the appearance of a devoted girlfriend.

At least, for her sake, he'd laid out the rules early and honestly. He'd not only opened the book for her, but flipped all the way to the last page so there would be no question on how he wanted it to end. She should feel grateful. Right?

While the radio whispered "Silent Night," Grace wanted to reconcile about the mistletoe, an enviable consequence if there ever was one. "Maybe you're right," she conceded on a huff. "If we're going to get through this, I guess it wouldn't hurt…getting to know one another, or parts of each other."

"Good," he said, so matter-of-factly she wondered if they'd just agreed to exchange recipes.

After a few motionless moments, with her still on the passenger side and him still on the driver's side, she realized he meant for her to make the first move. She might have been more inclined if he hadn't put in her head that she wasn't any good at kissing. Still, she leaned forward, and then stopped. *No, this is his idea to school her on the art of physical contact. She would sit and wait for him to come to her.* Only, he didn't.

After several moments of staring, he grunted and shook his head. "I can't even begin to imagine what's going on in that *pretty* head of yours."

She drew back, firing a response in his direction. "And I can't even begin to imagine how we're going to convince anyone we're in love."

She twisted back, closed her eyes, and let her head fall against the headrest. She believed if they didn't find some sort of common ground soon, he'd replace her with one of his twenty-six or so ex-girlfriends, and she'd have to leave Mistletoe without Danielle. One of those alternatives upset her more than the other did.

"Grace, for this all to work out, you'll have to relax."

His deep and instructive voice made her flip her

eyelids open. She angled her head and narrowed her gaze in his direction. "Is there anything else I'm doing wrong, Sensei?"

He chuckled, lifting his hand to rub at the stubble along his strong jaw line. Unable to stand being inside the cab with him any longer, Grace opened the door, stepped out, and slammed it shut. Emotionally exhausted, she pressed her back against the door and brought in a cold, wavering breath.

Yes, she was mad at Ayden. She was, however, more angry with herself. In the last twenty-four hours, she'd spent more time thinking of a man who only wanted a fake relationship with her than a man who might, someday, want a real relationship with her.

"So this is what happens when you move forward?" she mumbled to herself.

"What happens?"

She jerked her head up to find Ayden beside her. So engrossed in her own pathetic musings, she hadn't heard or noticed his approach.

"I came out here to sulk, so I'd appreciate a little privacy." She sent him an exaggerated smile. She then shivered, her noticeable discomfort prompting him to shift in front of her. His wondrous form blocked out the frigid wind and some of the trickling snowflakes.

"I believe I forgot to tell you, there's no sulking in Mistletoe, especially…outside…this time of year."

Grace clicked her tongue and dropped her forehead toward Ayden's chest. Despite their argument in the truck or how she felt about their situation, she longed to have someone to lean against, if only for a couple of days.

A few silent moments later, his arms wrapped

around her back, drawing her deeper into his sturdy embrace. Against her ear, his heart thumbed fast and strong. She wanted to believe she'd caused this physical reaction, but how could she when she'd been reminded, on many occasions, she wasn't even his type.

"Okay." She sighed, pulling back and making the mistake of glancing up into his cerulean blue eyes. In a matter of three loud heartbeats, heat spread from her toes to her face. The frosty breath she released made her reaction to him so noticeable

She relented to twisting toward the cab when he lifted his hand to her cheek and titled her lips up to meet his. Her stomach flipped, her pulse sputtered, and a car horn blaring behind her rattled the moment like a 3.5 earthquake.

"What the—"

Chapter Nine

They turned to see Neil waving from the driver's side of his 2011 Dodge Ram, his eyes frantic and his face a shade of a red summer rose. "Sarah's in the hospital, they say she's five centimeters," he yelled while powering down his window.

Ayden held up a hand. "Go. We'll meet you there."

"No." Neil panted as if he was the one having the baby. "Go get Maggie's tree, and I'll call when you can visit." The man rendered a stiff salute and sped away, fishtailing to the right side of the road.

"I hope everything's okay," Grace said, feeling a little foolish.

Ayden nodded. "Sarah's thirty-seven weeks, so I think everything is fine. As for the parents, now that's another matter." He sent her a wink, seeming to forget he was about to kiss her and she was about to let him.

Inside the cab, she huddled close to the heater as Ayden maneuvered his truck back onto the road. "So, does this mean we're on tree duty?"

He nodded in her direction. "How are you with an axe?"

Grace squirmed under the thought of such an unfamiliar endeavor. "They do make fake trees, you know?"

He sliced a disapproving glance before committing to driving up a winding road, the truck moving closer to the clouds than before. Grace forced her mind and body to relax, allowing the careful bounce over uneven terrain to dissolve any anxiousness she felt toward Ayden or their situation.

Around a quick bend in the road, a sign indicated the place as a designated Christmas Tree National Forest. On each side of them, snow-covered firs lined the narrow lane, the path getting smaller and denser the further they traveled. He finally halted the truck inside an empty three-space-deep parking lot.

"Just to make one thing clear." His features softened. "I was only kidding about the axe. I don't expect you to help me with this. You're welcome to stay in the truck if you'd like."

She drew back, insulted that he assumed her too fragile to help chop down a measly old tree. "Lead the way," she said, the sky darker than before with a coating of gray and snow beginning to fall fast and thick on the windshield.

He laughed before shaking his head and leaping from his side to stride around to hers. "Here." He reached behind her seat to pull out a navy blue crocheted toboggan cap, matching scarf, and mittens. With expert care, he placed the cap on her head and the scarf around her shoulders, leaning in so close, her lips almost touched his neck.

God, he smelled so clean and deliciously masculine. She held the air inside her lungs to keep from breathing on him. Leave it to a man to create a relationship born of physical needs as opposed to emotional ones.

As she wiggled her fingers through the cozy mittens, he leaned over to grab an axe from the back before leading them on their journey.

"Are these Maggie's, too?" she said, stretching out her arms.

"No, my nephew's."

"Oh. How old is he?"

"Four," Ayden answered without faltering.

Grace dropped her chin to glance down at her gloved hands. Rick always complained about them being too small.

"How can you bake anything with those things?" he'd tease her without smiling. She wondered why she'd stayed with him for so long. *Fear?* No. Familiarity. Why did she ever have to plan anything, be afraid of anything, when she knew what was going to happen one day, one year from now.

"Grace, are you all right?"

Ayden's concerned tone shook her from her self-conscious thoughts. "Yes, of course." She moved to stuff her fisted hands in her coat pockets when Ayden caught one to wrap in his, guiding her toward the tree forest. They tramped through the snow, she admiring the beauty of her surroundings and the reprieve from their earlier conversation. She inhaled deep, crisp mountain air and the fragrance of sappy fir filling her senses and some far removed memory.

So mesmerized by what lay ahead, she'd not paid one bit of attention to where she was going, until her feet refused to budge under a mound of clumpy brown snow. Ayden stretched out his arm, until he realized she'd haltered. He glanced back and then down to her shoes.

"I think…I'm stuck."

She glanced up in time to find his fist pressed over

his lips, a futile effort to keep from laughing.

"I'm so glad you find this amusing, McCabe."

He cleared his throat and lifted his hands, palm out. "Stay put."

"That's not even remotely funny."

He showed her a crooked smile and then handed her the axe. She waited with her back to him, missing his comforting presence in the lagging moments. She hummed a tune, finding "Foolish" stuck in her brain, before the sound of Ayden's easy footfalls sounded behind her. She shivered when he drew a few inches away, dropping a pair of small mountain boots at her feet.

"Are you ready?"

"Ready for what?" He wasn't thinking of lifting her out of her buried, second-hand, half-price ankle boots into the perfect pair of tan Timberlands, was he?

His strong arms wrapped around her midsection, causing her heart to catapult hard against her chest. "I really don't think this is a good idea." She wanted her voice to sound steady, unaffected. It came out as a high-pitched squeak.

"And I think you think too much," he said against her left ear. If he meant to shut her up for a few seconds, it worked. Too stunned to contemplate a clever comeback, he lifted her with ease, his own heart beating hard and fast against her shoulder blade.

Without a fight, she allowed him to ease her damp feet into the cold, but dry footwear. Then he let go, and she missed his strength and the spicy, clean scent of him.

"How do they fit?" he asked, stepping back.

"Fine, just don't tell me these are a pair your

nephew left in the truck."

"They're not."

"Good."

"They're actually a pair he grew out of last year."

He smirked and clasped her hand again, procuring the axe and swinging it onto his opposite shoulder. He didn't exactly resemble Paul Bunyan, although his woodsy attire did remind her of the looming character.

They traveled a little further before he stopped, let go of her hand, and presented her with the tree he planned to chop down. "What do you think?"

It stood seven feet tall with soft blue-green needles and a silvery mist to their fat and bushy branches. In all her life, she thought she'd never seen a more perfect Christmas tree. "Beautiful." She leaned in, inhaling the holiday fragrance she'd been deprived of for so long.

"Yes."

She thought he was speaking of the tree until she glanced in his direction and found his magnificent gaze steady upon her face.

Unused to such compliments or attention, she ducked her head to keep the modest blush hidden. Not the least bit cold now, except for her nose, which she guessed was as red as her cheeks, she stepped back to give him room. "Where should I stand?"

She waited for him to point, designating a spot to his left. She clomped backward and watched him handle the ancient tool with precision and skill.

He began to chop, his face focused and magnificent. She kept her gaze there until a glimmer in the tree caught her attention.

"Is that...wait! Stop!" she yelled and rushed forward.

"Grace, no!"

Ayden's panic-filled voice was lost with the splintering sound of wood echoing in Grace's ear. She glanced up to find the chubby branches hurtling forward, grasping at her like a seizing relative. She tried to retreat, but her feet, so unaccustomed to the boots, refused to move fast enough. The heavy fir, in all its grandness, toppled over her, shoving her deep into the snow.

She lay in a daze, the place above her right eyebrow stinging, her nose numb, and her pride severed. The reality of her foolishness settled upon her like an avalanche, and she dreaded the instant of settling her gaze upon Ayden's patronizing features. To avoid the moment, she squeezed her eyes shut until the heaviness lifted and muted daylight showed through her eyelids.

"Grace," he said in a low and concerned voice close to her left ear. His hot breath fanned across her frozen face and thawed her lips.

"If you're going to ask if that was the dumbest thing I've ever done, rest assured, it was not," she confided.

Caressing fingers brushed melting snow from her forehead, forcing her eyelids open.

He loomed above her, his eyebrows furrowed with worry, not condescension. "Dumb, no. Slow, yes." The corners of his mouth lifted before sending her an irresistible wink. God, he was magnificent. "If you're going to live up here, you need faster reflexes."

She didn't let the *live up here* slip from her mind without storing it in her consciousness. Still flat on her back, snow falling onto her lashes and seeping into her pants, she tried hauling herself up. Only, her ankles bent under her awkward footing, sending her grappling for the closest object, Ayden McCabe.

They both fell, his body, harder and less pliable than a seven-foot tree. The wind knocked out of her, she lay wrestling for a breath, the air thinner here than in California.

They remained in frozen astonishment, both staring into each other's eyes, neither having the fortitude to take advantage of the situation. The moment could have played out just like one of those romantic Christmas movies on Lifetime. Only it didn't. He didn't kiss her, she didn't kiss him, and the magic moment slipped away.

"I think we'd better get going." He pushed himself up, shook the snow from his coat, and presented her a helping hand. She wanted to smack it away, hurt by his aloofness. So what if her heart skipped a beat whenever he stood within a few feet of her? So what if she wanted to kiss him so bad, she couldn't think straight?

However, she reconciled with the strangeness of their situation and allowed him to help her stand. The adrenaline and warmth of his nearness gone, she began to shiver, a visible tremor causing him to glance down with piercing eyes.

"Are you all right?"

I'm fffffine," she said, her body trembling more.

He canted his head, and she understood when not to challenge him with another transparent lie.

"Do you think you can get back to the truck by yourself?" he asked, offering her the keys.

"Of course," she said, with more confidence than she felt.

"Good. As soon as you get there, turn the heater on and stay warm. I'll be right behind you." She nodded and turned, retracing their steps until they disappeared under the heavy falling snow. Several times, she stopped, backtracked, and started forward again. It wasn't long before she recognized nothing—not even the tips of the mountaintops.

"Ayden?" she called, her voice hoarse with alarm.

Despite the shivering, she was sweating, her heart reaching a crescendo of beats with each trudging step she placed upon the layer of new snow. "Don't panic," she whispered, moving forward, changing course and slogging back the way she came. She walked five more minutes before she saw the top of Ayden's truck.

She let out a cry of relief, half-tumbling, half-sliding down the small embankment to the all but empty parking lot. Numb and frozen, she fumbled for the keys and opened her door, slipping onto the cold, hard seat.

With her fingers and toes stinging from both her falls, she tore off her gloves and shoes and stretched to switch on the ignition. She huddled near the heater; however, no matter how near or how long she stayed in the position, the warmth never seemed to touch her.

"Th-think about San Fr-francisco," she mumbled to herself. However, some of her memories there were just as cold as she felt. Then her mind switched to Ayden. All she needed to do was remember that single kiss under the mistletoe, and her insides melted. If only the memory could thaw out the rest of her chilled body.

She blew out a wavering, unsteady exhale. This day had turned out nothing like she wanted or even expected. Having an impromptu boyfriend meant snowball fights and ice skating lessons where some sort of mutual affection formed over the course of a few days. Doomed to keep reading the same book with the same unhappy ending, Grace bent her head and cursed her sister.

If Danielle hadn't run away, Grace would be home, stuck but safe, and unwilling to move one way or the other. As long as she stayed in Mistletoe she saw possibilities, even if they were part of a man's plan to stay single the rest of his life. She sniffed, starting to feel sorry for herself when the truck shook, and a few moments later, Ayden joined her inside.

He glanced her way, doing a double take in her direction. "You don't look well."

"I'm fffffine."

"Yes, you've said that. Did you do what I told you to do?"

She nodded, "But I sort of gggot lost."

"Dammit!" he cursed.

His anger didn't make Grace feel any better.

"I should have made you stay in the truck."

She pressed her reddened fingers to the vents and tried to ignore the way he was staring at her. After a few relatively quiet moments, he shifted toward her, giving a command that almost made her faint.

"Take off your pants."

Chapter Ten

Grace's head jerked in Ayden's direction, the sudden action making her dizzy. "What?"

She blinked, afraid to move. Less than a foot away, he shrugged out of his coat and then scooted to her side to help her out of hers. His features stern and concentrated, she didn't realize what he was doing until his fingers fell to her midsection, grasping for the button of her khakis.

"Ayden, no!" She stretched out her arm, her hand pressed firm against the thin fabric of his T-shirt and the rapid beating of his heart.

"Dammit, Grace," he growled and reached behind her, producing a thick maroon and gray fleece blanket. "You're going into hypothermia." He threw the blanket over her before giving her a stern warning. "If you're not out of those pants in three seconds, I will be more than happy to remove them for you."

When she didn't budge right away, he exhaled and said the one word that sent her scrambling to get undressed. "Two."

Her arms trembled, making it much harder to slide from her wet clothes. She tried to argue with herself that he was wrong and she was just cold. "I'm not…getting…hypothermia," she said aloud, her teeth chattering and proving him right.

"Lie down."

She shook her head, and he wasted no time grasping her hips to pull her underneath him. In a blink, he had his coat tucked under her head and his body pressing her back into the leather seat.

"Th-th…this only wo-works in the mo-mo-movies." She stared into his fierce and worrisome features.

He brushed a piece of hair from her eyes and caressed her forehead with his fingertips. "You don't like it when someone takes care of you, do you?"

She turned away, his palm gently bringing her face back to his. She cleared her throat and lifted her chin higher. "I'm just not used to it," she said when she thought she could talk without stammering her words.

With his body longer than the cab, she realized he wasn't entirely nude and neither was she. He had lifted his T-shirt so his hard chest lay flush with hers, her black lace bra still fastened around her breasts.

She craved his warmth, shifting to adjust herself under him to accept more of what he had to offer. The woodsy and spicy scent of his skin comforted her mind, so much so she felt herself drifting in and out consciousness.

"Grace, no. I need you to stay awake, okay?"

"A little nap…I promise."

She floated toward the awaiting darkness, content to let the obscurity envelop her when she felt the crush of Ayden's mouth on hers, jarring her back awake. Welcoming and wondrous heat spread from her face to her stomach. Unlike the mistletoe moment, Ayden's kiss was full of urgency and promise. His lips, unyielding and delicious, teased hers further apart. She let go a whimper and then a soft gasp when he clutched at her hips, bringing her up to meet him.

No longer drowsy, she dug her fingers into the corded muscles of his flexed arms. Her blood now rushed through her veins like a thawing mountain river. With her heart booming against her breast, she glided her tongue along the seam of his mouth, drawing from him a deep groan and a hasty retreat.

"I…had to do that," he said, his voice husky and low.

"Do…what?"

He struggled on an answer until she realized he'd kissed her just to keep her from falling asleep. Embarrassed that she'd thought there was something more, she shoved at his chest, but her arms only shook the harder she pushed. With a frustrated grunt, he clasped her wrists, holding them so her palm pressed flat against his heated skin.

"Stop wasting your energy," he said.

She stared into his stern features. Since the falling snow had covered the windshield, it obscured the light inside the cab, turning his eyes an indigo blue.

"Have you ever had to do this before?" she asked.

He smiled down at her. "At least once."

The obvious questions sat on the tip of her tongue. With whom? Was he dating her? Did the situation turn into more than him administering mouth-to-mouth? The longer she continued to ask the silent questions, the wider his smile grew. She had no doubt, with his various superpowers, he had the ability to read her mind.

Of course, he didn't volunteer any information, and Grace didn't dare make any more mental inquiries. Instead, she quieted herself to the moment.

After a great deal of time had passed, Ayden cleared his throat and spoke in a deep and restrained tone. "I should get you back to the house."

He lifted above her, his gaze falling over her breasts and then quickly away. Her head hurt too much to interpret his sudden withdrawal, so she observed, instead, him jerking his shirt back on and trying to avoid glancing over to her again. Perhaps she *did* affect him more than he wanted her to know.

"Leave your clothes on the floor and the blanket around you." Ayden switched on the windshield wipers, his gaze shifting everywhere but to her.

Too exhausted to argue, she wrapped the polar fleece tighter around her bare skin. "I'm sorry," she said to break the quiet and initiate a conversation. Of course, she wasn't sorry, nor did she want to feel guilty about any of this. Not for trying to save a bird's nest, or getting lost, or forcing Ayden McCabe to tear off his shirt so he could lay on top of her and kiss her back to recovery. "I mean—"

"I should never have let you go back to the truck by yourself."

Before she could shake her head or say anything to make him feel less responsible, he changed the subject. "You're going to be sore for a while," he said above the squeak of the windshield wipers.

If she didn't feel so miserable, emotionally and physically, she might have harrumphed at his words. She believed one of the benefits of pretending to be his girlfriend was to fast-forward them through this awkward stage of pre-dating. She supposed if she were taller and blonder, Ayden McCabe would have no problem taking advantage of the situation and making her sore for an entirely different reason.

"Are you all right?" he asked after a long moment of awkward silence.

"No." She closed her eyes and tried to clear her mind of everything except the hum of the engine and the click of the dog tags on the rearview mirror. Afraid to fall asleep, however, she allowed herself to reminisce over the last fifteen minutes. It wasn't hard. Every time she inhaled, she smelled Ayden's heady, masculine scent. She still tasted him, still felt the pressure of his lips on hers. She imagined him kissing her, without the need to do so and without the unemotional pact between them.

What seemed like a second later, the jolting underneath her changed, and a familiar coldness whipped across her chapped face. She fluttered her eyelids open to find Ayden beside her on the passenger side. He bent down as if to scoop her into his arms when she pushed him away.

"I think I can manage," she snapped, unable to imagine him carrying her up a flight of stairs like a helpless child.

"Don't fight me on this, Evans," he said, lifting her up with little effort. Too tired to struggle, she let him carry her all the way to the room she'd occupied the last part of the previous night. It lay as she left it, cloaked in partial darkness, a single ray of daylight seeping in through a set of velvety blue curtains. He sat her on the bed, before stepping to an antique mahogany dresser. Under hooded lashes, she watched his rugged and disheveled form, her body so much more aware of him since they'd spent a few intense half-naked moments together.

When he returned to the bed, he sank down beside her and placed a pair of men's blue and green flannel pajamas next to her. "They might not fit, but they're a lot warmer than what you brought with you."

She thought about arguing, but the words stuck somewhere between her mind and windpipe. She didn't like being this dependent on anyone, or rather, she wasn't used to being this dependent on anyone. Since her father's abrupt departure from her life, she'd taken care of her mother and sister, diving into the role without question or resentment.

When Ayden left her, she shrugged into the heavy fabric and then laid her head on his cologne-scented pillow, wondering how any woman would ever let him go. Then again, she wondered how many hearts he'd shattered trying to break free. The answers continued to wreak havoc on her *emotional* state of being. She didn't have time to conjure up any more unsettling questions before he returned.

"I made you some chamomile tea." He set down the steaming mug and took a seat close to her hip. In his hand, he held a small first aid kit.

"Are you hurt?" she asked.

He reached up, and she drew back, sucking the air between her teeth as his fingertip grazed a tender spot above her left eye.

"You're the one who tried to fight a seven-foot tree," he teased.

"I was trying to save a bird's nest."

He nodded. "I know." When he lifted his hand to clean the cut, she tried not to flinch. After all, how many scrapes had she cleaned of Danielle's when their mother confined herself to her room for a full year after their father left?

"You should heal in no time," Ayden said, his warm breath skimming across her chafed cheeks. Despite the dangers, she relished the intimate moment, he taking his time to place a small butterfly bandage over her eyebrow.

"Are you warm enough?" he asked in a low and husky tone.

She smiled. "I'm okay."

He blinked his dark lashes, his gaze narrowing, as if waiting for her to add something more to the conversation.

"Thanks…for…you know, keeping me…alive…in the truck," she said, unsure of what to even call what he'd done for her.

He sent her a lazy wink, and she glanced away. It was getting harder and harder to pretend she didn't feel some attraction to him. Forget the forbidden emotional part of their relationship; the physical aspects consisted of two kisses, one of them under some mistletoe with an elderly couple cheering them with romantic enthusiasm.

"Well," she said, lifting herself. "This has been an adventure, but we've lost time trying to find Danielle." She pushed the blankets away and shifted her feet toward the floor.

He shook his head, bending down to urge her legs back onto the mattress and to throw the covers back over her. "Not today."

"But—"

"Grace, I have two of the most…meddlesome, yet intelligent, men I know looking for Danielle. You need to rest."

"But—"

"Say *but* one more time."

She opened her mouth and then slammed it shut when he lifted his fingers to unbutton his shirt. When he dropped his hand back to his side, she tried not to appear too disappointed.

"You need to rest, and since you're too stubborn to listen, I'm going to make sure you do exactly what I say." His mouth lifted into a crooked grin as he unlaced his boots and pushed them off next to the nightstand.

"What…what are you doing?" She knew exactly what he was doing, she just couldn't believe it.

Although she thought about protesting, she didn't have the energy or the inclination to deny him. She did, however, have to put up some sort of fight, even if it was a verbal one. "I'm not sure about all the other women you've bedded, Mr. McCabe; however, I'm positive none of them did much *resting* with you next to them."

This time, he laughed, sliding into bed and reaching over to cocoon her in a muscular embrace, her back pressed firmly to his chest and torso.

"For one, you read too many historical novels, and two, I don't *bed* women, I make love to them."

Heat spread like wildfire from her toes to ears. "God, how did I know you were going to say that," she mumbled, her insides tumbling over the thought of him making love…to her.

After a few moments wrapped inside his arms, and reliving their kisses once again, he gave her another command. "Grace, you need to relax."

"Relax," she said, mocking him. "Right."

He chuckled and pulled the hair from her neck, his

steady breath soothing on her nape and earlobe.

"I'm not usually this helpless, you know," she said, her gaze focused on the wall and the shadows growing larger and closer to the bed.

"I think you're too hard on yourself. It's okay to be dependent on someone once in a while."

Funny, Grace thought. Her friend Betsy said that to her at least once a week. With a bachelor's degree in psychology from Seattle University, Betsy counseled Grace, without charge, on her pathetic relationship with Rick and her impractical responsibility for her sister and mother.

"You need to break away, find a real man, and live your own damn life," Betsy would say and then make up insane scenarios on how to go about doing it. Grace's favorite scheme, so far, was Betsy signing her up for a mail-order bride advertisement from some ranch in Montana. Not that Grace had anything against cowboys, she just couldn't imagine marrying someone she barely knew.

Then again, as she lay in Ayden's arms, Grace wondered if time had anything to do with how well a couple knew one another. Regarding Ayden—in less than twenty-four hours, she knew how he liked his coffee and his women.

Chapter Eleven

Ayden brought Grace closer, cursing himself for being so careless as to expose her to the elements when she'd never lived in such extreme conditions before. So caught up in her presence, he wanted her with him today for selfish reasons. He'd lost his focus, and Grace ended up hurt because of it. He'd be wise, for both their sakes, not to forget why she was here and why he was helping her.

Regardless, he continued to hold her until she relaxed, until her tense figure melted into him. He thought she was asleep when she sighed and brought her hand up to caress his arm.

"Ayden?"

He braced himself for the onslaught of questions about his life and the moment where she'd expect something more than a physical agreement between them.

"Yes, Grace?"

"Thanks."

A few quiet inhales later, he realized this was all she'd meant to say. Still, he lay next to her, waiting for her to push closer into him, to give him the female sign that she was ready, physically. After a while, however, he realized she was asleep.

Disappointed, he adjusted her lithe form, turning to kiss her bruised temple and brush back a strand of her mahogany-colored hair. God help him, he liked her, attracted to her quiet strength and subtle beauty, so much so he looked forward to taking advantage of every intimate moment together.

For now, and with the day almost gone, he slipped out of bed and sauntered into the kitchen, still smelling her sweet scent on him. He smiled, stepping to the refrigerator to pull out some chicken to prepare his mother's famous Irish chicken and dumplings stew.

He enjoyed cooking, and he liked the idea of sharing some of his mother's recipes with Grace. Though, for her sake, he added a little bit more garlic and broth. With the meal almost ready, he sat and checked his phone, finding a text message buried between unsubtle offers to the Christmas Eve *Eve* Dance.

It's a boy, seven pounds, nine ounces, red hair, ten toes.

Ayden glanced at the scrunched babe held up by his excited father. Funny how Neil appeared to have aged ten years since the last time Ayden saw him. Unwilling to stare too long into the portrait of fatherhood, Ayden sent his friend a quick congratulatory reply and then deleted the random messages from girlfriends past. The very last message came from his sister. *Dinner postponed. Kids sick. Will try for later this week.*

Relieved not to have to explain what happened to Grace, Ayden responded right away with *OK*. The next hour he spent making phone calls and putting his second-in-command in charge of running his company while he stayed with Grace. He also placed her phone next to his in case someone decided to call her. Of all the people he thought might try, he dreaded Danielle's call the most. Then, Grace's phone rang with a normal tone, and he glanced down to find the name *Mom* over the picture of an older woman with similar features to Grace.

He weighed his options of accepting the call before he grabbed the device and swiped across the screen.

"Hello?"

"Grace?"

Ayden cleared his throat. "No, ma'am. I'm a...friend of hers in Mistletoe. My name is Ayden McCabe, and I'm helping your daughter find Danielle."

"Oh, thank God," the woman said, half laughing, half crying. "She did mention you when I talked to her earlier. Is she available to talk?"

"Uh, she's actually...sleeping right now." Ayden closed his eyes for a brief moment, wishing he'd thought of something a little more covert to say. He'd learned mothers could be even more matrimonial-minded than their daughters.

"But she's okay? I've been so worried about her. I don't think she's been on her own for this long before."

Ayden nodded. "She's in good hands. I promise."

"Thank you. Please tell her to call me when she wakes up."

"I will."

He ended the call and had no sooner placed the device on the counter before the phone blared a familiar tune. "Foolish."

Ayden didn't even hesitate to answer this one. "Hello."

"Grace?"

"No. She's sleeping, but if you'd like to leave a

message—"

The phone went dead, and Ayden smirked, not feeling the least bit guilty. Oh, he had no doubt Rick would tell Grace, and then Ayden would have to explain why he did what he did. Until then, he'd convince himself it was because he and Grace had an agreement. She was his girlfriend and no one else's.

Unwilling to reminisce and think too much more on the matter, he occupied his mind and time answering emails regarding the business and crunching numbers for the upcoming town bid. He also doubled back with Fitz, but the man had more questions than answers and nothing new to report since the last time they talked. Ayden tried not to smile at the little information he received.

At around seven in the evening, he made himself some coffee and lounged against the island, his mind reliving the panic he felt after the Christmas tree had swallowed Grace whole. He also recalled, with thundering clarity, the blood rushing through his veins as they landed on the snow together. She lay underneath him, stone still, her ingenuous gaze shaking him to the depths of his closed soul.

Now he stood trying to shake the emotional rippling of what she stirred inside him. Even in her weakest moment, as she lay beside him, he'd grappled between gentleman and jerk. However, from experience, he knew if he showed one too much over the other, she'd get the wrong idea and start making plans about their future.

He swiped a frustrating hand down his face and over his stubbled jaw, seeking to remind himself to keep things as he intended: physical. Although, he had to admit, he was more cautious than usual regarding this aspect of their relationship, as well. Something about Grace made him hesitate, and it wasn't about her not being his type. Yet the longer she slept, the more he remembered the sweet taste of her tongue and the exquisite scent of her skin. Unfortunately, he had plenty of time to reminisce over her attributes the rest of the night and most of the next day. During her hibernation, he slipped into her room every few hours to check her body temperature and pull the blankets back round her arms.

Now, despite the danger of thinking so, he missed her company and their conversations. As he reheated the chicken and dumplings, he heard her soft footsteps enter the kitchen behind him.

"What smells so wonderful?"

Ayden twisted to find Grace barefoot and wearing the enormous clothes he'd given her. With her dark hair pulled into a haphazard ponytail, he thought she was the most attractive woman he'd ever seen.

"You should have stayed in bed."

"The sheets were too cold," she said and then clicked her tongue.

He knew an excellent opportunity when he heard one. "I thought you liked cold sheets."

She swiped a long bang from her eyelashes and smashed her lips together. With his attention diverted to her mouth, he believed he would be unable to keep her at arm's distance for too much longer.

"A wise man," she said, her words cautious, "or rather a cocky man, once said, a warm body is preferable to a pair of cold sheets any day. After the Christmas tree fiasco, I'll have to agree with him."

He exhaled, imagining himself on top of her again, this time, bringing her temperature up to unleash the fire he saw in her eyes whenever she gazed at him. However, he needed, he wanted her to come to him. No matter what he imagined, he'd found it was better to stir a woman's passions as opposed to lighting them.

"And whose warm body did you have in mind, Miss Evans?" He raised his gaze without lifting his head.

"Wow."

He chuckled. "What?"

She opened her mouth, closed it, and opened it again. "Is that how you get women to fall in bed with you: suggestive words and flirtatious overtures?"

He sent her a wide grin. "No. Fortunately, there isn't much conversation at all."

A peach blush lit up her face, and he thought the color suited her very well. Her lips agape, he reached up and tapped her chin with the end of his fingertips. When she'd taken a seat at the counter and recovered from what he'd said, he stepped back and waited for her response.

She struggled at first, but he knew never to underestimate her ability to keep up with him.

"In that case, Mr. McCabe, if there isn't much dialog, I can't imagine how you'd know you were doing everything right."

The gluttonous grin she presented him prompted him to walk around and stand behind her, all too eager to demonstrate exactly what he meant. He realized she'd had enough rest to bear some instruction on what he *did* know.

****

From the seductive and amused look on Ayden's face, Grace knew when she'd roused a sleeping panther. Too late to take back what she'd asked, she sat there, owning her words and then contemplating having to eat them. Still, anxious to know what Ayden had in store for her, she kept her head forward. Her heart sputtered with excitement and restlessness as he stepped behind her and pulled the hair away from her neck. Then he braced his arms on each side of her, sheltering her in an encompassing embrace.

"You really don't have to prove—"

"Shhh." It was all he said. With skilled slowness, his hot breath fanned across her nape, the torturous but exhilarating contact sending goose bumps dancing all over her body. She closed her eyes and tried to relax, reveling in the feel of his soft lips skimming soundlessly against her bare skin. Where he touched her, she tingled. In control, he slid his mouth to the sensitive flesh below her ear. An ache of innate pleasure began to build at her waist, spreading deep and untamed.

When her arms dropped to her lap, he seized them and brought them up with his, placing his palms flat on top of hers on the granite countertop. He made her dizzy, drugged her senses, and caused a sensual twinge to grow stronger with each careful caress of his lips.

She began to lose herself to the moment when he swung her around to face him. Grace's lids flew open, to find his blue eyes glinting like dark blue obsidian.

With their noses almost touching, he asked in a soft and husky tone, "Did I do everything right, Miss Evans?"

The answer stuck in her throat as he pushed back

and stepped around to the other side of the island, leaving her forward. She waited until she thought of something to say before rotating around to face him. "Does it ever get…tiresome?"

"Does *what* get tiresome?" he said, lifting his coffee cup to his lips, and then pulling it away as if he should wait to take a drink until after she'd answered him.

"Your overconfidence regarding women? Do you think, maybe, the women you seduce are more than a football game, where at the end, win or lose, you move on."

He stuck with the NFL analogy and counteracted with his own toss of the ball. "Believe it or not, Grace, the women I know would much rather be in the game, win or lose, than sitting on the sideline."

Her lips clamped together, and she turned away. She realized when she'd been beat. She also realized she was no different from the other women in his life, wondering, waiting, for that devastating loss down the road.

To change the subject, she supposed, he rotated toward the stove. "I've made some chicken and dumplings. Would you like some?"

She stared at his back, her body still reeling from his arousing demonstration. She thought of saying no…until her stomach growled, loud and obnoxious. Before she could practice the lie of not wanting anything, he scooped the thick stew into a bowl and placed it in front of her.

The hearty smell reminded her of home, but not the home she remembered from her childhood. It was the home she always escaped to when the burdens of everyone's life became too much. And with each bite, she felt closer to the imaginary place she'd built for herself. Finally, when she scraped the bottom of the dark brown bowl and set down the spoon, she glanced up to find Ayden staring at her.

"You should go back to bed," he said, his features pulled into serious lines.

The last thing she wanted was to waste any more time lying down…without Ayden beside her. She blushed at her thoughts and quickly changed the subject. "I've had enough of sleep for one day. I'd really like a bath."

He hesitated to reply, as if waiting for her to volunteer something else to the discussion. When she said nothing, he furrowed his brows and harrumphed. She gave up trying to guess what he was thinking and slid off the barstool to go back upstairs. She'd managed to step halfway into the hall when she remembered Maggie's Christmas tree dinner. Had he decided to leave her alone and go to Maggie's without her? Somehow, Grace felt abandoned. However, as little as she knew of Ayden McCabe, him abandoning anyone didn't fit into his many creeds. Still, she had to know and ambled back into the kitchen, finding him staring out the glass door into the darkening horizon.

"I just realized I slept through Maggie's dinner…I think."

He turned and smiled. "No, Grace. The dinner's been postponed. Maggie wants Neil and Sarah to be able to bring the baby over."

"Oh, that's right. Sarah had the baby."

He nodded and pulled out his phone to show her the picture of Neil and his son. Grace stood and shifted against him, liking his warmth and virile energy. The picture could not have been more beautiful, and she folded her palm over Ayden's knuckle to bring the phone closer.

"Ironic, huh? Thank God that baby took after his mom."

Grace giggled and pressed closer to Ayden, a mistake she didn't anticipate until he withdrew and stepped toward the stove.

"I'll make you some more tea," he said over his right shoulder.

Grace tried not to show her disappointment at Ayden's cold departure from her side. Instead, she tiptoed upstairs and languished in the sweltering tub until she relaxed against the constant tide of emotional thoughts.

At least Ayden didn't pretend to want a committed affiliation with a woman. With him, she knew what to expect: flirtations, maybe a few lessons, and, perhaps, an unemotional night of making love. He'd perfected the art of the corporal relationship and sought to teach her. Only, she didn't know if she was teachable or if she was just tired of dysfunctional relationships without any depth.

"Grace?"

Thrown out of her reflection, she drew up and swept the curtain closed, unsure if she'd even thought to lock the door.

"When you're ready, I put a cup of lemon-ginger tea on the stand beside my…our…your bed. You will have to sleep there until I can get the window fixed."

She wondered if he'd not fixed the window on purpose. Maybe he'd expected for them to already be sharing his…their…her bed.

"Grace?"

"Yes, okay," she answered before he decided to barge in and make sure she hadn't passed out and then have to give her mouth-to-mouth again. She supposed the women in Mistletoe would have invited him into the tub by now.

But you're not his type. That statement echoed in her brain loud and jarring. Petite, not tall; pretty, not gorgeous; needy, not self-reliant. Hell, whose type was she? Rick's? She moaned, afraid to see too far into that answer.

With the water cooling, she sighed and stood, donning another pair of scanty California pajamas she'd packed for the trip. She thought Ayden would have ventured back downstairs. She should have known her assumption was as wrong this time as the last.

Still damp from her haphazard drying, she swung open the door and smacked right into Ayden's hard form. His arms wrapped around her as a gasp tore from her throat.

She stared into his blue eyes, a challenging glint lighting their cerulean depths. Her gaze dropped to his mouth, slightly open and inviting. His delightful breath fanned across her face, caressing her skin and awakening a torrent of unrequited wants.

She lifted her hands, pressing them into the hardness of his chest. Where his heart knocked at a furious pace, hers fluttered and flipped a dozen times, as if she'd been tossed upside down in one of those traveling carnival rides. This was insane. A kiss should not be this complicated. They'd shared two for God's sake. Albeit, under unusual circumstances.

Still, she hesitated as if she clung to the edge of a jagged cliff, the urge to jump nudging her chin upward. Just a whisper from touching her lips to his, in the heat of a semi-normal moment, an irritant tickle started to build inside her nose.

At the last moment, she turned her head away and sneezed, three violent jerks of her already sore body. She groaned and fell against him, squeezing her eyes shut to what she'd almost accomplished. Now, she wanted to crawl back into bed and bury her head in his spicy-scented pillow.

"Grace?"

"Hmm?"

"You might have forgotten you're not wearing much, but I haven't." His deep and hoarse voice resonated against her cheek.

Yes, she was more naked than clothed and smashed against him, her body straining for a closer connection. Through the thin layer of the fabric, she felt him harden and expand against her midsection. If kissing him was going over a cliff, then going any further was jumping out of a C-130 without a parachute.

She supposed she should have pushed away, feigning naive indifference, but no. She just stood there, unable to peel herself from him. To her rescue, his hands lifted, grasping her shoulders to separate them. She made the mistake of glancing into his face. His features showed no amusement, no amount of humility, and the muscle jumping along his jaw line gave her no indication he'd enjoyed the last few minutes at all.

She understood his need to stay in control one hundred percent of the time. Slow and awkward, she fell away, only to hear him curse under his breath and then seize her hand, pulling her hard against him.

Grace's stomach somersaulted as Ayden's hand curved around the back of her head, pulling her lips toward his. Their gazes locked for a moment. In one thunderous heartbeat, his mouth took hers in a wild, ravenous kiss.

With a soft moan of surrender, she lifted up on her tiptoes and wove her fingers through his soft light brown hair. Heat trembled through her body as his tongue parted her lips and began a provocative dance inside her mouth. Every rational thought before this moment dissolved under his silky prowess, his powerful and solid arms wrapping around her back and pulling her into his midsection.

The size of his arousal made her gasp, and she swore she heard a chuckle escape from deep in his throat. Then his kiss slowed and became tender and searching, the penetrating strokes of his velvety tongue teasing her into a knee-buckling surrender. She tasted the sensual sweetness of him, felt the solidity of his chest pressed against her. Every sensation opened to her, the fire of his kiss and the silkiness of his touch. She'd been with men, but none like Ayden, none so capable of sending a lightning surge of passion and need through every cell in her body.

Chapter Twelve

Ayden expected to coax Grace through the intimate exchange; he just didn't expect to be so aroused by it. As her timid fingers trembled at his nape, he rotated her so her back rested against the wall. Despite their difference in heights, she molded to him. He continued to kiss her, to taste her, and stir an invasion that was both demanding and gentle. Lost in the moment, his hands fell to her waist, his fingers sliding under her thin shirt to stroke her tight abdomen. Her skin quivered where he touched her, pulling a low groan from deep in his chest.

When he ventured higher by gliding his palm under her small, firm breasts, she tensed and drew back. For a few loud heartbeats, he stared into her blushing features. He kept his gaze steady on her face, on the gold flecks dancing in her kaleidoscopic green and brown eyes. He inched forward and slanted his mouth close to hers, relishing as her unsteady exhale glanced across his neck. He bent down and teased her with a whispering kiss, a protesting whimper sending a riveting charge up his spine.

He shifted his hand to cup her jaw, angling her head to nibble at the sensitive flesh below her earlobe. The sugary smell of her was exhilarating. He wondered, with his heart hammering against his ribcage, how easy would it be for him to guide her toward his bedroom and spend the rest of the evening making love to her? Then again, how easy would it be for her to forget what they'd agreed upon and then find herself lost in the charade?

Despite what he wanted, what his body wanted, he needed to know she understood that whatever they shared, ended as soon as they found Danielle.

"Grace," he murmured against her lips.

****

Grace lifted her hand to Ayden's chest, her pulse racing inside her veins. To her surprise, Ayden's features appeared mildly unaffected, as if he'd been here, at this moment, a hundred other times. She wanted him to say something, to differentiate her from the other woman he'd kissed in this hallway and maybe afterward led to his bedroom. Perhaps he'd even carried them. Her gaze wandered to the room he currently occupied, and he called her on it.

"No. You're not ready."

Grace's jaw dropped, unable to comprehend the insult. "Ready…ready for what exactly?"

He clenched and unclenched his jaw before answering her. "Going in there right now would be a mistake, for both of us. You have so much passion, but I want to show you how to feel it without holding your breath, to feel it without losing yourself."

She tried to say something, but nothing remotely coherent passed her lips. So, this is how he lived and remained so emotionally unattached, by staying in control of everything?

She shook her head, disappointed. "Do you mean, without me forgetting how I'm just here to pretend to be in love with you, Ayden?"

He didn't glance away, and he didn't deny what she said was true. She concluded, either she'd have to get used to the idea of feeling nothing but physical attraction for Ayden McCabe or she'd end up on the losing end of their agreement. With more confidence than she felt, she shrugged and imitated one of his obnoxious grins. "Your loss," she said and traipsed by him. She did turn to see his reaction, finding a smirk that unnerved and melted her at the same time.

"Your mind is a wondrous thing, Miss Evans," he said, before backing away, sliding inside the chilly room she'd first occupied and closing the door.

With the day gone, Grace resigned herself to retiring for the night and finishing her book. Unfortunately, she replaced the longhaired god of a man with a shorted-haired Irish American with cerulean-colored eyes and sensual lips. Oh, she wanted to find some damn mistletoe, and make Ayden kiss her again, and again, and again. Physical, not emotional. Well, she certainly understood the meaning of that phrase now.

The next morning, she woke to an empty house, a stack of pancakes on the island with a side of bacon, and a note in neat handwriting stuck to the plate.

Work emergency. Jolene said she'd be by to take you to town, if you want to talk to some folks about Danielle. I will be back soon. Try to eat something.

Grace stared at the note, memorizing Ayden McCabe's handwriting, every curve and loop, until she pictured herself as one of his desperate ex-girlfriends throwing a rock through his window at two in the morning. "No," she said, aloud, unwilling to fall in love with a man who knew less than Rick about what it took to be in a real relationship.

Instead of chastising herself, she gave in to spreading peanut butter on her pancakes and then laminating them with thick syrup. After inhaling the delicious breakfast, she cleaned the kitchen and took a quick shower in case Jolene was on her way over. Grace had no idea who she might talk to in town, but she couldn't imagine sitting at Hearth's Gate without Ayden there.

Thirty-five minutes later, at half past nine, Jolene's sputtering Jeep pulled into the semi-circular driveway. Instead of making the older woman step out in the bitter cold, Grace ambled down the porch steps already dressed in the various winter garments that belonged to one of Ayden's relatives. Jolene waved and beamed at Grace through the salt-dusted windshield.

"So, what's on the agenda for today?" the woman asked, maneuvering the vehicle onto the cleared road.

Grace glanced down at her tan boots, her mind dancing back to Ayden. *No.* She needed to think about Danielle and her mother. Of course, thinking about them brought her full circle back to Ayden. *Foolish.* She sighed aloud.

"Oh, don't get too discouraged. I'm sure your sister is just fine. She's a little lost, is all."

Ironically, Grace wasn't thinking about Danielle. She wasn't even thinking about their mother, who hadn't been able to handle anything since their father left. Embarrassed by her own selfish thoughts, Grace angled her head toward the passenger side window and let out a slow exhale.

To keep her mind on track, she tried to remember her and Danielle's last conversation. Danielle had brought up the possibility of Grace making desserts for her wedding reception.

"You have to make that custard chocolate sticky-bun piece of heaven you sneak into Neely's on holidays. Once everyone tastes those things, people will be asking you to bake them for their weddings."

Grace had told her sister she'd think about it, wondering if she was opening a door she wasn't able to walk through. Either way, it didn't seem to matter what Danielle wanted now.

"So, Grace, is Ayden bringing you to the Christmas Tree-Lighting Ceremony tonight?"

The question drew Grace's gaze back to the thin woman beside her. Jolene with her jovial demeanor, sat waiting patiently for an answer.

"I…don't…think…"

"Not that I'm one to pry, mind you, but I knew the two of you would hit it off right away." She shrugged her bony shoulders inside her heavy flannel coat. There was something so familiar about the woman, but Grace couldn't put her finger on it. "I'll admit though, when Maggie called to tell me he'd introduced you as his girlfriend, I thought, he's going to marry her someday."

Grace's inhale caught in her throat, making her cough. Jolene reached over and slapped her hard a few times between her shoulder blades before returning her hand to the steering wheel. "You see, when Ayden sees someone he likes, he doesn't waste any time with small talk."

Grace grumbled a "no kidding" under her breath as Jolene carried on with the conversation.

"So, are you thinking of moving to Mistletoe or continuing a long-distance relationship with Ayden?"

Grace clamped down on her lips, unwilling to give her opinion on anything that involved either her or Ayden's future.

"Well, you'd be a wonderful addition to the town. If you'd like, I can see about asking O'Shannon if he has any positions available—"

"That…really won't be necessary," Grace said on a heavy exhale.

Jolene rotated in Grace's direction, her eyes large and blinking.

"I mean, I'm thinking of opening my own bakery and café…in San Francisco…sometime…in the near future," Grace said, trying not to give away how *that* dream had vanished seventy-two hours ago.

"That sounds lovely. We could use one of those around here, especially if we get a few more tourists."

Grace shook off the comforting and fantasy-laden thought of staying longer in Mistletoe.

"Anyway, what kind of desserts do you make?"

Before Grace could answer, Jolene sucked in a lungful of air. Grace jerked around, thinking she might have spotted Danielle walking across the quiet street.

"What?"

"You should make something to bring to the Christmas Tree-Lighting Ceremony."

Grace dropped her shoulders started to shake her head when Jolene slapped the steering wheel and then maneuvered the Jeep into a small parking lot adjacent to a gray brick building that read Fresh Market.

"I need to pick up some things for my famous punch. You're welcome to purchase a few things to contribute to a dessert. I'll buy, you bake."

A few hours later, Grace was elbow deep in flour.

As she mixed and Jolene gossiped about who was taking whom to the Christmas Eve *Eve* dance in a few weeks, Grace baked her custard-filled chocolate glazed sticky buns.

Around three thirty, after Jolene left with enough to take to the lighting ceremony, Grace made a few more batches, one of them for Wilhelmina Hawthorne and her husband for being so helpful in finding Danielle a few days before.

"Danielle," Grace whispered. She and Jolene had gone to town and had spoken to zero people regarding Danielle. Too caught up in her own thoughts of Ayden and the opportunity to bake, Grace had gone grocery shopping.

Now, three—or was it four…she'd lost track—days had passed, and she wasn't any closer to discovering where her sister had disappeared to and why. She realized it had nothing to do with getting cold feet. Grace knew Danielle, and she'd never do something so irrational. Well, almost never. Furthermore, no matter how many times she forced her mind to stay focused on bringing Danielle back home, mostly for their mom's sake, it always strayed toward Ayden.

He was like no other man Grace had ever met. Despite his bachelor creed, there was something so domestic and spousal about him, something lasting and eternal. He held her hand in public places, gave her his undivided attention in others. Despite the fact he had more ex-girlfriends than she had excuses, she was still drawn to him.

Shaking her head to clear her mind of him, at least for a while, she closed the extra buns in a cake container and set them on the counter.

With the day already getting late and still no word from Ayden, she thought about going outside for some fresh air. Standing on the porch, the warm maroon and gray fleece around her shoulders, she gazed around at her majestic soundings. She breathed deep and exhaled slow, loving the way her breath crystalized in midair. Yes, it was a wondrous place, made for a man whose reputation and elusiveness exceeded him.

She stepped to go back inside when the stone house next door caught her attention. She stared at the whimsical fairytale building with its sharply pointed thatched roof and tall diamond-paned glass windows. Both boredom and curiosity pulled her along the cobblestone path until she found herself standing at the red door, hesitant to go inside.

"If it's locked, I'll go back," she said. Only, the knob turned easily and the wind pushed at her back, propelling her inside the capricious home.

The main area was quaint with plenty of light filtering in through a set of sheer curtains. Where a cozy sofa or high-back chair may have existed sat two powerful woodcutting machines with a mountain of sawdust piled underneath them. Above hung a wood beam ceiling, adding to its wistful comfort.

Without any heat, however, she only stayed long enough to pass the narrow winding staircase and a charming kitchen with a stone fireplace and baby blue-painted cabinets. She thought it would make an adorable shop, minus the sawdust and power tools, of course.

On a sigh, she pivoted and headed back to the main house. She'd barely stepped into the foyer when her phone rang. On purpose, she'd chosen not to talk to her mother since their last conversation, afraid to answer questions about Ayden or tell her she didn't have any further news on Danielle.

Grace let out a breath when the display screen showed her friend's number instead.

"Hello," Grace said, smiling.

"Hey, have you found Danielle, yet?"

Grace sank down on a bench next to the staircase. "No. It's the strangest thing, Betsy. No one's seen her." She left out the part about her having the opportunity to talk to people today and instead, made dessert for a Christmas Tree-Lighting ceremony.

"So, is Ayden taking you?" her friend asked, her voice steady and excited.

Grace shook her head, wondering if she'd somehow voiced her thoughts aloud. "I'm not—"

"Well, of course he is, right?"

Typical Betsy, Grace thought. Her friend hated Rick and was determined to set her up with any man who she happened to cross paths with, even desperate strangers."

"I don't know. He's sort of…unavailable."

"What? You mean he's married?"

"Um…he's—" Grace tried to answer, finally giving up when her attempt to explain Ayden McCabe failed. "It's complicated."

"Oh, God. Tell me you're not seeing a married guy, Grace. That's worse than the loser you can't rid yourself of now."

"Speaking of the loser, I mean, Rick." Grace rolled her eyes. "Has he stopped by any more?"

Betsy clicked her tongue. "Yeah, a few more times.

He's acting all pathetic…I mean, more pathetic than usual. He keeps asking about Ayden and how you met him."

"What did you tell him?" Grace shuffled into the kitchen to get a glass of water, waiting for Betsy to come up with a clever reply.

"Oh, that you answered some gorgeous guy's mail-order-bride advertisement and flew up there to test the sex out before you committed to anything."

Grace choked on her water, spitting most of it onto the kitchen floor. Why she chose to take a gulp and ask her friend questions at the same time, she didn't know. "Please, tell me you didn't?"

"No, but I wanted to. You deserve better than that jackass, Gracie."

At this point, Grace didn't know what she deserved, but she knew what she wanted, at least what she needed to change to get it. *Just breathe and remain emotionally detached so no one gets hurt.*

"Look," her friend said. "I have to go, but try not to worry. You might be surprised how this all ends up. Go Hawks."

Grace smiled, missing her most peculiar friend. "Go Hawks," she repeated, ending the call and going upstairs to put on her football jersey and a pair of comfortable pants. The game would be on soon, and she didn't want to miss kickoff, or Ayden when he returned. She only hoped, when he did return, he didn't smell like a woman's perfume and have a solid excuse of why he was wearing it.

Chapter Thirteen

Ayden parked his truck in the driveway with the snow flying and his watch showing a half past four. He had been called to a remote worksite where there was no phone reception, nor was there a way to contact Grace to let her know he'd be a while getting back.

It didn't help that Gregg Dunlap, his second-line supervisor and second-in-command, teased him endlessly about trusting a woman he'd just met to stay in his house alone. "Wait until you get there and find half your possessions stolen, then you'll never leave another woman alone again."

Ayden chuckled and reassured the man Grace wouldn't take a bar of soap from a hotel room, much less his family's silver heirlooms.

"Okay, but when you get there and find your TV missing, you can join me at O'Shannon's where I'll be after the lighting ceremony, watching the second half of the Seahawks and Niners game. I owe you a beer from last week, anyway."

Ayden declined the offer. He admitted to himself, though grudgingly, he was more anxious about finding a goodbye note from Grace than a missing expensive flat screen. He was sure she was mad as hell about not hearing from him all day and had concluded he was with another woman, or something else. With that thought plaguing him, he headed back to Hearth's Gate.

When he walked onto the porch, he didn't like what he saw. Every window cast a daunting shadow of abandonment.

Yanked into a foul mood, he drove his key into the lock and tried to blame his disappointment on her not holding up her end of the bargain. The truth was, he couldn't stop, for one minute, thinking about her careful smile or the kiss they shared the night before.

One minute timid, the next minute daring, she always kept him guessing. Regarding women, he admitted he demanded a lot from them, physically. If they wanted to stop at the beginning of making love to talk about how he felt regarding starting a family, he knew it was over.

With Grace, he couldn't stop thinking about how her gaze wandered to his bedroom and how he'd stopped himself from taking her in there. She fired up his soul, and he thought all day of how to get her alone once more, to teach her the many ways they could satisfy each other, without words or faithful promises.

Then again, he'd never seen his house so dark. Every light was off, as if the occupant had left in the middle of the day with no intention of returning. The thought hit him hard, his breath growing heavier the closer he drew to his door. If she'd left him a damn note, he wouldn't even attempt to read it. With his gut twisting and his heart thumping to an obnoxious beat, he entered the house and headed to the kitchen, flipping on the overhead lights.

What he saw there made him falter. There, on his island, sat a cake pan with a note attached. *Don't you dare eat these yet, Grace.*

Whatever they were, they smelled warm and sinful.

More willing to see her again than ignore her warning, he turned and stepped toward the stairs. He was halfway up when a flickering light coming from a set of French doors caught his attention. He didn't spend much time there, but he'd bought a sectional and an eighty-inch flat screen for Maggie and Collin whenever they came to visit.

He entered the dark and quiet room. The television was muted and the couch appeared empty until he peered over the back to find Grace huddled in the corner, her lashes fanning her cheeks, the navy blue afghan his mother had made tucked under her chin.

He remembered Rachel had once asked him if she looked like an angel when she slept. He'd been honest and said no, not even knowing what she'd meant by the question. Now, he knew. He dropped his hand to pull back a lock of Grace's brown hair.

He shifted closer only to have the wooden floor creak and jar his sleeping beauty awake. A shaky hand flew to her heart and her gaze darted around, anxious and confused. "Who's there?"

"Grace, it's me," he said, placing a reassuring palm on her left shoulder. "You must have fallen asleep watching"—he paused to make sure he was seeing the screen correctly—"the pregame show."

He didn't know many women who liked sports, and even less who were interested enough to watch it on TV. Every turn with Grace, he found another unexpected treasure.

She sighed and relaxed, pulling the blanket down around her waist, exposing her Seahawks jersey. He shook his head. "How the hell are you a Hawks fan?"

She dipped her chin to her chest before raising it

back up again. "It's a long story reserved for when we have absolutely nothing else to talk about." She adjusted the blanket back over her arms.

"Are you cold?" he asked, knowing she wasn't one to complain about anything.

"Oh no. This blanket is the warmest, most perfect thing I've ever had wrapped around me."

He stared down at her unable to keep his mind from wandering or his thoughts quiet. "Certainly not the most perfect thing, Grace. I seem to remember doing a fairly good job of keeping you warm."

She smirked at him. "But *you* weren't *here*."

Of course, he deserved that as an answer. "Look, I'm…I should have found a way to call you." He stepped around to take a seat beside her. She smelled heavenly, her vanilla and sugar scent intoxicating.

She answered him with a quick shake of her head. "I never expected you to quit your job to help me, Ayden." She then stood, drawing the blanket around her like a shawl.

Reluctant to let her go so soon, he reached out to grab her hand. He wanted to teach her to relax and trust him, but it was hard when everything they were doing was a damn show. Regardless, he kept his grip firm around her wrist. "I was wondering…would you like to go to the Christmas Tree-Lighting Ceremony? We don't have much time, so we'll have to hurry. They always like to start and finish before kickoff."

With a slow lift to the corners of her pretty mouth, she finally agreed. "Yes." He didn't realize how much he wanted to hear that word.

With the truck well heated, they drove away in the direction of the main square where a permanent forty-two foot Christmas tree stood in all its grandeur. He glanced over at Grace, realizing for the first time how he'd insisted she'd wear as many layers as possible to keep warm. Now, he couldn't help but chuckle at her cartoonish appearance: burnt orange toboggan hat two sizes two big, a thick aqua scarf covering her lips and nose, and enough garments under her coat so she had to twist her entire body to look at him.

"I look silly, don't I?" she asked.

He managed to decipher what she'd said under the scarf and chuckled. To see her better, he pulled the thick wrapping so it hung around her neck. "You look…warm."

She scoffed and then giggled, shaking her lovely head.

"Have you recovered enough from our last venture outside?" he asked, still cursing himself over what happened and how helpless he'd felt as it all unfolded. She laughed and nodded, touching the slight scrape above her eye. She'd taken off the butterfly bandage so all that remained was a tiny pink scratch and a small bruise.

"You know," she said after staring at her tan boots, "maybe I watch too much television or read too many unrealistic books, but I thought I'd know where Danielle was by now. My mom has called ten times since I talked to her at Hawthorne's. I don't know what to tell her."

He opened his mouth to reassure her when it dawned on him what she'd said. "You were talking to your mom in Hawthorne's?"

"Yes, I was talking to my *mom*. I tried to tell her we were close to finding Danielle, a lie she didn't believe, and then she asked who *we* were, and the conversation sort of went downhill from there."

He sank back and inhaled. "I thought—"

Grace cut him off. "I know." Then she gave into her nervous habit of tucking a loose strand of dark hair behind her ear. "If you're worried about Rick, I can assure you, he won't mess anything up regarding Maggie."

Ayden didn't want to admit that jealousy, not concern, was his first knee-jerk reaction to believing Grace had told another man she loved him. No matter his emotional response, he needed to stay focused and on course.

His thoughtful silence caused Grace to continue to reassure him. "Rick likes to 'find himself,' which usually involves some girl with a three-syllable name." She paused. "Re-bec-ca. Na-ta-lie. So-phi-a. I swear, if I have five children, all girls, none of them will have three-syllable names."

Ayden chuckled, trying to imagine her with five children, all with brown hair and brown-green eyes. He sobered as soon as he pictured himself standing beside her holding one of them.

"I have to ask…how often have you and Rick broken up?"

Ayden believed if a woman had to inhale and lift her head to the starry night to recall the answer, the number was more than she realized.

"Ten times."

"Ten?"

"No, twelve."

He felt his eyebrows furrow. "Twelve? Are you sure?"

"Yes. Wait, does it count if he calls it quits only to arrive three hours later with flowers and a bracelet?"

He nodded with his eyes closed. "Yes."

"Then sixteen."

"Jesus," Ayden murmured, lifting his hand to rub at his temples with his thumb and middle finger before diving back into the conversation. "So, you're saying you and Rick have broken up over a dozen times, and you let him walk back into your life as if nothing happened?"

She wrinkled her nose. "Well, more like crawl."

"And you don't see a problem with this?" He waited, with unusual patience for her to think of a way to answer.

"He's what I know, Ayden. There are no surprises with him. Disappointments, yes, but at least I know what's coming around the corner. I'd prefer that over a sucker punch any day."

He sat stunned by her confession. "You're like this revolving door."

She snapped back a response. "And you're like a closed one."

Their fiery gazes locked until a car horn jerked their attention away from one another.

"I'm so sorry." Her delicate voice rippled through the cab. "I shouldn't have said that."

He raised his hand to stop her from apologizing further. He was used to females crumbling under his inquiries, turning to him to help carry their baggage. Then there was Grace. Not only did she not want his help in patching up all the holes in her life, she stood firing off excuses why she wanted them there.

"Why don't we take a break on trying to

139

psychoanalyze one another, okay?"

Her shoulders dropped as she unfisted her small hands and pulled the toboggan off her head.

"I would ask what you did all day, but, um—" He pointed to the wrapped desserts sitting between them on the seat.

She grinned and drew away from him. "Yeah, when I should have been out asking questions about Danielle, I came home and made desserts."

She stopped talking, and he believed they realized, at the same time, how she'd used the word home, so easily. From his peripheral vision, she exhaled and then chastised herself with a shake of her head. Before she could apologize, he lifted his chin toward the square, and pointed to the lofty unlit Christmas tree.

"We're here."

Although most of the parking spaces were full, he drove a few more blocks and parked at O'Shannon's. "We'll have to walk…is that okay?"

Grace nodded, pulled the scarf above her nose, and pushed the door open with her shoulder. Before joining her, Ayden snagged the blanket he'd used to keep her warm a few nights ago. A shudder went through him, remembering her miserable and pasty appearance when he'd climbed back in the cab that day. He didn't want to let her know, but he'd almost panicked. For a moment, he felt helpless. All he could think about was his parents, the unit he'd abandoned in Afghanistan, and his buddy who never made it home.

He let out a shaky breath. For years, he'd tried to forget Lt. Mark Ramsey. They had graduated Officer Candidate School together and been assigned to sister units in Afghanistan. They shared stories and booze, and talked about what they wanted to do when they returned home. Then, Ayden's parents died, and Mark was transferred to take his place. Three weeks later, he and five others from his platoon were killed by an insurgent attack. Right after Ayden received the news, he made a pact with himself, believing as long as he remained unemotionally attached to anyone, he never had to worry about losing or leaving them ever again.

"Ayden?'

Grace's quiet voice yanked him out of his thoughts, and he turned to gaze upon her outrageous outfit. She rolled her eyes toward her hat and then down at her puffed-up appearance. "Do you think I could lose one of these things?" she asked, behind her scarf.

"Do you want to risk getting hypothermia, again?"

Her dark eyebrows rose over her gold-infused, multicolored eyes. Although they both shared a harrowing experience, he had no doubt; her mind was remembering what he'd chosen to do to raise her heart rate. They stared at each other, inching forward when the crunch of someone's boots forced them to separate.

"Howdy."

They turned to find Neil standing beside them, a Santa hat fitted over his Stetson. He gave Grace a once-over and then let out an ear-piercing whistle. "Well, ain't you a sight to see."

Grace lifted her gaze to his hats, pulled down her scarf, and grinned. "Yep," she said, imitating his heavy Texas drawl.

Ayden held a chuckle behind his fist as Neil sent her a slow wink.

"So, how's Sarah and the baby?" Ayden asked, pulling his friend's attention back to him.

Neil sent him a single nod. "Oh, just fine. She sent me here so she can watch the lighting via my iPhone. She didn't want to miss making her wish."

"Of course," Ayden said. Women and their wishes, he thought as he reached for Grace's gloved hand. He also thought to take the extra container of desserts she'd made before leading them toward the festive event.

Although the snow had stopped and the clouds had cleared to render a brilliant night sky of twinkling stars, it was still very cold.

"Are you warm enough?" he leaned down to ask Grace.

"She looks like the doughboy in those croissant commercials, Ayden. I'm sure as hell she's warm enough," Neil said, aiming a freckled index finger at her midsection.

"Don't you dare," Ayden warned with a stern glance in Neil's direction.

Neil's lopsided grin told Ayden he'd revealed more than a firm warning not to touch her. Then with a wink and a quick salute, Neil moseyed off in the direction of the tree, his gait assured and easy.

In the background, the local high school band began to play another Christmas song, this time, "Please Come Home for Christmas."

With Neil standing behind the conductor, mimicking him, but trying to get the band to speed up the tempo, Ayden maneuvered Grace toward Francis Tisdale's concession stand. Jolene stood beside the older woman, her wrinkled features beaming with excitement. As was tradition, Francis ran the charity auction for the children's hospital, making sure the young patients received plenty of presents on Christmas day.

"You *did* bring her"—Jolene handed both a paper cup of hot chocolate—"I think," she added, squinting as if to see if the woman dressed from head to toe in winter gear was, in fact, Grace.

Grace giggled and lowered the scarf from her mouth. "It's me."

The older woman sent Ayden a quizzical look before lifting her mouth in a secretive smile.

"I brought some more desserts." Grace took the container from him to hand to Jolene.

"Thank God," the woman said. "The ones I brought, we ran out of them about a half hour ago. I'm thinking of upping the price. Supply and demand, you know?" She sent Grace a smile. "Well, you better go find a seat, Ayden. You don't want Grace to miss making her wish, do you?"

Ayden smirked, *wishing* he hadn't forgotten about the damn custom before asking Grace if she wanted to come here. The last thing he needed was for Grace to make a wish regarding her ex-boyfriend.

"What's this *wish* thing everybody keeps talking about?" she asked after they'd rotated in the direction of the benches.

Ayden glanced down, and she blinked back up at him like a curious child asking about the meaning of life.

"Well," he said and then paused.

"You're not going to tell me, are you?"

Her question threw him off guard. "It's…just—"

He let out a big sigh and then turned to face her. "There are too many damn legends in this town to keep up with all of them, in my opinion. The one tonight says, if you make a wish in the exact moment between when the mayor calls the last number of the countdown and the lights are switched on, then whatever you wish will come true."

She blinked at him and didn't say anything for a few shallow and puffy cold breaths. When she finally found her voice, her next question was as challenging as the last one she'd asked. "Have you ever made a wish?"

If Ayden did, he didn't remember one of them. He was too sensible, caring more about tangible things, things he could feel with his hands and see with his eyes. "No."

Her glittering gaze narrowed on him before she rotated to stare at the tree. He wondered what she was thinking. For someone who read romance novels and whose favorite movie was a fairy-tale cartoon, he knew she was capable of wishing the most unattainable things in the world. Then again, even if her fairy-tale wish did come true, would she spend the rest of her life, wondering if there was an unhappy ending somehow attached?

"All right, folks. Are you ready?" called the well-dressed mayor into the microphone.

The crowd responded with loud cheers. Ayden needed to do something to keep Grace from wishing for what he thought she wanted: Rick back in her life.

"Five, four, three, two…"

So, he did the only thing that he knew would pull her attention away from the wish and to him: he kissed her.

Chapter Fourteen

Grace had her wish ready, and she couldn't wait to make it, until Ayden turned her head and brought his lips firm against hers. As the echoing voice announced the final number in the countdown, her wish flitted away.

Within another thunderous heartbeat, a cheer erupted from the crowd and a bright light penetrated through her closed eyelids. Tender and languishing, his mouth slid across hers, this kiss more drugging than the last. Lost in a cloud of elevated sensations, he parted her lips with his tongue. His hand cupped the back of her head, and his thumb caressed her cheek. Then, just as fast as the kiss began, it ended.

Ayden drew back from her, his gaze steady on her face. She blinked at him, a little dazed and a tad winded, her breath leaving her in quick, shallow puffs.

"We should go," he said after a long moment of silence between them.

Unable to think of a reason to stay, she stood when Neil ambled up to stand between them.

"So, what did you think when you first saw the tree light up, Grace? Wasn't it…magical?"

Grace canted her head toward Ayden and shrugged. "Sorry, Neil, but I think I had my eyes closed."

Neil agitated his full head of red hair. "It's the wish

that matters, as long as you thought of it in time."

Grace drew in a frigid inhale. She had no way of knowing, not with Ayden's mouth rendering her thoughtless for those few precious moments. Oh, she wasn't so daft as not to realize he'd tried to distract her enough to keep her from making a wish. This thought didn't bother her as much as how much his kisses were starting to affect her…emotionally. Either she needed to keep reminding herself of their peculiar relationship, or she'd be the one left with a devastating broken heart.

With a braver façade than she felt, she rotated toward the Christmas tree, the white lights glowing like a heavenly orb. Despite what she knew, she closed her eyes and made the wish she'd planned on sending out into the universe.

"Well, ya'll make sure you come by and see Sarah and the baby tomorrow." Neil tipped his hat before sauntering off in the direction of O'Shannon's.

For the next ten minutes, Grace walked beside Ayden, watching him wave to everyone he knew, stopping once when one man called out to ask if he was going to O'Shannon's to watch the game.

"I have other plans." He grasped her hand.

Ayden didn't let go until they were back at the truck, and he didn't say a word until they were settled in the cold interior of the cab.

"You can, you know," she volunteered before he shifted the truck into Drive. She remembered how Rick always blamed her for keeping him from doing what he wanted. She didn't want Ayden thinking the same thing.

To her surprise, Ayden said nothing until they reached Hearth's Gate, and he stepped around to help her out of her side. "I know, Grace."

Inside the house, his warm and deft hands spun her around, helping to untangle her from her winter garb. When he smirked down at her, her heart melted. This emotional feeling was the one sensation she feared the most. *God help her.*

****

Ayden wanted like hell to kiss Grace, again. So far, his creed of never making the first move had backfired on three occasions. His only solace was that the first time he'd been coerced, the second time was a life and death situation, and this third and final time was necessary to keep things going as he planned, without any interruption from her ex.

"Do you like rum cake?" he asked to keep himself from having to reevaluate all the reasons again. He admitted Wilhelmina Hawthorne's dessert was more alcohol than flour, but anything to keep Grace from leaving him to go check her text messages in case the damn wish somehow made it through…not that he believed in the folklore in the first place.

"Sure, but I'm not very good with liquor." She tucked a piece of dark hair behind her ear.

He chuckled, imagining her getting wild and disrobing on top of his antique coffee table. "So, what happens with you and alcohol?"

She smiled. "I don't take off my clothes, if that what you're asking."

"Damn."

She laughed but lifted a dainty finger as if to give him a warning. "I fall asleep, so I can have some cake, but keep in mind there's a very good chance my face will fall flat into the plate after my third bite."

"I'll take that chance."

"It's your call." She shrugged. He left her to retrieve Wilhelmina's prized rum cake, deciding to bring the entire Bundt-shaped dessert with two forks resting on each side. When he entered the room, he found Grace sitting in quiet contemplation, her attention focused on the dormant redbrick fireplace. Since he'd installed the gas furnace several years before, he'd not had any desire to light the fireplace up again, even when his dates hinted several times of how romantic it would be to cuddle before a crackling fire.

"Are you cold?" he asked.

She peered up ,startled. "No, I'm fine." She tried to stifle a shiver, and he sat the plate down and ambled away to retrieve some logs from his deck. Despite not using the fireplace, he understood the importance of keeping it ready for emergencies.

It took several minutes, but he managed to build a popping fire, the sweet aroma of sizzling sap filling the space with a comforting fragrance. She moved to sit beside him, bringing the blanket his mother made with her.

"This feels wonderful." Grace closed her eyes and let the flickering light kiss her cheeks.

"Yes." He sat captivated by her entranced features, realizing how he'd reminisced about kissing her, every glorious inch of her.

"Are you ready for some football…and cake?" He projected his voice above the tone of his own thoughts.

Her lids flew open, and he wondered where she'd been these last few moments, and with whom. The thought unsettled him.

"Are you ready to carry me up a flight of stairs?"

He cocked his head and narrowed his eyes. "Only if you're fully naked."

"How did I know you were going to say that?" She sighed and maneuvered around so the cake sat between them on the short coffee table. As he flipped the game on and muted the volume, she lifted a small bite to her lips when he reached out to stop her.

She gave him a quizzical look. "What's the matter?"

"How about we make this interesting?"

She drew back, and he knew she didn't trust his motives. "How…interesting?"

He laughed before pressing his palm into her back to bring her closer. "Since we are in need of learning as much about one another as possible, I say, for every question asked, the other has to take a bite. The more questions one has, the more bites the other takes."

She nibbled at her lip before answering. "You do realize I'm at a serious disadvantage?" After a few moments of deep sighs and headshakes, she finally stuck her hand out for him to shake. "Fine, who goes first?"

He pulled a coin from his pocket. "Call it." He flipped it high in the air and caught it in his palm.

"Tails!"

"Heads. You go first."

Like a child, Grace wiggled so her back sat against the pillow he'd propped against the mahogany table. As he watched her, mesmerized, she closed her eyes and thought of her first question. Damn, he wanted to kiss her again. He'd thought of the game to relax her, to put her at ease, not take advantage of her.

Of course, the longer she sat meditating on her

question, the longer he sat thinking about her lips or tasting the sensitive flesh just below her earlobe.

"Okay," she finally said, jerking him, again, out of his thoughts. "If your life was turned into a movie, what actor would play you?"

Caught off guard, he almost choked. He'd expected a question about how many sex partners he had or his favorite position. Thoughtful, he turned his head toward the fire and contemplated his answer. "Dead or alive?"

She tapped the end of her index finger against her lips, drawing his attention there. "Alive."

"Chris Hemsworth." He sliced a glance in her direction, satisfied to see her smile. "Now eat."

As promised, she lifted a spoonful in a mocking toast. He could tell by the thick bouquet of molasses and alcohol, he'd know soon how honest she was regarding the effects. "My turn," he said with a nudge against her shoulder. "What was your worst subject in school?"

"Uhm, wow. I…I guess it was drama."

"Oh, right," he said, wishing he hadn't wasted a question on something that was so obvious.

For good measure, however, he dug out a generous amount of cake, savoring the strong portion as it warmed a trail from his throat to his stomach. He'd barely had enough time to set the fork down before she lobbed another question at him.

"What was your worst Halloween costume?"

He threw his head back and laughed. Having indulged in this game before with at least a dozen women, he thought he'd know her questions before she asked them. He was wrong.

Offended, she drew up beside him. "What's so

funny?"

He cleared his throat and pulled his lips into a cocky smile. "I guess I expected a more erotic game of truth."

She nodded. "You mean, like, what was your worst date, or where was the craziest place you ever had sex?"

He sat there, with his mouth open, unsure what to even say now that she'd posed the obvious questions to him. "At the moment, I can't remember ever being on a worse date. As for the second, I would have to say—"

Before he could tease her with an answer, she stuffed a full bite of cake into his mouth.

"Now, where were we?" she said, daring him to distract her from the game again.

"Cheating," he answered simply and swiped the corners of his mouth with the tips of his thumb and index finger.

She blinked at him, innocent and quiet.

"All right, my worst Halloween costume was Little Tarzan."

She laughed, her eyes glittering in the warm firelight. "Oh, you must have looked adorable."

"Adorably cold," he admitted, his gaze narrowing.

He knew by the way she nibbled on her lower lip, she had more inquiries pertaining to his outfit. "Go ahead, but every one of them will cost you."

Her smile lit up with excitement. "How old were you?"

"Seven."

"Leopard or stripes?"

"Leopard."

"Do you have pictures?"

"No! I burned them." He pointed to the fireplace. "Right there, in fact. Now you owe me three bites."

She opened her mouth to protest when he scooped up a charitable amount and placed it between her lips. It proved a rewarding effort as her pretty mouth closed slowly around the spoon without protest.

Content to remain as sober as possible, he encouraged her to continue her interrogation until her movements and speech slowed. To make it somewhat fair, he pandered to his own curiosity, taking a bite off her plate for good gesture.

"I know your worst childhood memory, but tell me your best one," he asked, feeling her relax. She sighed and slunk her shoulder against his, her soft body molding to his side and her cheek resting on his arm.

"That one is easy. It was a few months after my dad left, and we were all suffering from the aftershock. My mom thought it would be a good idea to get us out of the city and decided to take us camping."

"Do you like camping?" He made sure to keep his voice gentle.

She sighed, her shoulders rising and falling like a gentle wave. "That's two questions." She held up two fingers and kept them out to exaggerate her point.

He brought his hand over hers, relishing in the suppleness of her skin. "In that case, put it on my tab."

"A tab, why didn't I think of that?" At this point, her words were methodical and deliberate. "Camping was okay, but both Danielle and my mother hated it. After about three hours of bizarre animal noises, a brief rain, and something slithering around my mom's feet, she packed us up and checked us into the nearest place with a bed that sat more than a foot off the floor."

"Oh, this sounds like a wonderful childhood memory, Grace."

She clicked her tongue, and he held a chuckle to keep from breaking her thoughts.

"We ended up staying in this quaint bed and breakfast somewhere in Oregon. The couple was very nice, and I remember we'd sit around, just talking. The owner's husband was tall with a full head of white hair and friendly twinkling aqua-colored eyes. He'd tell us these funny stories of other guests, while his wife served us tea and always with these delicious little desserts that just melted in your mouth. I guess that's why I wanted to start baking. I wanted to create a little magic, like she did."

Grace paused to yawn, and he waited for her to continue. Only she didn't. When he glanced down, her gaze was transfixed on the fireplace, a million miles away.

"Grace, tell me what happened to you that Christmas day."

Her head shook against him. "You really don't want to know. It's depressing and boring."

"Nothing you say is boring."

She exhaled and then cleared her throat. "It was an unusually hot night, I remember. I was sleeping and Danielle, who still believed in Santa, decided to wake me first and find out what he'd brought us for Christmas. She was so excited. By then, I knew the truth, so the magic of the day had somewhat faded."

For her sake, Ayden sat with a stealth-like silence, waiting for the rest of the story.

"But since I loved to see the sparkle in her eyes when she talked about her favorite holiday, I pretended to believe. So that morning, I grabbed her hand and led her downstairs, hoping, praying to see a normal Christmas morning. You know, the ones they show on TV with presents around the tree, the aroma of strong coffee brewing, Mom and Dad wrapped in holiday housecoats on the couch."

She paused, but not for long. "Instead, the tree lay in a mess on the floor and our presents were cast about as if a bear had gotten loose in our living room. Danielle crumpled on the stairway as my mom sat in a corner, her arms locked around her knees, her face swollen from hours of crying."

He'd heard enough, enough of the sadness and disappointment in her voice. "Grace, you don't—"

"I know. My parents had gotten in a horrible fight about the flavor of the week: money, his job, her gift, some woman named Theresa. He left and never came back."

Ayden brought Grace closer against him, unable to imagine her being a child or having to endure such heartbreak.

"After that day, my mom sort of just closed up and handed everything over to me."

"For God's sake, Grace. You were just a child."

She hesitated for a moment before continuing. "I felt so bad for her. I remember lying in my bed, listening to her crying across the hall. In the morning, when it was still dark, I'd get up to fix Danielle something for breakfast, and I'd find my mom sitting in the kitchen with the lights off."

"Oh, Grace." He bent his head to kiss her hair.

"So basically, we became nonparticipants over nonbelievers."

"Yes," he agreed and stayed silent. After a very long moment, he called her name. "Grace?"

She didn't answer. Like she'd said she would, she fell asleep. He glanced around him and realized they hadn't even paid any attention to the game. So far, the Hawks were on top by fourteen. With Grace still leaned against him, he turned off the TV, scooped her up, and carried her upstairs. Light as snow, he laid her upon his pillow, sat down, and brushed back a wisp of her dark hazelnut brown hair.

With the hall light filtering into the room, he noticed when her eyelashes flickered open and she smiled. "I hope I wasn't too heavy for you to carry."

"No, not at all."

She nodded and sighed. "So do you think you know enough about me, Mr. McCabe?" she said in a tired voice.

"I do have one more question."

She let her thick eyelids flutter and then rest against her check. "All right."

"Have…you ever thought of leaving San Francisco?" He thought it a safe enough question while she was slightly intoxicated and half-asleep.

Her lips curled upward. "Do you mean, like moving away?"

"Yeah, I mean, did you always want to live in California?"

"That's two questions."

He leaned forward. "I still have a tab, remember."

"Cheater," she teased and rolled onto her side, tucking her hands under her cheek. "No. I guess I never thought there was any other option."

That was all she said as she let out a breath. Ayden

155

sat, enjoying watching her sleep. Then, after some time he stood, unsure how many more nights of getting to know each other he'd have to endure. In the past, the answer and question game always led to one thing, with the outcome always being the same, them in his bed, and definitely not sleeping.

He chuckled to himself and ambled back to the spare bedroom, believing life had a clever way of mocking him.

Chapter Fifteen

Grace awoke with a throbbing headache. The last thing she remembered was reminiscing over her happiest and most tragic moments with Ayden.

Ayden! She jerked upward, afraid to find the bed occupied, his magnificent body stretched beside her, his irresistible grin burning into her conscience. To her heart's disappointment, the mattress lay empty.

"Oh, please don't fall further for Ayden McCabe," she chanted to herself between showering, dressing, and slipping downstairs. Believing he'd endured another night in the windowless room, she stepped into the kitchen, halting abruptly inside the doorway.

If she thought she'd escaped glancing upon Ayden's half-naked form this morning, she'd not remembered whose house she occupied. He stood, shirtless in a pair of forest green pajama bottoms and propped against the counter, a midnight blue coffee cup in his left hand and a folded paper in his right.

She glanced away, trying to cease the sudden swooping motion in her stomach. Unable to erase the image of his hard-sculptured chest and contoured abdomen tapering into a V below the drawstring waistband, she continued on a blind path to the breakfast nook.

On the round mahogany table, she found a stack of toast and a bowl of buttered grits. Between both sat a frosty glass of what looked like tomato juice.

"I thought you might want something light on your stomach after—"

"You shamelessly got me drunk? Thanks," she said, embarrassed how she'd indulged so much in front of a man she'd didn't know existed less than a week ago. She settled down, grasping a piece of rye toast.

"How do you feel?"

Grace closed her eyes, not wanting to admit she wished to crawl back in bed and sleep for another day or two. However, she needed to get back to work and she still didn't know how to find Danielle. "Never better."

"That's the spirit!"

She knew, even without looking, he stood smiling, his beautiful lips curled, behind a steaming cup of coffee. As not to appear obviously affected by his wondrous half-nakedness, she rotated around and settled her gaze on his amused face. "Do we find Danielle today?"

"Hmm," he commented before throwing the paper on the marble island and sauntering over to join her. "I asked the Hawthornes to locate the surveillance recording of the person who took the postcard. Maybe from that, you will be able to recognize him."

"Mistletoe needs surveillance?" she half joked.

"For insurance purposes, yes."

Grace nodded, finding optimism in his plan.

"Until then, I thought we'd go to the hospital and visit the O'Shannon clan." He reached over her to take a piece of toast from the plate. The warm, spicy scent of him made her imagine lifting her lips to his bare skin and tasting every bare inch of him. She felt groggy from the alcohol and the constant thoughts of falling in bed with him without both of them overthinking or ruining the moment with premeditated notions.

"Do you want to?"

Heat rushed to her cheeks as she forced her gaze to his face, unsure if she'd said her thoughts out loud. "Do—" she started to say, and then had to clear her throat. "Do I want to do what…exactly?"

Ayden chewed slowly on his food before asking, "Are you okay?" The sincere concern made her bow her head in embarrassment. While she was thinking of tearing off what was left of his clothes, he was probably wondering about their next step in finding Danielle.

"Yes, of course."

He sent her a lopsided grin, and she knew he'd guessed at her wayward thoughts. She shifted her gaze to the window and the brilliant sun glaring off the thick snow. Her reflections quickly turned to someday leaving this place: the snow, the cold, the falling Christmas trees, and Ayden.

"I don't know," Grace said, her mind suddenly remembering what he'd asked before she took a U-turn down the road of immoral contemplation. When she angled back to look at him, he was lounging in his chair, still shirtless, with an expression of perplexity. Now, *what* was *he* thinking? She shook off the answer. "I mean, I don't know Sarah or Neil very well, and I can't imagine they'd want me there."

Ayden pushed forward, his elbows resting on the table, his long fingers clasped together in what looked like prayer. She glanced down to see how close he came to touching hers. They remained a hair out of reach. "Sarah texted me and made me promise to bring you, and I don't break promises."

When Grace sat there, not giving him an answer, he tried another tactic. "Besides, it will give us a chance to work on Maggie. Between all our misadventures, we haven't had the opportunity to let her see us together and—"

Grace blinked at Ayden, knowing he stopped short of saying, *in love* on purpose. It was just as well. The things he said, or refused to say, no longer shocked her.

"Grace?"

She closed her eyes for a brief moment. "Still here," she murmured.

"Good." He tapped the table, stood, and left her alone, returning a half hour later dressed in a simple gray sweater over a white T-shirt and a pair of well-worn jeans. His dark-blond hair lay damp at the nape, and his face showed a close and careful shave.

"Are you ready to go?"

"If you promise I don't have to look like the doughboy in the croissant commercials."

"Fine, but you're wearing the hat and wool coat." She sent him a quick nod and followed him outside with what was left of the breakfast pastries she'd made. At the truck, she stopped for a moment, allowing flecks of snow to kiss her eyelashes. Like dandelion tails, they scattered with the wind, dancing to a silent wintry beat.

Lost in her environment, she lingered for a little while longer before settling inside the cab with Ayden beside her. From her peripheral vision, he appeared uncomfortable, turning his head toward her and back to the road at least a half dozen times.

"So," he finally said. "Have you given much thought to how we go about convincing Maggie we're…in love?"

If not for the seriousness of Ayden's tone, Grace would have burst out laughing. *Her…give advice on how to play the part of an infatuated lover?*

"Um," she said, making sure to keep her attention focused on the flying snow and the road ahead. "Maybe you can tell me the last time you found yourself, oh, I don't know, in love? How did you react?"

She made the mistake of glancing in his direction, his piercing blue gaze unblinking and avoiding hers. She waited, even allowing her fingers to tap against her pants before he dignified her with an answer.

"Well, I didn't get hives, if that's what you're thinking."

She drew back, offended. "I wasn't thinking anything."

His right eyebrow arched upward as skepticism spread across his handsome features. She let out a loud exhale and sank deeper into the leather seat. "I don't think it would be too hard to make Maggie think we're head over heels for one another. I mean, you just need to look at me all the time, and I just need to lean over and whisper in your ear every three minutes."

"Is that how you do it with Rick? Or is this how it plays out in those books you read, Grace?"

Her mouth fell open. She'd been wrong. Things he said still had the ability to shock the hell out of her.

"God, you're too much of a romantic, Grace, and that is how you will get your heart broken every time."

Astonished where the conversation was headed, she continued to gawk at him, lifting her hands in defense. She fought to keep the words from tumbling out. She fought in vain. "At least I'm willing to get mine broken. You on the other hand, have yours hidden away behind an impenetrable padlock where you've thrown away the key."

He raised his chin and scooted closer to the driver's side window. The tension inside the cab grew with each breath. "I'm starting to wonder if this whole thing was a mistake."

She didn't want to agree with him, but she did. They didn't say much more to each other until they entered the maternity ward at the county hospital. The first person they saw was Neil, a Santa cap still placed over his cowboy hat. Around his neck, he wore a pair of jingle bells that made a soothing little tinkle sound every time he moved.

"Damn, what happened to you two? I think I've seen happier faces in a dentist's office." He paused before his eyes grew large. "You brought dessert. God bless you."

He took the tray Grace offered as she braced for Ayden to confess their entire façade. When the only thing he did was grunt, she dropped her hand from around her waist, her fingers accidently brushing against his. She expected him to pull away, but she almost gasped when his palm pressed against her ungloved hand and his fingers interlaced hers in a locking grip.

The connection made her stomach flitter in anxious happiness. She knew, even if what they were doing was a mistake, she wanted to stop thinking and enjoy every moment of it.

"Lordy these are good…damn good. Honey, you gotta try these buns Ayden made," Neil yelled into the room.

"No, Neil, Grace made them."

The man chomped down on another bite and tried to verbalize his surprise. "Gwace...made dese?" Neil said, his mouth full and outlined in chocolate.

Grace nodded.

"You know, you should be a baker or something."

"Oh, for the love of God," Grace heard Ayden mumble.

"Anyway, Sarah is almost done feeding Nate. I'll come get you when you can see him."

The proud father jingled away, leaving Grace alone with Ayden.

When she tried to pull away, he tightened his grip on her hand, forcing her back to his side. "I'm sorry about what I said earlier. I'm not used to being called out on things." He lifted his thumb to caress her cheek. She thought he might try and kiss her again, but he stepped away and led her to a set of uncomfortable-looking chairs along the main hallway. It wasn't a big hospital, but she supposed it served the residents of Mistletoe well.

"Grace," Ayden said before Neil poked his head around and enthusiastically announced, "She's done."

With Neil shoving them both toward Sarah's room, Ayden never finished his thought, and Grace never seized the opportunity to ask him.

"Ayden, you brought her," Sarah said, her face glowing and her eyes bright with newfound motherhood. Grace's nervousness escalated with each quiet footstep forward. Neil, minus the bells, led them to a small couch nearest the window.

In wondrous fascination, Grace followed Neil as he transferred the sleeping bundle into Ayden's arms.

"He's so tiny." Grace caressed the baby's hand, his tiny fingers opening and squeezing her pinky in a firm grip.

"Smile."

Grace glanced up to find Neil with his phone. "Say, 'mistletoe'."

Grace and Ayden sliced a glance toward each other before repeating the word in forced unison. Neil clicked his phone and then checked the picture, sending Ayden an exaggerated wink.

"So, who do you think he looks like, me or Sarah?" Neil tucked his phone into his pocket.

Grace left the question up to Ayden to answer.

"Well, being as cute as he is, he definitely favors Sarah's side of the family."

"Thank you, Ayden. You are a complete gentleman." Sarah beamed.

"Rake is more like it." Neil snickered.

"Neil Cashel O'Shannon," Sarah scolded her husband.

Neil stopped and straightened like a prairie dog in his seat, his large-eyed gaze landed straight on Grace. She understood Ayden's reputation never escaped one's judgment, in one way or another.

"Don't pay any attention to my husband. He's been so worried, poor thing hasn't slept in two days. I think he's been reading all the dirty parts in my romance novels to stay awake."

Grace glanced up at Sarah, happy to hear that not everyone placed Ayden McCabe on an infatuated pedestal. For the next half hour, Grace sat in the room, enjoying the light banter between friend and co-worker. Sarah even let her hold Nate for a few minutes while she gobbled down two and a half pieces of pastry.

"You'll have to make this for the Christmas Eve *Eve* dance," Sarah volunteered.

Grace struggled with what to say when Ayden suddenly stood and extended his hand toward Neil. "Well, you have a beautiful son." Then he ambled over and laid a tender kiss on Sarah's forehead. "Keep that boy out of trouble," he whispered, receiving a wide and enamored grin.

They all waved their goodbyes with Ayden grasping Grace's hand and gently leading her into the open corridor. The glistening floor, polished to a buffed shine, reminded her of the place she worked. Funny how she hadn't thought much of Neece's. She even waited for the eagerness to return home to cause an anxious fluttering. When, after a few dispassionate moments nothing happened, she knew she was in trouble.

In disquieting reflection, she strolled beside Ayden and away from the bustling nurses, nervous fathers, and wailing babies. They'd not traveled too far before he stopped her just at the elevator, his stiff stance yielding an uncomfortable admission. "I'm sorry about Neil. He blurts out things without thinking."

Grace didn't know why Ayden was apologizing for a reputation he seemed proud to have built. "He didn't say anything I haven't already thought myself."

"Oh?" Ayden drew back, the casual bluntness of her reply surprising both of them.

She allowed him to mull over her comment, seeing no harm in him reflecting on how she saw him. "It's not a bad thing," she assured him. "Through the centuries, men have aspired to become rakes, and women have aspired to tame them."

The corner of his mouth twitched and his cerulean eyes flashed a challenging decree. "And how many *rakes* have you tamed, Grace?"

In one searing blaze, he'd managed to open a tender wound, one that left her vulnerable and frightened. She answered the only way she knew how, with blind sincerity. "Despite what you may think of me, I do not aspire to break the will of any man. As I've painfully discovered, I cannot force anyone to fall in love with me, whether by taming or otherwise." She ambled away, entering the elevator on the tenth floor, Ayden's footsteps close behind her. She was still facing forward when she heard the elevator close and felt his hand clamp down on her wrist, whipping her back around to face him.

In one crashing heartbeat, he wrapped an arm around her back, the vigorous motion locking her against him. She tried to move, but his free hand cupped the back of her head, pulling their mouths within a sliver of touching.

He smelled of scented soap and crisp air, a thrilling combination that drugged her thoughts and sensibilities. He didn't kiss her, his mouth hovering and taunting her to lean a hair closer.

"Give it your best shot, Grace." His voice was a hot, husky whisper against her cheek. Did he really mean to open this door, to expose them both to proving, one way or the other, impassioned philosophies? With her heart battering hard in her chest, she leaned forward and touched her lips to his.

He emitted a low growl and shoved her against the hard steely wall of the elevator. As it jolted into motion, he took her mouth with unbridled possession, draining her of any thought or energy. Wild and unchaste, his lips pressed hard against hers, forcing them to open for him. She delighted in the sweet taste of his kiss and the urgent command of his mouth.

She tried to keep up, to take what he offered and give what she thought he wanted. Then the elevator beeped, and he separated from her, pausing to plow a hand through this thick dark-blond hair. Rattled and trembling, she braced her hand on one of the elevator handrails waiting for the door to open. When they did, an elderly couple stepped inside.

For three painstaking minutes, patients and hospital staff entered and left with her sneaking quick glances in Ayden's direction. She wanted to know his thoughts and if they were as convoluted as hers. Of course, she'd often daydreamed of an elevator kiss. What girl didn't? Nothing, however, prepared her for the emotional and physical collision between her mind and heart.

Finally, the elevator jolted to a stop on the first floor, and Ayden secured her hand, guiding her into the corridor and toward the sliding glass doors. Outside, the snow crunched under their feet, and the wind snapped at their cheeks. She wondered if she should not have said what she did. What right did she have in spewing her ideas of love? Not that she didn't feel it, she'd just chosen to stick with a guy who had been as reliable as every other man in her life.

Chapter Sixteen

Ayden couldn't remember the last time he wanted a woman this much. She made him lose all sense of reason the longer he spent with her and the longer he stood fighting for control.

In the elevator, he'd kept his emotions in check until the satiny lushness of her tongue brushed across his lips. Control surrendered to obsession. She'd matched his fervor, exploring and teasing until, so sweetly, she'd opened further for him. At that moment, he knew he couldn't rest until he'd sampled every inch of her, his creeds be damned. For now, however, he needed to cool his blood, for Grace's sake…and his.

"So," he said, once they were settled inside the cab. "Are you ready to find out who might be behind your sister's disappearance?"

Grace sat quiet and contemplative, and he knew she thought about what he'd said and did in the elevator. Despite what he craved from her, he only hoped she didn't sit there planning a spring wedding, although, he did see her more as a fall bride, one with more reflection than spontaneity.

"Yes," she answered after some hesitation.

His heart hammered from both their kiss and her reply. Had he actually sat there mulling over the idea of marrying her? Damn, he cursed to himself, unused to losing track of his concrete beliefs on falling in love and matrimony promises so easily.

In a conscious effort to stay focused, he parked a few spaces from the store, the place hopping with customers. He saw Jolene who sent him a cheerful nod from the potpourri section of the store. Unfamiliar to most of them, Grace scooted closer to his side. The shop attracted many of Mistletoe's females, and he recognized all of them, one-third of which he'd tied himself to in one intimate way or another.

Whether there existed a history or not, at least six flickering glances remained fixed on him and Grace from the door to the counter. One of them, he cared not to see, not since she'd shattered Grace's bedroom window a few nights before.

To his rescue, Wilhelmina called from behind the cash register, a small paper bag clutched in her wrinkled hands. "I do hope you find what you're looking for," she said with profound sincerity. "Now did you happen to sample my rum cake?"

Her dark deep-set eyes shifted from him to Grace, at last landing on the most affected victim of the spiked dessert.

"Sample is a good word," he said, without chuckling.

Wilhelmina gushed and giggled like a teenager.

"Oh, and I wanted to make you something to thank you for all your help." Grace handed the older woman a plate of her dessert and backed away.

"Oh, my. These look delicious. I heard somewhere you were a baker."

Grace smile. "I work in a bakery, but I'd love to have my own place…someday."

As they continued to talk, several feet away, Ayden

leaned back and enjoyed the view. That was until El slunk up beside him.

"She's pretty."

Ayden suppressed an expletive, trying everything in his power to avoid the woman's sultry voice inside his right ear. He didn't move as she sauntered around to his front and grinned at him like an innocent child just about to raid a candy store.

"Yes," he agreed and lifted his head a little higher to avoid her searching lips. Her hands, long and hunting, dug inside his unzipped coat.

His patience exhausted, he bent to retrieve her fingers when her mouth clamped hard over his, her body twisting against him like a wild eel.

"Eloise Victoria Riley, unhand him this instant!"

El jerked backward, enabling Ayden a clear view of Wilhelmina and Grace. The latter stood wide-eyed and astonished but unmoving and silent. Although his and Grace's relationship was anything but real, he felt dirty and undeserving of her.

"I was leaving anyway." El sniffed and then spun around to direct her last thoughts straight at Grace. She was a harmless woman unless provoked. He loathed placing Grace in the middle of his mistakes and stepped forward to protect her when she sent him a subtle headshake.

With a few curious customers watching, El eased before Grace and lifted her chin at a haughty angle. "I actually feel sorry for you, you know. One day you'll be where I'm standing, pining away, while he's gone and left you behind."

Grace sent El a sympathetic smile. "You're very beautiful. I don't know what happened between you and Ayden, but I do know at least a dozen guys in San Francisco who would be tripping over themselves to ask you out. There's no reason why you should be left anywhere."

Ayden's jaw dropped. He'd expected a catfight, and so did most of everyone else in the store. After a few astonished moments, El leaned down to whisper something in Grace's ear.

She then turned and walked in his direction, pausing to give him a parting harrumph. When he lifted his gaze to Grace, she stood calm and poised. Not that he wanted her to fly off in irrational jealousy at what she'd seen, but some sort of annoyed reaction at seeing El kiss him might have fed his ego a little.

Instead, she sauntered forward, smirked, and lifted the bag from his hands. "I'm ready if you are." She turned her attention to Wilhelmina, who might have expected the same thing he did. "Thank you very much for everything."

Every single gaze followed them, with Grace keeping a safe distance ahead as they walked under the mistletoe, three seconds apart, and out the door. He refrained from saying a word until they had gathered in the cab and settled into the leather seats. He tried to look at her, but she had her face forward and her gaze straight ahead. With the temperature of the cab still comfortable, he thought it as good a place as any to talk. In one smooth movement, he grasped the lever and shoved the seat back to give himself plenty of legroom.

She didn't even act surprised as he lifted his knee and drew close to her. "Would you like me to explain what happened between me and El?"

Grace dropped her head back to lie against the seat.

"No, I'm pretty sure she summed it up very well in there."

He drew a hand down his face and up again. "You're angry?"

Her gaze shifted toward him first before she decided to straighten and rotate toward him. "I'm feeling a lot of *emotions* right now, but anger is not one of them."

She glanced down at her hands where they lay folded in her lap. Halfway through "Jingle Bell Rock," she inhaled and raised her chin level to his. In an unconscious move, she swiped at her bangs and dove into an explanation.

"I'll admit it was a little…jarring to see you kissing her, especially after what has or has not happened between us in the last few days, but I've no expectations of us, Ayden. I'm here to find my sister and fool yours. As far as we are concerned, whatever happens between us, the end will undoubtedly be the same."

She paused as something outside his window drew her attention away for a brief moment. He started to turn when her enchanting gaze flitted back to him. "And the sooner, the better, I think."

He didn't have much time to ponder her words as she shifted closer. Her eyes alight with uncertainty, her body trembling with nervousness; she touched both sides of his face with her small hands.

"Grace," he whispered, his heart starting to pound with expectation.

"Shhh," she scolded him and bent her head to place a warm, leisurely kiss against his lips.

Lost in the moment, he wrapped his arms around

her back, pulling her closer. Only, he didn't stop until she sat straddling him with the steering wheel pressing them closer together. He stifled a groan as the electrifying connection sparked between them again

****

Grace settled onto Ayden's lap, his thick arousal igniting a desire she could not control. Fire pulsed through her veins, consuming and ravenous. Together, their heartbeats pounded in thunderous rhythm. She became lost, enveloped in Ayden's embrace and the rapture of his kiss. She melted into him, accepting each delicious and lilting stroke of his tongue. She longed to draw closer so nothing, not even light, separated them. Her breath hitched when his hand cupped the back of her head and pulled her mouth harder against his. He took from her, his lips strong and controlling, gliding over hers with dizzying prowess. Underneath her, his arousal expanded. She almost cried out when his hands moved to grasp her hips and drive her deep against him. Trembling inside and out, she writhed on his lap, the tension of her desire building with wondrous sensations. Then a groan tore from his throat, and he broke the kiss in an agonizing revolt.

"Grace, stop."

Dazed, she leaned back to find his eyes squeezed shut and his face set in a severe pose. Although she'd been the one who initiated the kiss, he was the one who put her here. Still, afraid that she'd overstepped the boundaries of their phony relationship, she pushed away from him. Humiliation at her unguarded inhibitions made her stomach knot and the back of her neck break out in a cold sweat. Not that she was inexperienced with men, she'd simply never felt the rush of such physical passion, never heard her name called out with such hoarse frustration.

On her side of the cab, in her sudden puddle of insecurity, she tried to find an excuse for what she'd done and why. When Grace had spotted Maggie on the sidewalk, at least twenty feet away, she wanted to settle her and Ayden's counterfeit relationship for good. She believed that if Maggie saw them as a couple, Ayden would concentrate more on helping her with Danielle than falsifying her existence.

Only, she didn't anticipate losing herself in the moment. Now, as much as she dreaded it, she returned her attention to Ayden, finding him sitting on his side, his head bent back and resting against the rear window.

Before he rushed to draw any rash conclusions about why she climbed on him like an animal in heat, she said, "I saw Maggie, and thought it might be a good idea to show her that we were madly—" The words froze on her tongue. *In love.*

She realized getting through, however long it would take to find Danielle, was going to be like dancing through a field riddled with land mines. To make matters worse, Ayden's sister had disappeared into thin air, making Grace appear like she'd made up the entire episode to accost him in front of an innocent couple's drug emporium.

Her emotions began to snowball into disarray as Ayden stayed silent and sulking, shifting the truck into Drive and taking them home without saying a word. He even switched off the radio, forcing Grace to hum something in her mind to keep from thinking of how blatantly she reacted to him. If only he'd say something, even if it were a stern, "Don't ever do that again."

In the driveway, she leaped out of the cab and was halfway up the porch stairs when he joined her to open the door. Once inside, she contemplated packing her bags and returning to San Francisco, forcing Danielle to lie in the bed she'd made.

Only, when Grace took two steps toward the staircase, Ayden grabbed her arm and swung her around, slamming her hard against him. "What was that?" he asked, his voice deep and growling.

Grace stiffened. She knew exactly what he meant. "I told you." She'd hesitated to say the words again. His dire mood confused and troubled her. Distrusting his sudden disposition, she lashed back at him. "This was your plan, remember? Convince Maggie how much—"

"In love we are?" he finished for her. "Yes, we've covered that, and do you want to know what I think?"

"Will it do any good to say no?"

He ignored her, his blue eyes flashing danger and incitement. "I think you are wrong about drama being your worst subject, Grace. Your display earlier did a good job of making a pretty little liar out of you."

Her jaw dropped open, hurt by his brusque tone and callous insinuation. She wanted to say something to defend herself, but what? Acknowledge she hadn't pretended anything? That the emotional delight of kissing him, touching him, came as natural to her as...holding her breath. Well, he certainly didn't want to hear that confession.

"And I think I've had enough of you and Mistletoe, Mr. McCabe." She struggled to free herself, him letting her go a little easier than she expected or wanted. He stepped back, his shoulders stiff, his jaw jumping from having his teeth clamped too tight.

"Where are you going?"

"Home." She took a step up the winding staircase.

"So, you're running away."

She whipped around. "No, I'm quitting."

"What's the difference?"

Unprepared for the challenge of her answer, she wrestled with a reply. "Running away means you're afraid of something. Quitting is when you've given up on a ridiculous notion."

She saw the Adam's apple in his throat bob before lowering his voice and asking, "What notion would that be, exactly?"

Grace pressed her palms to her forehead and brought in a few therapeutic inhales. Unwilling to confess her disenchantment with love, she dropped her arms, deciding, instead, to feign indifference.

"Look, if you're concerned about Maggie, I'll write you a Dear John letter on the train. I'll make it so heart wrenching, you might even shed a tear over it."

She rotated back up the staircase when he reached up to stop her and then turned her so her back lay pressed against the angled wall, his hands planted on both sides of her head.

"I've touched a nerve with you, haven't I? You wouldn't be so angry if I hadn't!"

She felt her eyes grow wide with astonishment. "I'm not the one who's angry, you are!"

He opened his mouth with a reply when the doorbell rang. She glanced toward the door to find a shadow of a woman standing on the other side.

"Dammit!" he cursed, and traipsed down the few stairs to the landing. Grace almost expected another one of his ex-girlfriends, maybe dressed in nothing but a gray trench coat and holding a can of whipped cream. Who she didn't expect was Maggie.

****

Ayden stared down at his sister, half wanting to twirl her around and boot her back onto the porch. He and Grace needed to finish talking…or arguing. Oh, he'd had his fair share of fights when it came to women; he'd learned to walk away from them. With Grace, he found himself so absorbed and responsive to everything she did and said, he didn't know how to control what he was saying or how he was saying it. Regarding the incident in the cab, hearing she'd initiated the kiss just to give Maggie a show infuriated him. There he was, his blood pounding, his body rigid with want and unfulfilled satisfaction. Only, Grace had done exactly what he'd asked her to do. She was *playing* his girlfriend. He needed to be more careful. The last thing in the world he wanted was to get tangled up in something he couldn't leave. But God help him. Grace, in a matter of days, had managed to break down his concrete boundaries and intentions.

"Maggie, this isn't a good time," he said, in a warning voice.

"You always say that." She brushed by him to stop in the foyer, her attention drawn to Grace on the staircase. He shut the door on a loud sigh and rotated around to find both women, staring at one another.

"You're quite popular already," Maggie said, a hint of admiration in her voice.

Grace smiled. "I think it was inevitable, with your brother as my…boyfriend."

Maggie let out a soft laugh and then nodded. "Yes,

I'd say so."

Ayden relaxed his shoulders and walked around his sister to stand beside Grace. She had descended to the landing, her hands clasped together in front of her petite form. Wanting to feel her near him, he slid his arm around her back and pressed her against his side.

"How are the kids?"

Maggie jerked her gaze up to his as if she'd been in some sort of trance. "What?"

"I said, how are the kids? Are they still sick?"

His sister shook her thick dark-brown auburn hair and let her shoulders slump. "Oh, they're recovering. I thought I'd have everyone over tomorrow evening. I'm not sure if Neil, Sarah, and the baby can make it, though," she finished saying and turned again to gaze at Grace.

"Yeah, I should probably bring the tree over tonight and get it put up before it starts to dry out, don't you think?" he asked. Again, he waited for Maggie to respond, and again, she ignored him. He had no doubt Maggie had seen Grace accost him earlier and that she was, at this very moment, guessing what size wedding dress Grace wore.

"Maggie, would you like something to eat?"

"No, I'm not thirsty."

"Right." He nodded.

He lifted his gaze to Grace, her lips clamped shut and her shoulders trembling with quiet laughter. For selfish reasons, he wanted Maggie to leave, but he didn't want to hurt her feelings. Remembering the tape Wilhelmina gave him, he pulled away from Grace and stepped toward the door.

"Well, it's been an…unusual visit, Maggs, but

Grace and I were about to…sit down and…discuss something."

As soon as those words left his mouth, he knew he'd just let the gates of his sister's romantic notions swing wide open. Her arms flew around Grace so fast, he didn't have time to recant or explain what he meant.

Maggie squealed and wrapped her arms around Grace, squeezing and agitating her like a washing machine. "Okay, okay. I'm leaving." She let go and backed away, smiling.

"Maggie, wait, why did you come here in the first place?"

She sent him a quizzical look, shrugged, and then beamed. "I can't remember. See you soon." And she was gone.

He took his time shutting the door before rotating around to find Grace with her gaze pinned to the floor at his feet. She didn't look up as she whispered toward him. "I feel awful."

He had to admit, part of him did, too. Still, he was more concerned about her leaving than crushing Maggie's expectations. "So, are you still thinking about quitting?"

Grace let out a long exhale and sank onto the second stair. She placed her elbows on her knees, her chin in her hands, and closed her eyes. He didn't move, soaking in her quiet and reflective form for as long as she allowed him. For the first time, he noticed how his heart beat in a battled rhythm at the mere sight of her. No matter if his mind wanted to wave off how much she affected him, his heart did not.

Unsure of what to say, he joined her on the staircase. "I'm sorry, about earlier. It's just that when you kissed me in the truck, it was so…unexpected and…real."

She scoffed and clicked her tongue. "Is that male code for bad?"

He laughed and then cleared his throat. "I'm not sure what a male code is, but no, it's not bad. It was as far from bad as anything I've ever…" He stopped short of explaining and changed the subject. "You didn't deserve how I reacted or what I said."

"It doesn't matter if I deserved it or not, you still believe I lied."

"No, I believe you underestimate yourself."

"Thank you…I think."

He wanted to reach out to her, but kept his hands to himself. "Grace. I don't want…I don't want us running away half-cocked, without at least trying to work through it."

"I told you, I wasn't running away."

He inhaled and drew his hands down his face. "You were quitting, I know. Damn, you're the most infuriating female."

"I hope that's not one of your pickup lines, McCabe," she grumbled in a sarcastic tone.

Chapter Seventeen

Grace didn't even have time to think before Ayden's mouth smothered hers in a kiss that made the hairs on the back of her neck dance. His lips caressed hers with one erotic stroke after another, making her want to forget the emotional tug-of-war taking place between them. Still, with his silken tongue driving her mad with wanting, did she dare consider there existed more behind this kiss than physical unadulterated lust?

Then, as fast as he pressed his mouth to hers, he pulled away. "One of the hardest things I've ever had to do was tell you to stop." His lips brushed across her brow. "And for the record"—he paused, shifting his mouth down to her ear to whisper—"I don't need pickup lines."

Her pulse shuddered and her heart raced, wishing they weren't with each other solely to provide a means to an end. At last, he let go and stood before her, tall and magnificent. She understood what took place between them was only the beginning.

"For now, we should go explore some clues to find your sister." He held out his hand, and she accepted his offer, not even sure she remained in Mistletoe for Danielle or herself. Regardless, she walked with Ayden to the living room and sat down, her outer thigh pressed close to the warmth and strength of his.

"Are you ready?" he asked, his features giving

nothing away as to what he wanted to find in the video.

Grace nodded and concentrated on the television screen, her eyes squinting at the mind-numbing and grainy image of "A Day in the Life of Mr. and Mrs. Hawthorne."

They fast-forwarded through the slow times until a half-hour passed, and Grace sighed and fell back against the billowy couch, discouraged. "Are you sure she gave us the right day?"

"Wilhelmina Hawthorne has an imaginary cat named Gunther. At this point, I can't be sure about anything."

Grace bent her chin to her chest and closed her eyes. It dawned on her the woman might have made up the entire story of someone coming into the store to purchase the postcard.

Leary of raising her hopes for nothing, Grace stood and began pacing. "Oh, what am I doing? I've come all this way, risked losing the only job I've ever had, for what? I mean, what if we do find Danielle? Do I drag her back to San Francisco?" Then a practical conclusion hit her like a ton of concrete. "What if she's met someone like you and fallen madly in love with him?"

Grace froze over her own words. Catching her meaning, Ayden lifted slowly from his perched position on the couch. She was thinking aloud, throwing out scenarios, hoping something would stick. Only, she didn't expect to reveal how close she stood to her last concern for her sister.

Frustrated and tired, she lifted her index finger toward his chest. "Don't you dare ask me what I meant by that; I'm not in love with you, Ayden McCabe, nor am I plan on falling in love with you. The last thing I want, or need, for that matter, is to wind up as one of your statistics."

Grace held her gaze on Ayden's stern lips and stoic expression. They'd only spent a few days together, but she knew enough to deduce he wanted nothing to do with emotions or commitment. He responded to her physically, but she wondered how long it would be before she wanted more, just like the rest of them. Whether he saw them as an albatross or nuisance, she didn't want him to remember her attached to either.

She supposed when the silence became too much for him to bear, he closed the distance between them and lowered his voice. What he said left her speechless.

"My mother loved my father. My father gave up everything to make her happy. I'm sure he had dreams, but they became buried under the obligations of this house. There was no compromise there. I believe they'd still be alive today if he hadn't been so weak as not to tell my mother he wanted to go back to Ireland."

Grace stood astounded at Ayden's fierce confession. Not only did she think his aversion to love came from somewhere else; she'd imagined his parents as the most fortunate of loving couples. Now to hear Ayden tell it, he appeared to resent what his mother and father meant to one another. She realized at that moment, she'd never be able to reach him, no matter what she did or didn't do.

"I'm hungry," she said to change the subject and pull the scowl from around his lips. He was much more handsome when he thought he had things under control.

He stepped back, his eyes narrowing. "So that's it?"

Confused, she shook her head. "What's it?"

He scoffed, pulling both hands down the length of his handsome face. "Come on, Grace. You mean to tell me you don't have some antidote bouncing around in that wistful mind of yours about how to cure my cynicism regarding love?"

Rising to his challenge, she crossed her arms over her breast and lifted her chin to a haughty angle. "No, McCabe, I have no antidote or potion or whimsical notion that will cure you of your cynicism. If I did, I'd reverse the recipe and use it on myself."

In the glowing sunlight cascading through the window behind them, his mouth lifted in a breathtaking, infectious smile. "Do you like ham and Swiss?"

She dropped her arms to her side and nodded. "It's my favorite."

A few minutes later, they settled back on the couch, a tad closer than they were before and drew their attention to the wide screen. Grace's gaze began to blur when the man the Hawthornes had described ambled into view.

Alert and cautious, she pushed forward and stared at the unfolding scene. With her heart drumming hard in her chest, she saw the faceless man the older couple described. He took less than five seconds to pick out the card before ambling toward the counter.

Ayden sighed. "One thing's for certain…he sure as hell didn't want anyone to know who he was."

Grace agreed, realizing they weren't any closer to locating Danielle now than they were five minutes ago. "So, I guess we're back to square one," she said, unable to hide the fact she wasn't entirely disappointed in finding herself there, again. As she struggled with the guilt of placing Ayden before her sister, her phone began vibrating in her pocket.

Half expecting Rick and half expecting her mom, she glanced down and gasped. "Oh my God."

"What?" Ayden laid a hand on her shoulder.

Grace blinked and then blew out a long breath. "It's a text message from Danielle."

Beside her, Ayden stiffened, an immediate reaction he quickly recognized and corrected. "What's the message?" he said in a more detached tone.

Grace read the cryptic text, her mind trying to decipher and process it at the same time. "*I'm fine. Isn't Mistletoe lovely? Wilhelmina is a hoot. Love, D.*"

"She knows I'm here," Grace whispered.

"She must have talked to your mom," Ayden volunteered, trying to make sense of it in his own way.

Grace nodded until a ding sounded and she glanced down to find a new text from her mom. Grace lifted her phone and read, "*Any word yet? I'm running out of things to tell people.*"

Grace inhaled and tapped her fingers to text her mom a response. *No word. Still searching.* She hit Send and then replied to her elusive sister. *Where the HELL R U?*

A heartbeat later, her screen lit up with a one-word answer. *Mistletoe.*

Grace lifted her hands to her face and dropped back on the couch. None of this made sense, and certainly not the fact that Danielle claimed to be in a town where no one had seen her. "Is it possible to track her location?"

The solemn glance Ayden sent Grace gave her little hope. "Only if she has the app, and even then, it's highly likely she's already had it disabled. Someone who doesn't want to be found will find a way to cover their tracks."

For Grace's sake, Ayden placed a comforting arm around her and brought her against him. She closed her eyes and allowed her head to fall on his chest. She loved being this close to him, hearing the steady and solid beat of his heart against her right ear. "I'll see if Fitzy can determine her location, somehow. He has connections."

Grace didn't say anything, unwilling to break the normal moment between them. They sat like this for a while, not talking, just breathing. She'd almost drifted off into a peaceful sleep when his voice reverberated against her cheek. She jerked herself awake and lifted up to see him.

"Grace, I have to take the Christmas tree over to Maggie's. You're welcome to come."

She didn't know if that was a good idea. She and Ayden still had fake relationship problems to iron out before an evening in Maggie's company. "I like your sister, but it might be best if I see as little of her possible."

His face remained unreadable in the dim light. "In that case, I'll be back as soon as I can. Help yourself to whatever's in the fridge."

He hesitated at the door, giving her a perplexed grin. For whatever reason, she felt his reluctance to go and wondered if he'd had the same thought of seeing his sister again and having to react to questions with no legitimate answer.

****

Ayden swung into Maggie's driveway, his mind still on Hearth's Gate and the guest who dwelled there.

186

It had been less than fifteen minutes since he'd left Grace, and he already missed her. Like a windswept flower, she danced about in his mind, clueless of what she was doing to him. He hoped, however, his obsession did not show so obviously on his face. Maggie knew how to read him, sometimes too well.

The first to greet him was his young nephew Collin. "Uncle Ayden," the boy said, running and wrapping his small arms around Ayden's knees. He was a child who desperately missed his father.

"Hey there." He ruffled the boy's hair with his free hand. "Where's your mom?"

"On the phone. I'll go get her." Like a cannon shot out of a rocket, Collin spun around and ran, full sprint, through the living room. He disappeared into the kitchen, appearing a few seconds later, pushing his mother from behind.

Maggie waved with a spaghetti-stained child on her hip. Ayden grinned at Ciara, his one-and-a-half-year-old niece, before turning to haul the rest of the tree inside the house.

"Where's Grace?"

Ayden paused to grimace at Maggie, wishing he had thought of a good excuse regarding Grace's absence. "She's not feeling well, but she says hello," he said, lying outright.

Maggie sent him a skeptical smirk. "She doesn't like me, does she?"

He threw his hand out. "For the love of God, Maggie, she likes you. She's just…having…a stomachache."

"What kind of stomachache?"

He drew a hand down his face as Maggie covered

Collin's ears before whispering in a loud manner in Ayden's direction. "You didn't get her pregnant, did you?"

Annoyed beyond reason, Ayden yanked the rest of the Christmas tree through the doorway, shut the door with a firm smack, and then dropped the bristly object at her feet. "How in the hell did you deduce that from what I just said?" He then tore off his gloves and threw them on a nearby end table.

"Well, I just thought—"

Ayden closed his eyes and lifted his head toward the ceiling in an exaggerated inhale. He hated overreacting, especially with Maggie so emotional with her husband away and raising two children by herself.

"I'm sorry, Maggs. It's been a long day."

She sent him a tired grin. "You can make it up to me by putting up the tree and then taking a peek at my washing machine. It won't spin. Kyle is always so good at that sort of stuff."

For the next five hours, Ayden found himself repairing a slew of household problems. Between fixing the washing machine, a leak in the upstairs bathroom, and a squeaky door in Ciara's room, he called the house to talk to Grace.

"Are you checking up on me?"

He smiled. "Yes. I was afraid you might have taken off with my big screen."

There was a pause. "No, it cost too much for a rental truck, and the darn thing's too big to carry through the front door."

He chuckled and then imagined her tucking a piece of hair behind her ear. "Why do I ask?" he teased.

"I don't know," came her sweet answer.

He closed his eyes and rested his head against the door of the kitchen. "I'll be home soon."

"Okay."

He hung up the phone and turned to find Maggie staring at him, a whimsical expression on her tired face. "Don't," he said before grasping Collin by the hand and leading him to the kitchen sink, a toy screwdriver secured in his toy construction belt. By the time Ayden checked his watch, it was half past eleven. "I have to go, Maggie. I'll see you tomorrow."

"Give Grace a kiss for me."

He opened his mouth to say something, but quickly decided against it. The hour had grown too late and his mind too weary to go another round of questions from her. He kissed her and a sleepy Collin and drove home.

A little less anxious than the night before, he entered Hearth's Gate with quiet and careful steps. After a long shower, he lay awake, exhausted and freezing from the window he'd neglected to fix. For fifteen minutes, he rotated his head from Grace's room, toward the ceiling, and back again. At last, he sat up with a relenting grunt.

Before he'd put one foot on the ground, a soft knock sounded at his door. "Ayden?"

"Come in." He waited for the door to open. She appeared, scooting to stand in a splinter of moonlight, several feet away. He started to push himself out of bed when she held up her hand to stop him.

"How was Maggie?"

"Nosy," he answered.

"Hmm, does she think I'm—"

"Pregnant? Yes."

"What!" The distance Grace had tried to keep

between them disappeared in a blink as she sprang toward the bed. With eyes as big as the sun, she gazed down at him. "You cannot be serious?"

"Oh, I'm dead serious," he said, unable to hold back a chuckle.

She grasped him by the shoulders. "Tell me you don't think that's funny?"

For the first time, he noticed what she wore under the blanket, and it wasn't much. The slinky tank top she continued to tease him with rose to reveal a powdery pale midriff. He lifted his hand, grazing his fingertips against the velvety smoothness of her skin.

"Grace," he whispered, closing his eyes, unsure if the blood rushing through in his veins came from his physical attraction of her or some emotional need. Either way, he wanted her; he just didn't know the consequences that would follow.

Chapter Eighteen

Grace's plan was to say hello, keep her distance, and *pretend* she didn't want to jump in bed with him so he could make love to her the rest of the night. When he hauled her underneath him, however, her plan disintegrated like a sand castle under a tidal wave. Clean, masculine heat radiated from his body, and she ached to connect to him, to feel his bare skin pressed against hers. Impatient and shaking, she lifted the ends of his T-shirt, breaking their kiss to pull it over his head.

Above her, his dark blue eyes changed to an almost black hue. If she wanted him to stop, she had to say something now. She didn't. Instead, she lifted her fingers up to weave through his thick hair and to pull his lips back to hers. Her eyes closed, and her head spun as if she'd eaten too much of Wilhelmina's sinful rum cake.

Despite how they met or the physical versus emotional terms of their agreement, he kissed her with an eternal promise. For this moment, they had no reason to ever part ways. She clung to the thought, opening to him, welcoming his velvety tongue and the whimpers of pleasure he elicited with each stroke. She believed they'd evaded each other for too long, the urgency to get to know one other pulling them closer.

Under his deliberate and careful prowess, clothes

fell away, leaving Grace naked underneath him.

"You don't know how much I want you," he said, his voice hoarse and breathless. She did know because she felt her own want for him pulsing deep inside her.

With his kisses driving her desires deeper, he cupped her left breast, his thumb teasing her nipple into a hard bud. She arched upward, every sensation heightened, every sensible thought gone.

Adrift in his wondrous and warm caress, she allowed herself to let go of the past and the future. This was her time, their time. He seemed to read her thoughts, his mouth growing more possessive and his hand sliding down below her waist. Her legs opened, allowing his fingers to explore and taunt the soft flesh between her thighs. She cried out when he found the most sensitive place at her core, her body trembling for a shuddering release.

"Please," she begged, sucking in a shallow breath.

He withdrew his hand, eliciting a protest deep in her throat. "Not until I'm inside you." He shifted their bodies, their hearts pounding with anticipation. "I can't wait," he whispered, his voice hoarse and trembling. She nodded and stared into his dark blue eyes.

"Ayden," Grace said his name on a tattered exhale. He brought his mouth to hers, kissing her with a fervency that drugged her senses. She wanted to give back to him, to make him feel the same delicious pleasure. Unbridled, she glided her tongue over his lips before plunging inside his mouth. She matched his intensity, moving in and out in a tantalizing dance.

"God, Grace," he rasped, moving his knees to spread her legs further apart. She dug her short nails into his back, pressing him closer to her. He lifted his hips to push forward when she froze underneath him.

"Grace, are you all right?" he asked, lifting his beautiful face above hers.

"I…I think there's someone banging on your door," she whispered, wishing she had chosen to ignore it. There was still a blissful place she wanted Ayden to take her, a place she might always wonder about if they found Danielle, and she had no more reasons to stay.

They lay perfectly still until the banging started again. "Son of a—" Ayden hissed. "I have to go."

"I know."

He kissed her lips and pushed himself up, reaching down to pull his discarded pajama bottoms on with a quick, forceful jerk. Before he crossed the threshold into the hall, he stepped back with a warning. "Don't. Move."

Of course, Grace lay alone, not flinching, and aching for Ayden's return. Unavoidably, she strained to listen, praying she didn't hear a muffled female voice drifting up the stairway. Of course, five minutes later, she did. After spending a frantic moment finding her shirt and shorts, she lay back down and pulled the pillow from behind her head, burying her face into the spicy scented down. Loath to eavesdrop on a conversation she had no business hearing, she brought the heavy pillow to clamp around her ears.

Feet shuffled, furniture moved, and doors opened and shut until she felt the bed wiggle.

"Grace?" Amusement settled into his subdued voice.

She shook her head, afraid to come out of hiding, afraid to glance over and see a woman wearing a trench coat and holding a dreaded can of whipped cream. With little effort on his part, Ayden gently pulled the pillow away from her face, a devilish smirk touching his lips. "Afraid of the dark?"

She blinked. "Something like that."

He kissed her nose and rotated on his side, propping his head in his hand so his elbow rested on the bed. "I wanted you to know we have company."

She scoffed and then shrugged, trying to feign indifference. "So, is it one of your many admirers?"

He nodded. "Hmm, three actually." He lifted the covers and then scolded her in a mocking tone. "I thought I told you not to move."

Dazed he'd take his charismatic reputation so lightly, and her gullible presence for granted, she pushed away from him, only to find herself pinned underneath his solid form for the third time in four days.

"What are you doing?" she whispered, bemused by his words and actions. The dark room outlined the devilish grin spreading across his enthralling face. Entranced by him, she let his hand brush back a wisp of hair from her lashes.

His features softened. "You're so beautiful." He bent to kiss her, and suddenly remembering who lay next door, she angled her head away from him. How could he think of making love to her now?

With his hard body pressing her into the mattress, she expected him to coax her into submission, to slide his mouth to the sensitive part below her ear and murmur words of pleasurable promises. Only he didn't, and after a few moments, she felt a rumble start to build in his chest. Was he actually laughing?

"Unbelievable." She pushed at his chest. "I think I

should go sleep on the couch." She didn't have to shove too hard before he relented and let her go—too easily she thought. She scrambled off the bed and stepped toward the door before whipping around, walking back, grabbing his pillow and yanking it from under his head.

"Oh, you are a sight to see when you're jealous."

Too incensed to notice the chilled air touching her skin, she spun toward him, charging at him with purpose and annoyance. "I'm not jealous!" She tried to keep her voice low, but her throat hurt from either the whispering or the truth of his words.

Even in the muted light, she could see his eyebrows lift above his blue eyes. "No, I'm fairly certain that what I'm witnessing is jealousy."

Grace opened her mouth to say something and then clamped it shut. It hit her like a tumbling Christmas tree that he'd been playing her the entire time and loving every minute of it. She closed her eyes and brought in a calm breath before addressing him.

"Maggie and your niece and nephew are over there, aren't they?"

She flipped her eyelids back open in time to see him nod. She struggled to understand her feelings. Embarrassment? No. Exposure? Yes. He'd made her reveal just how…what? How much in love with him she'd fallen. In the dark, in a matter of a few minutes, she'd bared her heart and soul to him without thinking. He, of course, appeared no worse for wear.

"Are you quitting on me, Grace?" His smooth, tranquil voice washed over her. She held back a shiver, forcing herself to remain impassive and aloof. He was her teacher, nevertheless.

After several quiet moments, she puffed out a

response. "No, I'm running."

He grinned wide, and she knew the more she stood staring at him, the further in love she fell.

"Stay with me."

She clicked her tongue, unsure of what to do. While her heart wanted one thing, her mind screamed another. "You're just saying that to keep me from waking Maggie or making her suspicious."

"No," he said, his gaze serious. "It's freezing in here, and you're a hell of lot warmer than my blankets."

Despite the turmoil of their relationship twisting inside her, she smiled. "There's always an ulterior motive with you, isn't there, McCabe?"

He held out his hand, and she walked to the edge of the bed. Without a word, he pulled her down so they lay sideways, him closest to the window and her back flush against his front. His muscular arms curled around her, protecting and possessive. Although the opportunity for them had passed, she delighted in his nearness, his heat and the rhythmic beat of his heart. She wondered how many more times they had together: one day or maybe two. Her disappointing sigh echoed in the shadowed stillness of the room.

"Grace?" he said against her right ear.

"Hmmm?" she answered.

"What are you thinking?"

She stared at the fireplace, the glow from a low fire, pulsating under the grate. "I'm thinking," she began, unwilling to tell the truth. "Why haven't you fixed the window, yet? It's been almost a week, you know."

"Clever diversion, but all right," he said, pulling her closer. "I've been a little occupied lately." He said the words with a more pronounced Irish lilt.

"Oh, women problems?"

"One stubborn and alluring woman, to be exact."

He brought his hand up to caress her shoulder, the light and rhythmic movements causing her erratic heartbeat to slow and her mind to drift.

She didn't know how she'd been able to fall asleep, but she awoke the next morning, finding the place beside her empty. Unsure how to face the day, whether head on or guarded, she padded to the bathroom, showered, dressed, and wandered downstairs.

From the foyer, the rich aroma of coffee steered her straight into the kitchen. Disappointed not to find Ayden leaned against the counter, shirtless, a paper in one hand and a large mug in the other, she strode to the cupboard to search for a coffee cup for herself.

Typical of a bachelor's domain, it sat a fingertip out of range, forcing her to rise on her tiptoes and stretch with extended fingertips to grip the loop of one handle. She almost had it when the front door slammed shut, startling her.

Out of reach, the mug teetered on the edge until it tipped, sailing to the marbled floor and breaking into seven or eight jagged pieces.

"Grace!" Ayden burst into the room, his face masked with worry.

"I'm really not this clumsy," she assured him, her heart pounding from the noise and his reaction.

"Are you hurt?" He ran toward her, dressed in the same pajama bottoms from the night before. His tan coat opened over his washboard torso, and she wished she'd paid more attention to his question than the way he was dressed.

197

"What?"

He threw down the paper she assumed he'd retrieved from the porch and maneuvered around the broken pieces to her side.

"What happened?" he said, grasping her wrists to pull her arms away, his intense gaze searching for blood or injury.

"There she is. See, I told you she was pretty."

Grace glanced around Ayden to find an unfamiliar character, flanked by six other men. All rugged in appearance, half with beards, half clean-shaven, some wearing ball caps, and all of them in jeans, nice shirts, and department store ties.

"Grace, this is my crew. Gregg, Chad, Pete, Kevin, Scott, Dave, and Steve," he said without turning to look at them.

They either tipped their hats or graced her with a nod, one of them even rendering a casual salute. The one who saluted her appeared the oldest out of the group with a few lines crinkling at his gentle eyes when he smiled. She straightened back to Ayden now, and he glanced down, silent, his thick lashes blinking a string of unsaid thoughts.

Grace sighed, knowing yet another delay stood a few feet away from her. "You're leaving, again?"

He peered up and then shifted closer to keep their conversation as private as possible. His hot breath teased her lips and sent her pulse thumbing against his hands where they still held her wrists. "The city moved up our bid to today. There's no way around it."

She nodded. She couldn't hide the fact she was disappointed. Not disappointed that she hadn't found Danielle, but that she missed spending time with

Ayden, talking and getting to know him better. She even looked forward to their arguments.

"Look, as soon as I get back, we'll start piecing some things together. I shouldn't be too long, okay?"

She didn't want him to know how much she missed him when he wasn't there, so she pressed her lips together and said nothing.

"Don't worry about the mess, and don't worry about entertaining them. They pretty much amuse themselves." He sent her a wink and sauntered toward the door.

She nodded before realizing he was leaving her alone with them. "Wait," she called, frantic. "Where are you going?"

"To take a shower.

She stared after him until she remembered she was not alone. Heat rose in her face, most likely the shade of a Washington apple cocktail. She tamped down the embarrassment of having a handful of men witness her ogle their boss and ambled shyly in their direction.

"Would you like some coffee and pastries?" she asked toward the group, ignoring Ayden's instructions as she swept up the mess and opened up the very last of her breakfast pastry.

"Sounds great. Yes, ma'am. I'm trying to quit," came several answers at the same time. The tallest of the group, Chad, offered to help take down the cups as she prepared them three-fourths full. She'd stepped around to retrieve the sugar and evaporated milk when Steve opened the door into the closed dining room, the other men eager to follow.

"Wait!" Grace called, unsure if Ayden wanted them in there, but it was too late. The youngest-looking one, Pete, complained about the darkness and threw open the heavy curtains, allowing a brilliant stream of sunshine inside.

Kevin, the most athletic and certainly the most handsome, complained that the room was too cold and went to the patio to retrieve some dry firewood to build a fire.

In the midst of the gaiety inside the forbidden dining room, Grace tiptoed around, trying to gather someone's attention. She just didn't have a good feeling about this. That was until all the men settled down at the enormous table with their coffee cups and her pastry and began talking. She blushed several times when Scott, the man who said he was trying to quit, raved about her baking skills and begged her to teach his girlfriend how to bake. Otherwise, he said, "I'm going to have to stop by every morning now for coffee and breakfast."

She never corrected his assumption that she'd be here after next week to make the coffee or teach his girlfriend how to do anything. Instead, she sat, mesmerized by the easy and lulling conversation. It reminded her of the B&B in Oregon and why she'd thought about baking in the first place. After several minutes, she began to relax and enjoy their stories. Pete, the narrator of the group, had them bent over laughing about duct taping one of the new guys inside a port-a-potty the day before Thanksgiving.

"What the hell is going on here?"

Grace jumped up, heart pounding and a sick feeling trickling to the bottom of her stomach. She blinked, unable to wipe the image of Ayden's flaring nostrils and clenched jaw. "Um…" was the only thing she could think to say. The severity of Ayden's features literally left her breathless.

"What are you doing?" His tone was harsh, his voice shaking; she knew he'd never believe this was not her idea.

"I—"

"I want everybody out now. This isn't a break area," he yelled across the large space.

The men rose in quiet unison and filtered out into the hall. She wanted to say something, to defend them, to defend herself. "Ayden?"

He stood, his lips pulled into a thin line and his finger pointing to the space behind her. "You had no right to open this door, Grace. You're a guest here, and nothing else. Do you understand?"

Tears sprang to her eyes, his words stabbing hard into her chest. She managed to send him a weak nod, her throat so constricted and unable to form a comprehensible sound.

For some minutes after the front door slammed shut, she couldn't move. She'd never felt so stuck in her life. At last, she recalled the harshness of Ayden's words, the hurt of their meaning wrapping around her heart like a barbed vice.

Convinced she'd made a mistake by staying here, she ran out of the kitchen and up the stairs. She didn't think of how she'd reach the train station until she rounded the corner and smacked straight into Maggie.

The woman glanced up and then down, her assessment of the situation astute and quick. "Ah damn, what did he do now?"

Grace closed her eyes to keep from bursting into tears. The fact that his sister knew he'd done something to drive Grace away did not bode well with her pride. How often did Maggie find one of Ayden's broken-hearted women, their bags packed and their hearts in pieces?

"It's a long story, Maggie. Would you be able to take me to the train station?"

"No, no, no. You're not leaving that easily." Maggie wrapped an arm around Grace and led her into the cold bedroom.

"I don't think you understand." Grace tried not to hiccup a sob.

"No, I don't think you understand. I've never seen Ayden like this before. Last night he came over, and he was like this teenager. He couldn't stop smiling. I've been waiting for that expression for years, Grace, and you gave it to him."

"But—"

"I know I'm a little overbearing, but I just want him to be happy like Mom and Dad were. He's so stubborn. I thought if he found someone he loved, he'd not want to sell this place, that he'd keep their memory alive. That he'd forget all the pain he's suffered."

Grace's intention to tell Maggie everything, melted like ice on a Miami sidewalk.

After a few moments of silent bonding, Maggie pulled away. "I'll make a deal with you. If, after some lunch, you haven't changed your mind about leaving, I'll take you to the train station."

Positive Ayden didn't want any more to do with her, Grace agreed, packed her bags, and met Maggie outside in her black-with-rusted-out-trim SUV.

After Grace let Maggie believe she might stay, she'd return home and tell her mother that Danielle was old enough to make her own mistakes, just like the rest of them.

Chapter Nineteen

Ayden sat in the administrative building in the heart of Mistletoe, with Gregg on one side of him and Kevin on the other. His men hadn't talked to him since he left the house and for good reason.

They continued not to say anything through the questions and PowerPoint presentation as he and his group received odd glances from the mayor, Hank Winslow, and economic development director, Dalphi Lewis.

Dalphi, Ayden groaned inwardly. She was Rachel's sister, and he had no doubt it would play into the final decision.

"We'll talk it over with the board and get back to you in a week or two. Good luck," Dalphi said with no hint of his company winning the bid one way or the other.

At this point, he didn't even care. All he saw during the entire presentation was Grace's face, and the tears glistening in her eyes as he unleashed a decade of pent-up pain and resentment.

No matter what, she didn't deserve his wrath. He hated himself now, hated the fact he'd come to care so much for her. He was breaking every rule he'd made regarding women and relationships and walking over the remnants barefooted.

It didn't help how he'd lain awake all night holding

her, feeling each soft breath she took. Despite his aversion to cuddling in the past, he craved this closeness with her. She fit against him perfectly and ironically. He always thought they needed to be tall.

Now, however, he didn't want to think if she hated him or if she'd rushed out of the house back to San Francisco and into Rick's awaiting arms.

"Damn." His curse drew attention from every corner of the room.

Gregg was the first to saunter forward.

"I'm sorry about earlier." Ayden extended his arm toward his friend and the mediator of the group. Gregg accepted his apology without hesitation.

"I'm not the one you need to apologize to, boss. That woman of yours tried to stop us from using the room. I guess she knew more than us how you didn't want that door open."

His men fell away as Ayden brought up his thumb and index finger to rub at the throbbing behind his eyes. Hoping to catch Grace near his phone, he punched the numbers and waited. Since he'd dismantled his answering machine a few days ago over Maggie's damn flyer, the house phone continued to ring without Grace answering it. He then tried her cell phone number. No answer.

With his patience stretched to the point of snapping, he told his crew to take the rest of the day off and drove back home, praying Francis Tisdale's grandson wasn't running radar behind the O'Shannon billboard sign.

He raced up his porch two steps at a time and tore open the door. "Grace!" he called, his throat closing around the word. The house sat so quiet. Too quiet. He

faltered, knowing, this time, she'd quit him for good.
****

Grace sat biting her lip every time she wanted to cry. Her sulkiness grew worse, having Ayden's niece and nephew staring at her from the back seat of their mother's SUV.

"Are you Uncle Ayden's girlfriend?" the young boy asked after a long silence. With his head leaned forward as far as it would go in the seat restraint, he waited for Grace's answer.

"Collin, leave Grace alone."

"Why—is she sick?"

"Um, no, she's not sick…we hope." Maggie leaned over to pat Grace on the kneecap.

Grace stifled a moan, knowing Maggie still believed she'd become pregnant with Ayden's child. The thought, despite seeing his angry face repeatedly in her mind, made Grace's stomach flip. Unconsciously, she placed her palm there, catching Maggie's attention and worrisome headshake.

"Then why do I have to leave her alone?"

Maggie let out a frustrated exhale and sent a sympathetic gaze toward Grace. "He's at that age, you know."

Grace didn't know, and at this stage in her life, twenty-five without any hopeful prospects of a good, much less lasting relationship, she wondered if she ever would know.

"Is he going to marry you?"

"Collin!" Maggie scolded from her rearview mirror, causing Grace to jump and turn to the boy. He stared at his mother with a *what did I do now* expression before realizing his insistent questions were not worth getting yelled at.

Oh, if only Grace had made Maggie take her straight to the train station four hours ago. Prolonging her dramatic exit from Ayden's life was not only making her feel worse, but also causing more time to slip away between now and her sister's uncertain wedding.

"Do you feel like stopping in at the Hawthornes', Grace? Collin wanted to go shopping for some new ornaments for the tree," Maggie volunteered brightly. "And then I have to stop at the supermarket to get some groceries for tonight."

Grace fell to pieces inside, remembering the Christmas Tree Dinner she and Ayden were supposed to attend, together. Christmas, she scoffed to herself. Here was another reason to hibernate for the holidays.

Swallowing the lump in her throat, she nodded. Why couldn't she just tell the woman no? *No, I have to go home. I have to go and hope Rick is there to…what?* Grace thought long and hard for an answer as Maggie parked the vehicle on the curb before the sentimental store.

For more months than she cared to count, Grace had been there for Rick. She was his landing pad, waiting patiently as he hovered, touched down, and then took off again. Grace had been the slab of concrete, remaining steady, strong, and in place. It started when she was nine, and she'd done nothing to change it. When she returned home, she had to cut the cords starting with her mother. Danielle needed to learn to stand on her own, and Grace needed a parent to help her, a role their mother abandoned all those years ago.

Of course, going back meant leaving, and that

meant she'd never see Ayden again. For the hundredth time that morning, she wanted to bury her head in her hands and cry. Instead, however, she followed Maggie into the store, enfolding Collin's hand in hers as his mother carried Ciara. They shuffled inside, the tinkling bell announcing their ungainly arrival.

Too eager to pick out his ornaments, Collin bolted toward the row of Christmas trees in the corner. The aroma of cinnamon-scented pinecones and vanilla candles infused the festive shop.

Determined to make this her last stop, Grace wandered around, halting at the display table of intricate snow globes she'd admired a few days before. As a child, she'd been drawn to them. She loved the security of such a place, where there were no surprises, only a small world where nothing changed but the falling snow. She picked up the one she admired the most, and shook it with careful hands. Before her, white flakes descended upon a tiny cabin surrounded by two large snow-covered trees. A warm glow of light shone from the cabin's side windows.

"That's one of my favorites, too."

Wilhelmina stood nearby, her soft, wrinkled face radiant from years of happiness.

"I'll let you have it for free if you bring over some more of those delicious pastries," she said with a joyful clap of her hands.

Grace opened her mouth to kindly inform the woman she was leaving, when Maggie answered a call on the other side of the store. All the blood rushed from Grace's face when she guessed the person on the other end.

"No, she's not, she's right here with me. At

Hawthorne's," Maggie said in a reprimanding voice.

"Is that Ayden?" Wilhelmina asked, already making her way to Maggie's side. "Tell him he needs to buy Grace this snow globe she's been admiring."

In horror, Grace shook her head at both women, but they ignored her, especially Maggie. "What? You're darn right you need to talk to her."

Grace groaned, searching for the closest route to the door.

"Ayden wants to talk to you." Maggie extended the phone, some fifteen feet away, in Grace's direction.

Unwilling to break her heart further over the situation, Grace waved away Maggie's offer and headed outside. She expected the cold wind and a few flurries whirling about her. She even expected someone she'd never met to raise their hand and send a cordial wave. What she didn't expect, however, was to find Ayden leaned against his truck, arms crossed and his face cast in troublesome shadows and narrow lines.

He pulled the phone from his ear and straightened to his full height. "We need to talk," he said in a low and rocky tone.

Grace turned back toward Hawthorne's, finding the front window decorated with Maggie and Wilhelmina's encouraging faces. Grace sighed and closed her eyes for a moment, wondering how she'd talked herself into Ayden's life in the first place. Not knowing how to say no was her answer.

Relenting, she walked toward him and stopped. Braver than she felt, she lifted her chin and disclosed her terms. "All right, but only if you promise to take me where I need to go, afterwards."

"No deal," came his quick response, his expression

stiff, his gaze never leaving her face.

"Then, I'll walk." She stepped away only to have him gently grasp her arm and haul her back in front of him.

"The hell you are. It's more than five miles to the train station, and you don't even have a decent coat. Do I need to remind you what happened the last time you braved the elements?"

She drew back, lifting a finger to his chest. "Yeah, you let a tree fall on top of me." It wasn't the complete truth, but she knew when she was losing an argument.

His rigid form drew closer until she had to crane her neck to look at him. Oh, he was a beautiful man. "Are we going to talk or not, Grace?"

She scoffed at him. "Not. I think we've said all we need to say to one another."

A muscle twitched in his jaw, and she knew she'd pushed him a little too far. "You know, I'm not averse to picking you up and putting you into the truck myself."

Afraid he might carry through with his threat, she pressed her palms into his chest. "What, in front of all these people who think you walk on water? You wouldn't dare."

He sent her a breathtaking grin. "I would dare, and I would love every second of holding you while I do it."

Grace's pulse jumped as she backed up an inch. Oh, she should have known: never dare a gambling man. "I swear, Ayden, if my feet leave this ground, I will disclose the entire agreement between us at the top of my lungs."

He paused and canted his head, cocking one eyebrow above his dark blue eyes. "I hate to be the bearer of bad news, but no one will believe I had to blackmail a woman into being my girlfriend."

Frustration pulled Grace's hands into small fists; she wanted so badly to pummel them hard against his chest.

"As well," he said. "It will be a little hard to confess anything, believable or not, when I'm kissing you thoroughly enough to render you speechless."

Grace swallowed hard, torn between wanting him to follow through with his threat and doing what she set out to do. When she realized she had nowhere to go, she dropped her shoulders and huffed out a puff of cold air. "Damn you, McCabe."

He lifted his hand to touch her chapped cheek. "Do you concede?" His eyebrows rose above his azure gaze.

She stared up at him, his vaporous breath, like hers, stirring the charged air between them. Inadvertently, she glanced back at the window to watch Maggie and her cohort send them a cheerful wave.

Grace straightened in Ayden's direction, dejected and afraid. "I tried to tell your men not to go in there. I tried—"

He surprised her when he lifted his other hand to cup her face and tilt it up toward him. "I know. I was a complete ass."

"Yes," she agreed, astonished he admitted to such a thing. "And—"

"Grace, I can't promise I won't say or do something totally idiotic tomorrow, or five minutes from now, but know that I have never run like a madman all over this damn town in order to apologize for it. You didn't deserve what I said, not at all."

Grace smashed her lips together to keep from

smiling. When he was sincere, his slight Irish accent became more prominent. "You know, you really should have your own line of greeting cards."

He smirked at her, warm and endearing. "Do you forgive me?"

She wanted to say no. His words had shaken her world and flipped it upside down. "Can I think about it?" Grace understood there was nothing else to say about what happened between them. He'd apologized in his own way and demonstrated how he wanted her to stay, at least until they'd used each other for their own gain. At this moment, her world felt balanced and full. Whether it would stay that way, she didn't know.

"Is your suitcase in Maggie's car?"

She nodded, and he left her to go retrieve it. Inside the cab, he gave her a play-by-play of what had happened during the bidding process and told her that he'd heard from Fitzy regarding Danielle.

"He wasn't able to trace her call, but he has a hunch that she knows someone here who's keeping her whereabouts a secret."

Grace thought for a long time before giving him an answer. "I know all Danielle's friends. They're either from California or Arizona."

"Then is it possible you might have a mutual friend from here, or who's lived here?"

Grace opened her mouth to tell him no when she froze and just sat there.

"Grace?"

She shook out of her trance and turned to Ayden. "Betsy. We've been friends for a long time, and she did go to school in Seattle. That's why I like the Hawks."

Rattled by what they may or may not have

discovered, Grace closed her eyes and let her head fall back. She thought about her friend, and how she may or may not be involved with Danielle's voluntary disappearance. Grace also thought of how she and Ayden had come close to crossing a treacherous boundary in their relationship. However, she didn't know how far they were willing to go to explore it. She understood five months, much less five days with a man like Ayden McCabe, didn't change his staunch perspective on anything, especially love.

"Grace?"

She jumped when he said her name and angled her head to find him standing at her door, concern pulled across his handsome features. She agreed with a heavy sigh and let him guide her into the house, a firm hand pressed at her lower back.

"I'm going to put your suitcase in my room, but I thought we might want to"—he paused to take a deep breath in and out—"prepare for Maggie's dinner tonight."

Whether he meant it in an intimate way or not, she pointed to the French doors, leading into the living room. "I'll meet you in there."

He gave her a quick nod before leaving her to shrug out of her thin coat. Braver than she felt, she ambled into the cozy living space and settled into the corner of the sectional. As she waited, she grabbed the navy blue afghan and wrapped it around her shoulders.

"That blanket looks good on you."

She jerked her head to the doorway surprised she hadn't heard his assured approach in the hall. She wrapped it tighter and smoothed her hands over the soft material. "It's so lovely."

He stepped further inside the room. Although it was late afternoon, the room was dark with the shades closed and the curtains pulled together.

"I'll make a fire," he said and disappeared before she could convince him they didn't need one. As he stacked and lit the wood, Grace sat back and memorized everything about him. When he set his mind to do something, he did so with focus and poise. Nothing distracted him. No one distracted him.

Despite having to leave Mistletoe soon, she wanted to allow herself to fall helplessly and tragically in love with him. This meant, however, giving up the notion of him falling helplessly in love with her. For once, however, she wanted to do something irrational. Always the responsible parent, she wanted to know the exhilaration of not having her feet stuck firmly in the ground.

As the glow from the fireplace flickered over his intense and wondrous features, she brought a deep breath in and let it out. She *would* let him teach her how to touch and feel. Whether she lost her heart forever in the process, well, that was another matter.

After a few minutes, he joined her on the couch, rotating so his knee was propped up and almost touching her outer thigh. He rested his chin on his fist, his gaze straight on her.

"So, what did you have in mind?" she asked.

Chapter Twenty

Ayden sent Grace a wolfish grin, charging her nerves.

"Okay…why don't we start off with a conversation and go from there," she volunteered. She believed if he kissed her again, they'd never get around to figuring out where they met and why…at least where Maggie was concerned.

"That's safe enough, I suppose."

"Good." She nodded. "First question: Where did we meet?"

He sent her a quizzical glance. "O'Shannon's?"

Grace lifted her shoulders in a shrug, but he'd already changed his mind. "No," he said, glancing down to take her hand in his. "Maggie's too much of a romantic to believe I picked you up in a local bar."

Grace twisted around several different scenarios before offering up the only one that made sense between them. "Maybe…you saw me broken down on the road somewhere, and being the perfect gentleman that you are, on most occasions, you stopped to help."

One side of his mouth lifted. "Go on."

"Um," she said, trying to keep fantasy and reality separate. "We met about six months ago, and had a whirlwind romance for the weekend. We exchanged phone numbers and email addresses with the secret intent of never seeing each other again."

"That sounds like me," he interrupted.

"Shhh!" she scolded and returned to her story. "We went our separate ways, only *you* couldn't stop thinking about me. Every night you'd lie in bed remembering how well I…kissed. So, you wrote me this long sappy email with an invitation to come visit."

"I don't write long sappy emails. Hell, I don't write short sappy emails. Besides, men don't write down their thoughts any more, it's too incriminating."

She ignored him. "It was so like Jane Austen's *Persuasion*. You told me how much you missed me and how you couldn't go another day without seeing my pretty face." She smiled and batted her eyes at him. "Which reminds me, my car wouldn't make the trip— back in the shop, you know—so I had to find an alternative mode of transportation."

Grace paused, suddenly realizing there was one person who could disprove their entire relationship.

"What's the matter?" Ayden touched his fingertips to her cheek.

"How well does Maggie know Jolene?"

Ayden shrugged. "Like a second mother, I guess. Why?"

Grace chewed on her lower lip before answering. "Because that day she drove me to O'Shannon's, she knew we'd never met, and yet the conversation about us being strangers has never come up between her and Maggie. Why do you think that is?"

Ayden straightened away from Grace and rested with his elbows on his knees. "Unless Maggie knows the truth and has chosen to remain oblivious."

Grace had to force her mouth to stay closed. She had a feeling, if what Ayden said was true, Maggie was waiting for them to fall in love for real. Grace had to wonder how many hearts were destined to break at the end of their agreement.

She clicked her tongue. "There sure are a lot of people who either want to marry you or see you get married, Ayden McCabe."

He didn't even blink before offering her the proclamation. "Then let's give them what they want."

Grace stared at Ayden, unsure if she'd heard him right. "What?"

He stood and paced between the coffee table and the fireplace. The fire danced across his meditative features, frightening her a little. "Ayden?"

He met her with three hurried strides, reaching down to grasp her upper arms in order to lift her up to face him. "We'll get married."

All the blood rushed from Grace's face, only to have it come gushing back as soon as she understood the meaning behind what he said. "Are you insane?"

He smirked, still holding her six inches away. "Don't worry. It won't be real."

Grace's heart plummeted clear to her knees. What was it with Ayden McCabe and his unemotional and closed existence? She dropped her chin to her chest and stepped away. She'd already started to fall in love with him. She had no doubt, walking down an aisle strewn with fake roses and false intentions might finally drive her off the cliff she'd been desperately clinging to most of her life.

"I can't marry you, pretend or otherwise." She rotated and stood with her back toward him.

For a long moment, she heard nothing but the popping of the fire and the rampant beating of her own heart.

"Is it because of Rick?"

The vehement way Ayden said Rick's name forced Grace to swing around, her fists thrust toward the floor.

"No, Ayden, it's because a marriage is sacred and forever and should not be used to fool people into believing something that…isn't true!" She hiccupped the last word and tried to step past him before a sob tore from her throat.

She'd stumbled as far as an elbow's length away before he snagged her wrist and pulled her hard against his chest. She lifted her palms to push away when his mouth seized hers, possessive and impatient. Her lips parted in surprise, allowing his tongue to plunder and stroke and dissolve her willpower to soft sighs of surrender.

He broke away for a breathless moment. "I'm sorry," he said. "I thought—"

He didn't finish what he wanted to say, but he didn't need to with her. With her whimsical ways, he must have assumed she'd jump at the chance to create a fairy-tale ending to their forged relationship. Did he not realize just how far she was falling in love with him? She thought if he kissed her any more, she'd never be able to deny anything he wanted. Then, she'd leave with her heart stuck at Hearth's Gate. *Oh, and she thought Danielle had created a hell of a mess in coming here.*

Grace sobered to his touch, unwilling to follow in her mother's footsteps. "I should probably go get ready," Grace said, without moving an inch one way or the other.

"Is that what you want?" he asked, his tone low,

his hands lifting to cup her left cheek.

Grace sucked in a shuddered inhale as the pad of his thumb glided over her lips, parting them slightly. What she wanted didn't exist.

With her throat tight and thick, she managed to give a reply. "What I want is to someday look back and think about Mistletoe and wonder what you're doing." At least, then, she'd know she'd moved forward.

Her words caused the muscle in his jaw to flex. After several moments of waiting, she thought he'd nod and let her go. He didn't. Instead, he bent forward, his mouth finding the sensitive part below her left ear.

Her body tingled from the softness of his touch. "I guarantee you'll find me…thinking about you."

She angled her head so their lips brushed. She squeezed her eyelids shut, afraid to take it any further but more afraid to *look back* and always wonder. "That's good," she whispered, allowing him to cup her face and draw his mouth against hers once again.

He tasted like he smelled, delicious with a mixture of heat and spice. As he tormented her with dizzying and erotic strokes of his tongue, she lifted her fingers to the buttons on his shirt. Eager to begin where they'd left off the night before, she dropped her hand to the zipper of his jeans. He continued to kiss her, slow and drugging, until he lay naked over her, his hard body pressing her into the soft cushion of the sectional.

"I feel like I've waited forever for this moment," he murmured, sliding his lips over her collarbone and to the base of her throat. Her fingers fanned through his thick hair as he covered his mouth over her right breast, sucking her sensitive bud until she felt the lifting wave of pleasure build inside her.

She languished in a sea of glorious sensations, need and hunger coiling tight and spiraling through her. She knew no greater want, no greater bliss than his touch.

"Ayden," she breathed.

He brought his mouth back over hers as his thumb massaged the flesh at her core. She gasped, his gentle strokes lifting her to a euphoric and maddening place.

"Come for me, Grace," he whispered. She clung to him, the rhythm of his deft caress, driving her to a shuddering and exultant end.

She arched upward and cried out to accept the tidal wave of release. She floated to heaven and drifted back to earth, both shaking and winded. In the moments she took to catch her breath, Ayden rose to tear open a ready condom.

"Open for me." Ayden sank down and nudged her legs further apart. Still dizzy from where he'd taken her, she did as he asked and lifted her hips to feel the throbbing heat of his arousal.

He paused above her, his gaze intense and his features serious. "Tell me you want this. Tell me you want me, Grace." His hot, raspy breath sent tingles all over her body.

"I…I want you, Ayden." *I love you.*

He closed his eyes and wrapped his arms around her, cradling her in a tender and possessive embrace. In one sensual and powerful movement, he sank deep inside her.

She gasped from the emotional *and* physical shock of their union. He filled her before retreating, only to plunge forward again. In pure rapture, she touched her tongue to his earlobe, tasting the heady scent of him. Pleasure, like she'd never experienced, pulsed through every nerve of her being, growing stronger, higher, with each cadenced lunge. He grew thicker inside her, the summit of her desires tensing for the imminent flight. Unable to hold on any longer, she lifted her hips to accept the full length of him.

"Oh…God," Ayden murmured, his body shuddering as her tight, pulsing flesh gripped him, drawing him further inside with each rhythmic thrust. They rocked together in perfect cadence. She fit him like no other woman, the ecstasy of her exquisite body bringing him closer and closer to a convulsive release. He didn't want to finish, but the blood pumped at a raging swiftness through his veins, building to a storm of sweet, delirious rapture.

He bent to seize her mouth. Only the taste of her tongue forced him closer to the maddening end. When he thought to slow things down, she lifted to match the thrust of his hips, accepting all of him. Breathless, he felt her come around him, and his restraint snapped. He drove into her one last time, burying an intensely satisfied groan against her throat. His body shuddered with a violent and exhilarating release. For a few moments, he lay spent, unable to move.

Glorious silence passed between them. He raised his head and stared down at her glittering eyes. She was the loveliest creature he'd ever seen, and he wished things could be different. Despite what he knew, he leaned down and kissed her damp forehead before discarding the condom and sliding on his side to gather her against him. It still amazed him how perfect she fit.

He closed his eyes, memorizing the silkiness of her skin. Yes, he'd lain with plenty of women. However, he'd never known a more satisfying experience than the one he'd shared with Grace. She was his, and until the day she left, she'd remain his.

"Foolish."

Ayden tensed, his heart ramming hard against his already beaten ribcage. Without thinking, he tightened his hold around Grace, but her willingness to answer the phone was somehow stronger than his willingness to keep her there. She fished for her jeans and swiped to accept the call.

"Hello."

Ayden didn't have to strain to hear the conversation.

"What's the matter with you, Grace? Why aren't you home, and why do you make me wait to answer the phone every time I call?"

Grace just sat there, blinking and shaking her head. He'd heard enough. He lifted the phone and brought it to his cheek. "Because she has better things to do than wait around for your sorry ass."

He ended the call and dropped the phone back onto the pile of clothes on the floor. When he turned to Grace, he wasn't surprised to see her staring at him. If she asked why he did what he did, he wouldn't have an answer.

However, she astonished him by slipping out of the room and upstairs. They avoided each other for the next half hour, he unable to explain what he'd done, she unable to ask why he did it. Fortunately, Maggie sent him a text begging him to talk Grace into making one of her desserts for dinner. This, at least, gave him something to say without having to apologize for something he knew he'd do again given the chance.

After a shower, he found her in the kitchen, staring

out the bay window next to the kitchen nook. He loved the view from here, majestic and breathtaking with the snowcapped mountains and an endless swell of evergreens below.

He believed she sensed his presence and spoke with her gaze still pulled to the view. "It truly is the most beautiful thing I've ever seen." He grasped at the olive branch, reaching out with both hands. "It's why my father decided to build here. He wanted to give my mother the best of everything."

"Lucky woman." Grace swiveled to face him.

He exhaled, not wanting to add anything else to her comment. He chose, however, to change the subject. "Maggie begged me, literally, to ask if you'd make a dessert for the dinner tonight. I think she wants to show off your talents."

Grace's eyes lowered, her perfect complexion a glorious shade of pink. He thought she was one of the most modest women he'd ever met. "Um, okay, but I'm not sure you have all the ingredients I'll need."

"Whatever you don't have, I can pick up at the supermarket."

She agreed, and they sifted through his cabinets, she pausing to survey the montage of items they placed on his island counter. "Well…" She tapped her chin. "It looks like you have enough here for me to make some apple streusel cream puffs."

"Perfect."

Forty-five minutes later, after an impromptu flour fight, Ayden allowed Grace to instruct him around the kitchen. As he sautéed the apples in melted butter, they played the rum cake game, without the rum cake. The phone call forgotten for now, they shared, teased, and laughed about their most embarrassing moments and their most humble ones. He believed he'd never known anyone like he knew Grace, realizing he wanted to know much more.

"May I have one?" He attempted to snag the biggest piece off the corner plate.

Grace slapped at his hand. "No, you'll spoil your dinner," she said, her mouth lifting into a wondrous grin.

Before she pulled her hand back, he grasped her wrist and hauled her against him. His arms snaked around her small body, feeling every part he'd made love to not more than three hours ago. A surge of longing shot through him, and he tried to shake it off.

"You have flour on your face." He smiled down at her.

Her dainty eyebrows rose, amused. "Where?"

"Here." He leaned down to kiss the dusty powder from her right cheek. "And here." He skimmed his lips across her silky skin.

"I think you missed a spot," she whispered, pointing to the sensitive flesh below her earlobe.

He nipped playfully, finding the erratic pulse at the base of her throat and drawing from her a soft moan. His hand lifted to cradle her head, his mouth trailing sensual kisses until his lips found hers. The sweet taste of her drove him mad, and he wanted nothing more than to carry her upstairs and reacquaint himself with her delicious body.

He stepped back to maneuver her toward the stairway when he remembered the Christmas Tree Dinner and broke away in a rush of breath. "God, I can't get enough of you." He lifted his head to find her eyes glazed with the same want and desires. "I'm sorry about answering your phone. I would have been furious if a woman had done the same thing."

Grace sent him a slow smile. "We should get going," she said, trying to hide her emotions from him as she retreated into the kitchen to retrieve the cream puffs.

Inside the cab, he attempted to keep his mind focused on the road, but it continued to trail off, his thoughts consistently on the woman sitting beside him.

For more years than he cared to count, he'd learned to switch his feelings on and off like a light switch. It was easy then. He felt little connection. Oh, the sex was great; he couldn't lie. However, with Grace he wanted to discover more than what position she liked or what was her first broken bone, if she'd ever had one. Only, he didn't know how much more time he had with her since he'd gone and placed an ultimatum over another man's head.

As he relived the moment of the call and the look of shock on Grace's face, Maggie's decorated door swung open with Collin standing there grinning. As his nephew clasped Ayden's left leg, Maggie met them inside with a hurried hug and a bottle of stout. Over the threshold, he inhaled deep, the house smelling of pine needles and fresh-baked bread, comforting and familiar. To the left, a fire blazed in a stone hearth and a few of Maggie's young co-workers gathered around with spiked eggnog in their hands. In the mingling crowd stood half his crew, all grinning at him like drunken teenagers.

On the couch sat Jolene Watson beside Mrs. Hawthorne. Mr. Hawthorne had snagged the most comfortable chair next to the empty tree and was taking a short nap. Every year, the couple closed their store early just to be here for Maggie.

"Oh, these look incredible, Grace. I can't wait to have one."

"Me neither," Ayden said to his sister before sending Grace a covert wink.

Maggie grabbed the dessert before pointing a finger toward the basement. "Can you be a great big brother and go help Gregg with the decorations?"

Ayden hesitated, not wanting to leave Grace by herself or alone with Kevin, who couldn't stop staring at her. "Kevin is more than capable of helping Gregg," he started to say when Maggie waved her hand to shush him.

"I'm trying to fix him up with Belinda," his sister said in a harsh whisper, discreetly pointing to a cute strawberry-blonde, wearing a tight festive Christmas sweater.

"Of course you are," Ayden mumbled, wanting nothing more than to get Grace alone.

Within a second of asking Grace to follow him into the kitchen, a familiar slap between his shoulder blades stopped him. He turned to find Neil and all his ruby red grandeur.

"Mighty glad you could make it," he said with a tired twinkle in his eye. He then thrust a thumb over his right shoulder. "Sarah's in the bedroom feeding the baby. She'll be out soon."

Ayden, surprised to find him there and not still in the hospital, chuckled to himself. "They kicked you out, did they?"

Neil sent him a wide, lopsided grin before lowering

his gaze to Grace and elbowing her in the arm. "Still with 'im, eh?"

"I…guess you could say that."

"Good for you." Neil beamed. "It might take a woman like you to bring Ayden here to his knees, or knee."

She opened her mouth to say something when Neil nudged her in the shoulder and clucked at her.

"Ah, don't be modest, now." He ambled away to join the crew on the other side. They all gave him high fives and slapped him on the back with congratulatory whoops.

"He's like that Energizer bunny, isn't he?" Grace stared after him.

Ayden laughed before turning her to face him. Although they'd had a fun time in the kitchen and a lustful moment after, there remained the subject of the phone call. As if reading his mind, she brought up a finger to warn him.

"Yes, what you did was idiotic, don't get me wrong, but it took you two seconds to say what I've been trying to tell Rick for the last few months. I should have been the one to do it, not you."

Somehow, she didn't make him feel any better. Wanting more privacy, he grasped her hand and pulled her into the quaint kitchen. Every counter space was full of food, the sweet aromas making his mouth water.

He settled onto a tall chair and pulled Grace between his legs so they were more at eye level. "Hear me out, Evans." He lifted an index finger to give her fair warning. "I had no right to come in between…whatever it is you and this guy have. When you and I started this, I was relieved you had a boyfriend. Now—" He stopped to plow a frustrated hand through his thick hair. "God, I don't know."

Chapter Twenty-One

Grace raised her small hand to touch his cheek. "You're a good man, Ayden, despite your temper and Neanderthal ways." She bit down on her bottom lip to keep from laughing. "You know, I used to practice what I'd say to Rick whenever he came crawling back to me. It was usually with a tube of cream cheese, though," she said as an afterthought. "Only, when he did, I just stood there, nodding and welcoming him with open arms."

It stunned Ayden how someone so beautiful and amazing could stay with someone so undeserving. "Why?"

She dropped her gaze, her eyebrows furrowing. "I'm not very good at saying no, or saying what I want out loud." She closed her eyes and concentrated on her thoughts. "I guess I've been so scared that if I disrupted the flow of things, my world would break apart."

"Like Christmas morning?"

She nodded and opened her eyes.

Overwhelmed by her confession, he hauled her into his arms, wishing he had a good life to give her. For whatever reason, she seemed to understand the agreement between them, cherishing every moment without demanding another second from him.

He kissed her sweet-smelling hair, memorizing what he liked so much about her: how she fit perfectly against him, how her soft breath caressed his neck, how her small hands lay across his chest. "How are you not furious with me?"

She shook her head and then pulled away. "Oh, after the initial shock wore off, I was furious, but not at you. I don't think Rick has ever called me this often in one week, and it's all because he thinks he might lose me."

Ayden closed his eyes, unsure of what to say or even how to say it. His body went cold at the thought of her with another man. He felt trapped between his growing feelings for Grace and the pact he'd made with himself. In the past, he'd been able to get away without a moment's thought.

"Knock, knock."

Maggie poked her head through the swinging door. "I hate to disturb you two lovebirds, but dinner will be served soon, and Gregg still needs help with the ornament boxes. I sent Neil down after him, but I think he got lost."

"No, he probably found the extra mattress and is trying to sneak in a nap," Ayden said, regretting the instant he pulled away from Grace's side. "I'll go help Gregg but keep Collin away from her." He held up a straight index finger. "His magic shows have cost me more in ruined clothes than what you have saved in his college fund."

Downstairs, he met Neil, several strings of Christmas lights wrapped around his thin body and shimmering tinsel dangling from his red hair.

"Were *you* thinking of becoming the tree this year?" Ayden held back a laugh while finally taking a swig of his now-warm beer.

"Hilarious, boss. Just hilarious…" Neil mumbled as he peeled off the lighting display. "Gregg was helping me until Collin decided to spray him with disappearing blue ink."

"Hmm, let me guess, the ink didn't disappear."

"Nope. Now, he just looks like he peed his pants. He went back upstairs to see if Maggie has a pair of Kyle's jeans he can borrow."

For the next fifteen minutes, Ayden helped Neil weed out the bad lights from the good lights, tying them all together before heading back to join Grace. They both had reached the second to the last step when Maggie's raised and reprimanding voice sliced the jovial air.

"Collin, no, she's off limits."

Ayden sprinted into the dining room where Grace sat at a table, Collin standing beside her with milk pouring from her lap and dripping like fat raindrops onto the tiled floor below.

The crowd gathered, Maggie standing with her hand over her mouth and a wide-awake child in her arms. Sensing Ayden close by, she twirled around and mouthed the words, "I'm so sorry."

Ayden canted his head and sent her a harrowing glance, believing Grace might find her voice and tell them to all go to hell. He certainly wouldn't blame her.

However, in the hush of the room, she smiled and patted Collin on the head. "With a little more practice, you will become a great magician."

With those words, Collin raised his head, his cherub face beaming. "Did you hear that, Mama? Aunt Grace thinks I can be a great magician."

Maggie nodded and handed Ciara to Ayden. "She's

right, but for now we're going to show everyone how a magician cleans up his messes."

"Aww," Collin said, his bottom lip protruding out past his top one, his shoulders hunched in a defeated pose.

As Collin grabbed a towel and began mopping up the milk, Maggie motioned for Grace to follow her. Before they left, Ayden grasped her hand. He squeezed it, hoping she'd sense how much he admired her for what she had done.

She paused, a tranquil smile touching her soft lips. "I remember blowing up a few Easy Bake ovens at that age. I wanted someone to tell me to keep trying." She walked away from him then, a beautiful, sopping mess.

****

Grace knew what would happen; she just didn't have the heart to stop it. With Collin's eyes like windmills, she'd waited as the milk saturated her pants and drenched her skin. Neither did she think beyond the moment of needing another set of clothes or everyone's reaction. She only cared about the dreams of a young boy whose life revolved around the magic of imagination.

Still, she sloshed behind Maggie, wondering what they all thought of her. Inside a twelve by ten room, not large enough for more than a full-sized bed, a dresser, and a few scattered toys, Grace waited for Ayden's sister to pull a few things from her small closet.

"Tomorrow's laundry day, so I don't have much for you to wear."

"I'm not picky," Grace assured her.

After rifling through a few outfits, Maggie found a pair of jeans, a belt, and a Seahawks jersey.

Grace smiled, grateful.

"The bathroom is across the hall, and there is a washcloth and towel under the sink. There is nothing less appealing than the smell of sour milk."

Grace accepted the items, wishing she didn't feel so at home everywhere she went in Mistletoe. "Thank you."

Maggie ambled away until she thought of something she wanted to say. "I don't know what's going on, but I know Ayden. He's never been about substance when it comes to dating. Before I warn you not to hurt him, I might advise you to guard your own heart. Although he plays a great romantic, he's about as cynical as they come." She sent Grace a sympathetic smile and shut the door.

Grace wondered why Maggie had chosen to warn her. After washing and dressing in Maggie's clothes, Grace emerged from the bathroom to find Ayden standing next to the fireplace checking his messages.

"There you are," said a familiar voice behind her. Grace turned to find Sarah cradling her infant son. "Do you want to hold him?"

"Well, I—"

"He's such a good little thing…hardly cries, if you can imagine that." Sarah placed the baby in Grace's arms.

Mesmerized, she stared at the sleeping infant. His wisps of thin hair matched his father's, and his skin was a perfect shade of pink. He smelled of lavender lotion and fabric softener, and Grace wasn't sure if she wanted to give him back.

"Come." Sarah led Grace to a loveseat close to the naked Christmas tree. Grace brought in a deep breath, remembering how she and Ayden had found it and then all the intimate moments in between.

"I think he likes you," Sarah whispered.

Grace yanked out of her reflection to blink at Sarah.

"He usually senses he's not with me and squirms."

Grace felt her cheeks warm, embarrassed and disappointed Sarah hadn't been talking about Ayden, but her infant son. To divert her thoughts, Grace caressed Nate's perfectly round cheek. His skin felt like the smoothest velvet. She held him tighter, the urge to lay a kiss on his forehead, overwhelming.

Since spending so much time mothering women her age or older, she'd forgotten how much she wanted to have children, eight of them, to be exact. Of course, she'd let go of that dream, along with a dozen others. Rick, who was still a child himself, had yet to find his way.

Then, her mind turned to Ayden. He was a man so determined to block himself from whatever constituted a true commitment. He'd not only found himself, but placed a concrete barrier around his perimeter to keep people from getting in, or himself from getting out.

"I think you and Ayden should start a family as soon as you're married."

"I agree."

Grace glanced up to find Jolene's smiling face tilted down at her. The woman had a way of making a person blush, even without saying much.

"I see everything's working out between you and McCabe. I told you he was a fine catch."

Grace nodded believing Jolene knew more about Danielle's visit to Mistletoe than she wanted anyone to know. Did Jolene, somehow, have a stake in Ayden not selling Ida and Connor McCabe's dream home, too? Perhaps Jolene, a surrogate mother of sorts, wanted to see him happily settled as much as Maggie, by whatever means possible. Ambushed. Poor Grace didn't have a chance.

****

Ayden gazed at Grace holding Nate with keen interest. It appeared so natural for Grace to have a child resting in her small arms, her lips curved into a smile, her angelic face luminous and awestruck.

For today, he didn't want to think about her leaving or why she came here. He just wanted to get her alone and memorize every delicious curve and cherish every intimate moment. For this reason, he chose not to take the call from Fitz. If he had answers about Danielle, Ayden didn't care to know them until after he'd made love to Grace one, two, ten more times. Giving her up wouldn't be easy, but it was inevitable, unless he stood willing to propose. That, he could never do.

Still, the guilt of what he was doing gnawed at him. He'd made a pact with Grace to find her sister, and all he'd done was ask a few questions and toss the job to Fitz and Hogan. Despite the fact that Danielle was a grown woman who'd left California on her own accord, he should have done more, instead of placing the responsibility on someone else.

Nonetheless, he continued to gaze at Grace, fascinated by how easily she fit in with everyone. Even Jolene sat and talked with her for a few minutes, something the woman said causing a blush to creep in to Grace's smiling cheeks. He wondered about their conversation, good ole Jolene not shy about anything when it came to men or relationships.

Deciding a rescue was in order, Ayden stepped across the room, leaning down to give Grace a tender kiss on her forehead.

"There you are," Jolene said with more energy than a caffeinated teenager. "I was just talking to Grace here about the Christmas Eve *Eve* Dance, and was wondering if you had the chance to ask her yet. As pretty as she is, you'll have someone whisking her away from you before you ever knew what happened."

He sent the woman a warning glance. He loved her, but sometimes, she was as meddlesome as Maggie. "I'm afraid Grace has a wedding to attend to at the same time." He didn't mean to bring up Danielle, especially since Jolene was the only one who knew exactly why Grace was here. However, instead of commenting, the woman clamped down on her lips and then shot Grace a quick smile.

"Well, I'm going to go see if Maggie needs help in the kitchen," the older woman said with a quick slap of her knees.

At that moment, Nate woke and rooted around for something to eat. Grace, unable to help the child, handed the baby back to his mother. "I think he's looking for something I can't give him."

Sarah giggled. "This little guy eats more than Neil, and I thought that was impossible."

With that said, the young woman ambled away, allowing Ayden to sink down in the empty space on the loveseat beside Grace. He wanted to get her alone and play the rum cake game again.

Then, she shot him with the inevitable question. "Have you heard from your friend, yet—the one who's trying to find Danielle?"

He hesitated before shaking his head. "Nothing yet."

Beside him, Grace dropped her shoulders in defeat. "I think you were right."

He canted his head. "Right about what?"

"Danielle. She *is* leading me on a wild goose chase. It doesn't make sense. None of this makes sense." She closed her eyes for a brief moment, adding, "I don't even know why I'm still here."

Ayden brushed her cheek with his knuckle and then leaned in to whisper in her ear. He loved the delicious smell of her skin. "Don't tell me you've forgotten about our pact already?"

She shivered before pulling a few inches away from him. "Maggie. Right. It's just that it feels so natural to be with you and to be here, I keep forgetting."

He never had the chance to ask her to explain what she meant. Behind him, Maggie announced dinner in her usual way: with a silver spoon and a bottle of champagne.

At the large table with mismatched chairs, Grace settled beside him answering a bombardment of questions about her family, San Francisco, and her job as a baker.

"Oh, you must tell us how you two met, Grace."

Ayden halted his fork of pumpkin pie at mid-bite, unsure if Grace could pull off telling the lie of the century. It was almost like the moment in Hawthorne's store where she stood lifting her lips toward his, her body shaking, unsure and afraid of what the next moment might bring for them.

"Um, well, I." She gave up and exhaled a loud breath.

At the last possible minute, Ayden flew in to save her, telling everyone the truth and not some made-up story. "Believe it or not, we met at O'Shannon's. I saw her across the room, and…the rest is history, you might say."

Sarah sighed next to Neil, placing her arm around his neck and giving him a kiss on his freckled cheek. "I remember the first time I met Neil. He drove by and splashed my clean uniform full of black sludge. It was love at first sight. Then he invited me to the Christmas Eve *Eve* Dance, and I knew we'd spend the rest of our lives together."

"Come on, baby. Lay one on me." Neil paused the drumming with his fingers to give his wife a sweeping kiss on her lips.

The place erupted in whoops and claps as Ayden turned to Grace. She was staring at the affectionate couple, and he wondered what she was thinking. Instead of asking, he touched her arm, caressing the velvety softness of her skin. "You can repay me later for bailing you out a few seconds ago."

She scoffed, and he chuckled. He liked having her here, sharing her with his family and friends. Still, he believed he accepted this because she would be leaving soon. The thought pulled him into a foul mood, immediately.

"It's time to decorate the tree, Uncle Ayden. Hurry!" Collin jumped up to grab his hand. Everyone laughed and stood, chairs scraping across the hardwood floor and feet shuffling to follow him and his enthusiastic nephew into the living room. From his peripheral vision, he watched Grace glance at the tree and then touch her index finger to the place the branch had made its mark above her eye.

"Are you all right?" He stepped close beside her.

She jumped, not hearing him approach, and then nodded. If she had anything to say, she never got the chance as Collin pulled on her shirt, calling her Aunt Grace and asking if she could help Ciara put one of the ornaments she'd made for her dad on the Christmas tree.

With ease, she lifted Ciara to place the homemade reindeer, shaped like her tiny foot, on the side closest to her. The little girl giggled and hugged her before waddling over to the box to retrieve another ornament.

"You're very good with children," he said, absently.

She sent him a sideways glance. "Well, since I planned on having eight of them, I should be."

He hadn't expected that reply, and he realized too late the extent of his temper. "Eight? Is that how many you and Rick plan on having?"

It didn't take long for Grace to turn on him. "No. Eight is how many *I* wanted before my life fell apart. After all the women you've dated, Ayden, you should realize by now that we hold on to false childhood fantasies until there is no hope left."

By this time, their conversation had gained some attention, and he wanted nothing more than to turn back the next few minutes and enjoy having her there. As Maggie jumped in with a nervous offer of spiked eggnog, he grabbed Grace's hand and pulled her into the empty kitchen. He let go and paced between the steel stove and refrigerator, decorated with fingerprint art and smiling portraits of a happy family.

Time passed without him volunteering why he'd brought her all this way. He supposed she filled in the silence with her own interpretation of why they were there.

"Are we here to talk about the break-up?

He exhaled and stepped backwards until his back stood flush with the narrow pantry closet. He crossed his arms and canted his head, curious to see what she'd say. "All right, since you brought it up, what do you think we should do?"

Too late to hike back on this slippery slope, he waited for Grace to give him an answer. "I…I guess we could start with something we seem to do best."

"What's that?"

"Argue."

He drew back. "We don't argue that much, Grace. Even if we did, what do you suppose we'd argue about?"

She shrugged, and it irked him how she'd learned how to disguise her feelings. "I don't know," she answered. "I could accuse you of cheating on me or something."

He glared down at her, insulted. "I'd never do that."

She opened and closed her mouth several times before bringing in a long inhale. "What if I demand you marry me?" She jutted her chin out, defiant and challenging.

He didn't hesitate to give her an answer. "Too predictable. Think of something else."

Her arms fell straight to her side. "Fine, what if you ask me to marry you, bent on one knee, and I-I…do we have to talk about this now? I've had too much to drink to fight over what we need to fight over in order to never see each other again."

She cupped her hands over her face. Helpless. He hated that feeling. He also hated that Grace depended on him to provide her with answers. Frustrated, he lashed out.

"Christ, what do you want from me?"

Chapter Twenty-Two

Grace closed her eyes, taken aback by Ayden's temperamental mood and the weight of what he'd asked. She wanted to believe he was falling in love with her, just as much as she was falling in love with him. She'd tried to play his game, using his rules, and had come up the loser. She believed ABBA sang it best.

Hurt, she pushed away just enough to glance up into the hardened lines of his face. "I want, when this is all over, to have a good night of drinking to make me forget all about you."

The corners of his mouth lifted. "I will not let you forget me, Grace."

She shook her head. "You can't have it both ways." At that moment, she didn't want to leave Mistletoe angry or bitter. Ayden had done nothing wrong. From the beginning, he'd been honest about what he wanted and what he expected.

Cautiously, she lifted her hand to his cheek. "I don't know how to separate the emotional from the physical. God knows I've tried with you." She paused to swallow the lump in her throat. "Ayden, I don't know how many more nights we have together, but I don't want to spend them arguing over things we are unwilling to change. You might not like it"—she paused to bring in a deep, courageous breath—"but I've fallen in love with you."

He stared at her, unblinking. She expected that reaction and didn't want him to say something out of pity. When his lips parted on a reply, she rushed to silence him.

"I didn't mean for it to happen, and I don't expect you to say something to make me feel better about it. Until I leave, I'm going to love you without boundaries or limits." She exhaled, feeling some relief to her confession. "Then, I'm going to go home, throw away all my romance novels, and take charge of *my* life for a change."

She finally relaxed and stepped away. Just as she shifted toward the door, he cleared his throat and spoke, his words full of raw emotion. "I don't think I've ever been less deserving of anyone in my life."

She kept her back to him. "I'll get Maggie. She might need some help with…something." To her relief, everyone stood or sat, talking to the closest person to them. She noticed they all had a plate of her apple streusel cream puffs.

"Oh my gosh, Grace. You have to give me this recipe. Neil's on his third one." Sarah finished her last bite.

Not trusting her voice, Grace said nothing. For the remainder of the evening, she stayed busy clearing the table and organizing leftovers into Tupperware bowls for people to take home.

"Please be patient with Ayden," Maggie said, drying the same plate she'd started on a few minutes before.

Grace forced a smile before raising her head toward Ayden's sister. She was such a pretty woman: young, thin, and optimistic.

"You scare him to death, I think," Maggie continued. "He's so afraid of losing you that he can say the most reckless things to see what you'll do, to see if you'll run or stay."

Grace wanted to laugh at Maggie's assessment of their bogus situation. She wanted to tell the woman, so badly, how Ayden didn't care whether Grace walked off a cliff or walked out of his life. Well, not as dramatic as that, but it felt like it, sometimes.

"Anyway, thanks for doing the dishes. Sarah always helps, but with Nate, well, you know." Maggie finally placed the dish in the cabinet and gave Grace a long hug.

Adopting one of Ayden's tactics, Grace tried keeping her emotions under lock and key and followed behind Maggie into the living room. The lights were off; it was time for the McCrery tree-lighting ceremony. She didn't see Ayden until he slid in behind her. Despite the way they had left each other earlier, he wrapped his arms around her waist and drew her firm against him. Unafraid.

"Countdown," someone called out.

"Five, four, three, two, one," the congregation said in unison.

Grace blinked and found the room lit with the most beautiful Christmas tree she'd ever seen, the tree she and Ayden had found together. She brought in a heavy breath and placed her hands over her mouth. Everyone clapped, Ciara hopping up and down in front of the tree, excitement causing her to twirl and giggle like a dancing fairy.

Maggie quieted the gaiety by going to the middle of the room to make a firm announcement. "Now, everyone knows in Mistletoe, there's a lot of kissing that goes on. So, for those of you who came with someone, or found someone"—she paused to send a wink in Kevin's direction—"find your significant other and lay one on them.

Unsure of Ayden's reaction at this point, Grace turned inside his arms. "We really don't—"

"Shhh." He cupped the side of her face.

Grace closed her eyes and waited for his firm lips to find hers. The contact made her heart sputter and her knees knock. For a brief moment, she even thought her feet lifted off the ground. She ignored the warning bells and sirens, allowing him to lure her in again, understanding the consequences and accepting them without regret.

"Ayden," she sighed against his mouth. Then, as quickly as he kissed her, he pulled away. On shaky legs, Grace waved goodbye to the gregarious crowd and stepped into the night, the frigid air whipping across her heated skin.

As routine, he helped her up, walked around, and slid onto the hard leather seats. They didn't talk much, and she wondered if her confession had made things more awkward between them.

"I have to stop by Hawthorne's for something," he said. "Would you mind waiting out here?"

Surprised to see the store's lights on and Mrs. Hawthorne standing at the counter, Grace shook her head. He pulled to the curb and strode inside, the woman beaming at his approach. While Grace waited, the radio played "Silver Bells," one of her favorite holiday tunes. When the song ended and another began, she dug into her pocket to check her phone. No sooner did she go to put it back when it vibrated with an incoming call.

Grace's heart gave a strange beat, unsure what conversation awaited her on the other end. Hello," she said, in the darkened cab.

"Hello, Grace. I think you should come home, now." It was her mother's voice, and it was different from the last twenty or so calls she'd received from her.

Grace's stomach sank to the floor. Not so long ago, she couldn't wait to hear those words. Tonight, they turned her cold and numb. "What about Danielle? Don't you want me to find her?"

Grace knew she sounded desperate, as if grasping for any excuse to stay one more day with Ayden.

"Danielle purchased an airline ticket for you. She'll send you the details. I'll pick you up at the airport tomorrow and explain everything when you get here, okay?" Her mother paused. "For the life of me, I can't figure out what got into your sister's head."

Grace didn't know either, but instead of saying she wanted to stay in Mistletoe a few more days, she gave in. "I'll call when I land."

Grace pulled the phone from her ear just as Ayden opened the door and hopped inside. He didn't ask whom she'd talked to, and she didn't volunteer.

At Hearth's Gate, she left him in the foyer, ambling upstairs to begin packing.

In a daze, she folded his shirt and stuffed it under a few of her things. The window remained broken, the night air chilly on her back.

"Are you leaving me?"

She glanced up to find him standing in the doorway, his magnificent and powerful form resting against the doorframe, arms crossed, and his features unreadable. No matter how many times she looked at him, her heart still fluttered like an infatuated groupie.

"My mom called. She says it's time for me to come home."

He pushed away from the wall, walked inside, and sank onto the bed close to her suitcase. She stopped what she was doing, stepped around, and plopped down beside him. Before he could say anything, she pressed her mouth to his and kissed him with more emotion and physical contact than she'd ever allowed herself to give.

****

The urgency in Grace's kiss rattled Ayden to his core. He wanted to take it slow. However, his own eagerness to bury himself deep inside her had him pushing her to the mattress and disrobing both of them quickly, almost frantically. He lowered his lips to hers, craving the warmth of her mouth and the sweetness of her tongue. She teased and tormented him until a euphoric fervor pulsed through his veins.

"I've wanted to do this all night," he murmured, his hand gliding to the side of one pert breast.

She responded by wrapping her legs around his hips and positioning herself to accept him. The plan to take his time shattered in a thunderous heartbeat. His need spiraled upward, until he drove inside her, his body trembling, his blood pounding. Never before had he felt such uncontrollable desire for a woman. It frightened and liberated him at the same time.

As one, they created the perfect rhythm until her soft moans grew louder and her breathing more erratic. His passion for her escalated when she lifted up to meet his powerful thrusts, driving him further inside her small, tight body.

"Grace, no," he said, breathless, not wanting this to end so soon.

"I…I can't," she exhaled. Her muscles tensed and her hands lifted to wrap around his neck. He clung to her as her spasms gripped his swollen manhood.

"Oh…God." He surrendered to the explosive pleasure and uncontrollable spasms. Exhausted, he collapsed atop Grace, his body shaking from the aftershock. She ran a soft hand down his back, her touch sinking straight into his soul. To bring her closer, he shifted on his side. In the stillness, he kissed her damp temple and traced a finger over her petite curves.

She flattened her palm on his chest, his heart still pounding at an erratic rate. They lay awake for a while, caressing and memorizing this moment.

The next morning, Grace awoke to a fire-lit room and an empty bed. Morning had yet to peek through the quilt still hanging from the window. Missing Ayden already, she slipped on the shirt he'd worn the day before and tiptoed downstairs. In her mind, she kept remembering what he said. "I want you."

No, he didn't love her, but she grasped what he gave her and held on tight. Her entire life, at least the parts she remembered, she'd read the back of a book before she committed to reading all the pages. If it ended badly, she'd put it back on the shelf and reach for another. How ironic she'd seen the end to this story and was still willing to live every moment of it without regret.

From the bottom of the staircase, the French doors lay open in the living room. Unsure why he'd be there, she rounded the corner and froze.

"Oh God." Rick.

Her heart gave a sickening thud. She turned toward Ayden, finding his stance rigid in form and his face stoic in emotion.

"I don't want to know why you're wearing this man's shirt," Rick said with a nervous laugh. "What I do want to know is…" He paused to pull a small black box out of his brand-new winter coat. "Will you marry me, Grace?"

Grace's mouth went dry and she tried to say something—anything to keep the moment from getting any more awkward. How many days did she dream of him asking her this? How many of those days did she imagine saying yes, before changing her answer to no?

"I…" Sweat gathered between her breasts and her heart sank a little deeper inside her chest. She needed to tell him it was over between them. She needed to start saying aloud how she felt about the situation when it was happening. She closed her eyes, and in a firm voice, said, "No."

"What?"

Her eyelids flew open when both men exclaimed with the same question. She glanced from Rick and then to Ayden, realizing both held twin expressions of astonishment.

"May I have a word with you, Grace?"

This came from Ayden, and she knew what awaited her in their private conversation. He'd probably even ask for that grateful kiss now that Rick had come to whisk her away.

To save them both time, she slipped in front of him, her shoulders pulled back and her chin lifted to a daring angle. "No," she said. It felt good to say the word, so she said it again. "No, Ayden, you may not have a word with me because I know what you're going to say, and I'm not in the mood to hear it. I love you, and that's how it is. You can run from it if you want, but it's how I feel, and nothing you say will make me change my mind." A loud heartbeat later, she rotated back to Rick. "No, I will not marry you. You're only here because you're afraid to lose a backup when you get lonely. Well, I'm no one's backup. Not any more."

She smiled at her bravado, not even wondering how long it might last. For now, she'd spoke her mind and her heart. With Ayden, he'd expected her to say yes to Rick. From his reaction, she had no doubt he'd wanted her to say yes. Furthermore, for a man who remained unemotionally attached to any human being, she understood he needed her to say yes. He stepped toward her, and she backed away, swallowing a lump of tears that gathered at the base of her throat.

"I told you how it was going to be, Grace. I told you from the beginning."

Yes, and she'd ignored every warning bell. "All the reason to blame no one but myself."

He exhaled and shook his head. "In that case, you should probably know I just talked to Fitz." His gaze locked on her face. "He said your sister is in San Francisco, and that she has been there the entire time."

A cold wave of shock fell over Grace.

"Of course she has," Rick interjected. "This was all some damn joke by your friend to make me believe you ran off to be with another guy."

Grace couldn't believe what either of them were saying was true. This time, Ayden reached her, and her feet didn't move. He braced his strong hands on each side of her arm, the warmth of his palms seeping through his thin button down shirt.

"I'm afraid what Rick said is true. While you were sleeping, I made some calls. Your friend Betsy happens to be Jolene's great-niece. Jolene told me she coordinated bringing us together—with Danielle and Trevor's help, of course."

The blood rushed from Grace's face, and she slumped down on the sectional in a state of numb astonishment. She cupped her hands over her mouth, embarrassed that a group of women—a sister, a friend, and a stranger—saw the pathetic direction of her life and sought to intervene. They knew in the beginning, when her mother turned desperate eyes to her to fix the situation, she'd say yes.

"Grace, are you all right?"

Through the fog of her thoughts, she glanced up to find Ayden's features full of concern and disappointment.

"I'm sorry they pulled you in the middle of this."

He bent down and placed his palm on her bare knee. She let it rest there, unwilling to break the last moments of connection between them. "I'm not."

Remembering what he told her during their first morning together, she cupped her hands on both sides of his face and pulled his firm lips to hers. It was one of the most emotionally charged kisses she'd ever let herself feel. When she pulled away, she was shaking. She glanced up at Rick, his mouth open with silent shock.

"Rick, would you wait out there? I have to talk to Ayden about something."

Rick hesitated a step before shuffling out beyond

the French doors.

She laid a palm on Ayden's face and brought in a deep, stuttering breath. A cold tear slipped down one side of her cheek and landed on her bare knee. "I won't ask you to ask me to stay, and I won't ask if you love me."

His gaze lowered, and she understood he struggled on what to say to make this easier for her.

"Please don't do this." His voice was hoarse and trembling.

"Tell Maggie I broke your heart in a thousand tiny pieces, okay?"

"Grace—"

She smashed her lips together to keep from sobbing, stood, and walked out of the room. She talked Rick into taking her to the train station that would then take her to the airport. Of course, he had no problem leaving her without a word or conversation.

Chapter Twenty-Three

Like a zombie, Ayden walked around the house cleaning what needed cleaned and refusing to throw away any items Grace had left behind. There wasn't even a chance to get used to the idea. One minute they were making love, and the next she was gone. Hell. If he knew she was leaving so soon, he would have made himself last longer, a lot longer. His heart clenched every time he thought of her, every time he thought of how he'd allowed her to leave.

Then again, what sort of life could he provide for her when he planned to sell Hearth's Gate and live in his construction trailer until he found a small enough place? He even thought about moving in with Maggie until Kyle returned, but his sister refused to speak to him after he told her the truth of what he'd coerced Grace into doing for him.

Even Jolene tried explaining things, leaving Maggie confused and furious. His sister, of course, didn't blame Grace, seeing her only as a victim to his continuous run of bad choices and his idiotic determination not to commit.

Unfortunately, Sarah *did* talk to him and gave him a good scolding whenever she came by the worksite to drop off Neil's lunch.

"You should be ashamed of yourself, Ayden McCabe. Poor Grace. She's probably so heartbroken she ran back to that other guy just to get over you. She's going to end up married to him and miserable for the rest of her life, and it's all your fault."

Hearing this threw Ayden into one of his worst moods. He brooded and stalked around the house until he'd forgotten Rachel's visit regarding Hearth's Gate.

She'd traded in her jeans and O'Shannon's four-leaf-clover T-shirt for a pair of cherry-red stilettos and a matching thigh-high dress. She greeted him with a kiss on the lips, sashaying inside and handing him her black wool coat and leather purse.

"Where shall we do this?" She touched the tip of her tongue to her glossy mauve-painted lips and sent him a sly smile.

He wanted his body to react to her, to forget Grace and carry on as if she didn't plague his mind every second of the day and night.

"The kitchen," he said toward Rachel, knowing he didn't have to show her the way. However, for the life of him, he couldn't remember one memory of their time here together. Hell, he couldn't remember being with anyone except Grace.

As he tried to shake the haunting memories, Rachel sauntered her body so her curved hips glided with a rhythmic invitation. He followed her and sat down beside her, she scooting her chair closer to his, too close. She reeked with celebrity perfume and hair-care products.

For a distraction, he glanced out the window into the darkening horizon. The sky reminded him of his mood. While he brooded, Rachel pulled a stack of papers from a collapsible briefcase and placed them on the table before him. "I've taken the liberty of drawing up a seller's contract. You can take some time to look over it, or you can sign, and we can get things rolling right away."

He clenched and unclenched his jaw. "Just tell me where to sign the damn thing."

He heard her intake of breath, and he realized he was still an ass, with or without Grace. Slowly, he placed his palm on her arm. "I'm sorry."

Rachel's long, painted fingertips came up to caress his face. It tickled more than aroused, and he drew away.

"Ayden, I don't think I've ever heard you use those words before."

He glanced up at her, knowing what she was going to do and having neither the will nor the substance to stop her. She kissed him, grappling for something he had no power to give.

When she began unfastening the buttons, he cleared his mind of everything and everyone. He focused only on the zipper of her dress and the laced bra that clasped in the front. Her long fingernails dug into his back, and he seized her open mouth. She tasted of artificial sweetener and flavored coffee, turning his stomach.

"Don't stop, Ayden," Rachel whispered, her panting hot and damp against his cheek. At that point, he knew his heart belonged to one woman and one woman only. He was madly in love with Grace. God help him.

"Rachel," he grunted, righting her dress and pushing her gently away. "I can't."

She clicked her tongue before shrugging back into her clothes. "Believe it or not, I didn't come here to seduce you. I still need you to sign the papers, if you plan on selling this place."

"I'll get a pen." Of course, he couldn't find one when he needed it. Not one place in the entire house had a pen. Even Rachel, who'd searched her bag, came up empty.

"Dammit," he cursed, knowing where one might be and dreading having to open the door to retrieve it. Before going in, he grabbed a small flashlight and strolled inside, trudging to the large cabinet of heirloom china. He searched through every drawer, his temper growing hotter by the time he reached the last one. Every fiber of his being stretched taut with unsettled frustration. The drawer opened halfway, before snagging on something and refusing to budge.

Annoyed with the world, he yanked at the brass knob, the drawer giving way and spilling a Pandora's box of contents on to the dusty floor.

"Are you all right in there?" Rachel asked from the kitchen.

"I'm fine," he called back, lifting his friend's dog tags from underneath a pile of letters. He remembered the day he'd received the manila envelope, a hand written note from Mark's young widow tucked inside.

"He talked about you all the time and asked if anything ever happened to him, that I send these to you. God bless. Rose."

Ayden clutched the tags, squeezing the thin metal until he felt them bend. He knew, by keeping his friend's memory locked up, Ayden had not given himself the chance to accept what happened. As well, blaming his parents' circumstances did not change anything or bring any of them back. For so long, he'd been a coward, hiding behind a shield of indifference, an armor of resentment. Now, what had his staunch ideals and stubbornness cost him? Grace?

His heart hung heavy in his chest, stealing his breath. Before he left the room, he needed to reconcile with his pain and his loss. He believed it took being with her to see this. Although he appeared to keep moving forward, he'd remained as stuck as her. He let out a shaky exhale, allowing the weight of regret to fall from his shoulders. Reconciled to allowing his heart to heal, he stood and began to walk away. He'd taken three steps before his foot crunched on an object halfway toward the door. He stooped down, put the small flashlight in his mouth and inspected the unopened package, tied with a gold ribbon. A tiny discolored envelope was taped to the top. He opened the flap, his heart jolting at the hand-scribed note inside.

To my greatest love who made all my dreams come true. Will you marry me again?

Connor

Ayden's stomach sank to the floor. His mouth dry and his hands shaking, he untied the ribbon. Inside, on a bed of purple velvet, lay a white diamond ring stuffed with a rolled-up parchment paper.

He unrolled the stiff letter, his eyes watering as he read his father's timeless words, dated two days before his parent's accident.

Ida,

I will never forget what you said to me when I asked if you'd like to open up a Bed and Breakfast. You said, Yes. Then, when I asked if you'd like to open one in America, you said, "All right, but will I need to learn to cook?" From that moment, I knew I'd fallen in love with the right woman. You believed in my dreams and made them your own. And I know I've been the most difficult ass to live with at times, idiotic, in fact, but there will never be another man to love you like I do.

Connor

Ayden swiped the tears from his face. Ever since he'd lost his parents, abandoned his unit, and lost his best friend, all in a matter of weeks, he'd swore to himself not to have anyone depend on him again. It had cost his heart too much pain and resentment. "I'm so sorry," he cried, his shoulders trembling from years of pent-up emotions.

"Are you sure everything's okay?" Rachel called again.

Ayden dropped the light into his hands and glanced up to find Rachel standing in the doorway looking into the room as if it had appeared from out of nowhere. "Yeah...yes." He cleared his throat and stood, placing the ring and letter back into the box. He needed to talk to Maggie, to someone who would forgive him for the misguided grudge he'd held onto for so long. He also wanted her to tell him how to fix what he'd broken, because he wasn't sure he knew how.

Deciding to hold off on signing Hearth's Gate over to the realty company, he coaxed Rachel to her car and called Maggie. He supposed the tone of his voice made her quit work a little early. She agreed to meet him at Bethany's Ice Cream Shoppe with Ciara and Collin. Of course, the first words out of Collin's mouth were, "Where's Aunt Grace?"

Maggie narrowed a warning stare in her young son's direction before hurriedly ordering him a banana split to keep him occupied. "I'm sorry to hear about your friend. You never talked about him, I didn't know."

Ayden nodded. "He was a good man and a hell of an officer." Ayden spent the next few minutes telling his sister about Mark. "For so long, I didn't want anyone to care about because I felt like I'd let everyone down in my platoon…and in my life."

"You didn't let me down," she said, quick to take his hand and give it a squeeze.

He had to disagree. "If you remember, little sister, you didn't want anything to do with me when I came back. You were a rebel without a cause, never home and defying everything I said. When you met Kyle, I was even less important. Then you got married, and well…" He paused to ruffle Collin's already disheveled hair.

"God, I forgot what I brat I was," she said with her chin tilted toward her chest. "But you have to know, Ayden, without you coming back here, I probably would have ended up in a really bad place." She stopped talking for a moment and swiped a stray tear. "Anyway, I wanted to thank you and thought the flyer was a good way. I guess…I thought…if you found someone who deserved you, you'd find a way to keep Hearth's Gate and everyone would live happily-ever-after."

"Like Mom and Dad?"

She sighed and shifted Ciara into his lap to clean off the mix of chocolate and strawberry ice cream running down Collin's chin. "They weren't perfect. They argued about the silliest things, but they loved and adored each other, and they loved us. When you left for the Army, they were so proud of you. They didn't care if you came back to take over the business. They just wanted you to come back safe."

Ayden nodded, leaning over to give his niece a gentle kiss on her feather-soft blonde hair. "Why didn't I realize it was Dad's idea to open Hearth's Gate?"

His sister shrugged. "It did appear for the bed and breakfast to be Mom's idea. She cooked, and cleaned, and enjoyed every moment. Dad was temperamental and talked of returning to Ireland because he thought she was working too hard."

"I miss them."

Maggie's lips trembled. "I miss them, too." She then reached over to transfer her daughter back into her arms. "Again, I'm really sorry about the flyer. I thought…I wanted…I hoped you'd find someone who might be worth taking a chance on."

He gave a thick-throated chuckle. "I did, Maggie. I did."

****

Grace lay staring at the ceiling in her bedroom for so many minutes, she lost track of the time. Useless to go back to sleep, she trudged through a shower and then tiptoed to the kitchen. Instead of flipping on the light, she poured some orange juice into a glass at the refrigerator door and sat down in the dark.

Despite the blackness, she closed her eyes until a bright light forced her to open them again. She found her mother and Danielle at the doorway—one dressed in a flowery long gown, the other in short shorts and one of Trevor's T-shirts.

"It's not good to sit in the dark, Grace," her mother said with a rare smile.

Grace shrugged. "Like mother, like daughter."

The older woman clicked her tongue. "Not any more. When I didn't have either you or Danielle here, the dark scared me so much, I slept with most of the lights on."

Grace's gaze followed her mother's lithe form as she made a pot of coffee in an ancient coffeepot and joined her at the table. She was taller than Grace with short graying hair and emerald-colored eyes.

"Would you like some coffee?"

Grace held up her hand to decline. The strong aroma reminded Grace of Ayden and Hearth's Gate.

"I talked to Trevor." Danielle plopped down at the square retro diner table, the silver edging pristine and polished. "For all the trouble we put you through, he's agreed to name our firstborn after you, boy or girl."

Despite wanting to cry, Grace laughed. Since landing in San Francisco, her sister had apologized and explained over a dozen times why they did what they did. For one, they hoped to give Grace a great adventure, without Rick, of course. Danielle believed her older sister needed to spread her own wings and fly. Grace just wished someone had given her a damn parachute first. The original plan had Danielle leading Grace to San Diego for a few days. Then, Betsy told Danielle about Mistletoe. Soon after, Jolene masterminded the plan to bring Grace and Ayden together. Not once did the trio believe Ayden would let her go so easily. And Grace thought *she* read too many romance novels.

"You still love me, right?" Danielle asked, her eyes sad and remorseful.

Grace gave in to a rare giggle, as of late,

remembering the video of Trevor dressed like Randy from a "Christmas Story." "Apparently not as much as your fiancé."

Danielle presented Grace with a sheepish grin before lifting to give her a kiss on her cheek. "Betsy loves you, too."

Grace dropped her gaze to the table. Although Betsy had tried to apologize, Grace wasn't ready to forgive her part in the fiasco. When Grace rose from the table to get ready for work, her mother sat down and wrapped her hand around Grace's wrist.

"I'm sorry, too."

Grace settled back in her seat, so ready to move on and off the subject that reminded her of Ayden. "Sorry about what?"

"I haven't been a very good mother. You were always so much stronger than me, even at such a young and vulnerable age. After your dad left, you jumped in and took care of us, and I let you, but I can't do that anymore."

Grace pulled forward and brought her mother's hands between hers.

"No." Her mother scooted her palms to wrap around Grace's hands instead.

"Right before I called you to come home, Danielle showed up with Trevor and Betsy and told me what they'd done. They're right. You need to live your life, Grace. You need to not be afraid of what might happen if you take a chance. Don't sit in the dark like I did. I've watched you for too long, flipping to the back of the book before you read the first page. Don't be afraid anymore, because one day you might wake up and realize you've missed out on all the good stuff in between."

Grace scoffed at her mother's wise words. "Does that include suffering a broken heart?" she asked, her throat closing on a lump of unshed tears.

Her mother nodded. "Yes, because a heart can only mend if you accept how it was broken and then allow it to heal again. I know you love that man, but he isn't worth thinking about if he isn't brave enough to take a chance with you."

Her mother then stood, kissed Grace on her cheek, patted her on the head, and ambled out of the room.

No matter what her mother said, Grace couldn't stop thinking of Ayden McCabe or all the moments, good and bad, they shared together. He'd moved on, and she was stuck trying to figure out what everything meant. She missed him, she loved him, and she ached to feel him hold her hand one more time.

Thank God for her sister's wedding in a few days. Then she'd have her mind on bridesmaid duties and not the Christmas Eve *Eve* Dance. Despite her efforts, however, she wondered whom he might take. From a quick call she received from Sarah, Maggie was making him go alone. She called it punishment for what he'd put her and Grace through.

As the day wore on, Grace found her spirit sinking lower. When all she wanted to do was go to bed and force herself to sleep, the doorbell rang, her mother calling from downstairs for her to answer it. For whatever reason, she imagined Ayden standing on the other side, a bouquet of flowers in his hands and an apology on his tongue.

She glanced in the hall mirror before opening the door, only to find Betsy with a bouquet of flowers in *her* hands and an apology on *her* tongue. Despite her spiraling state of depression, Grace smiled.

"We need to talk," Betsy said, wearing an elf hat, elf shoes, and peppermint striped tights under her green skirt.

"Do you promise to never interfere in my life ever again?" Grace asked.

"No," Betsy said with a sincere grin.

"Good enough." Grace swallowed her pride and hugged her friend in the doorway. She smelled of ground coffee and cherry lip-gloss. As if nothing had transpired between them, Betsy grabbed Grace's hand and led her to the porch swing, both breathing deep the breezy night air.

"I know what I did was wrong, Grace, but you have to look at it from my side."

Grace sent her friend a skeptical smirk. "And which side is that?"

"The one that wanted to see you happy. Ayden McCabe is a legend in Mistletoe, and I just thought if he knew you he'd fall in love with you." She paused to crinkle her elf-like nose. "I also knew if you wanted to marry Rick, he might get jealous enough to come after you. I kept imagining him showing up to whisk you away and Ayden punching him square in the face out of some fit of jealousy. I really wanted him to punch Rick in the face, though."

"What made you think I ever wanted Rick to marry me?" Grace asked after a long moment of thinking of Ayden.

"I don't know."

"So, you fixed me up with a guy who not only wants to remain single all his life, knowing there was the remote chance I might fall in love with him?"

Betsy sighed. "There was no method to our madness, Grace. Danielle and I thought it would be a good idea to show you what else was out there, and Jolene thought Ayden might change his mind on settling down when he got to know you. She thinks of him as a son."

Grace sniffed, remembering how the woman had talked Ayden up in the first few minutes of their meeting. "How was that even supposed to happen, Bets? I wasn't even his type."

"According to Jolene, you were exactly his type."

Grace closed her eyes, finding it hard to forget how much her heart stayed in Mistletoe. She purposely maneuvered around the subject of Ayden McCabe, talking about everything else under the San Francisco moon. She even laughed when Betsy told her of seeing Rick outside Neece's arguing with his new girlfriend.

"Thanks for stopping by, Betsy."

"Don't mention it." She leaned over to give Grace a hug. "I'll see you at Bistro 118 tomorrow for lunch. Danielle thought it would be fun for us to get together before the rehearsal dinner."

Grace nodded and watched her friend climb in her rusty hatchback, the engine sputtering alive and hissing down the quiet neighborhood road. Grace sat for a little while longer trying to piece her life back together. Tomorrow, before lunch. Grace thought about walking down to the quaint shopping area to see if there were any places for sale. If she wanted to start her own company, she needed to do it now before she thought of all the excuses on why she shouldn't.

However, whenever she thought about the people

entering her bakery, they all resembled the friendly faces of Mistletoe, Washington.

At lunch the next day, she sat with her friend and sister poking at a Caesar salad, trying to put on a brave face. By noon, it had already been a long day. Had Ayden decided to take Rachel to the Christmas Eve *Eve* Dance? Yes, she'd called Sarah in a relapse-of-reason moment to ask how everyone was doing.

"Oh, everyone misses you, Grace."

"How is Maggie?"

"She's still very upset with Ayden, especially since he seems to have picked right back up with Rachel—"

The conversation had ended abruptly with Sarah apologizing and then backtracking clumsily over what she'd said.

Since then, Grace's stomach remained tied into a nauseous knot. So many times already, she wanted to run home and block out the pain of falling in love with an emotionally detached man.

"You have to stop thinking about him, Grace. You're going to whittle down to nothing," her friend warned.

"Have you heard from him?" Danielle asked, receiving a headshake from Betsy.

"No, and I doubt I ever will. He's one of those men who, even if he takes a wrong turn, will never get out and ask for directions. He keeps going, never looking back, never admitting his mistake and never regretting his decision."

"For God's sake, Grace, you weren't a destination."

It didn't matter what Grace was to Ayden. He had moved on, and she was determined to do the same.

Chapter Twenty-Four

"Grace, do you have a sewing kit in your purse?" her mother whispered, a little too loud.

Sitting in her beautiful wedding gown, Danielle, of course, panicked and began searching her dress to discover the reason for a needle. "Is something torn? Oh, God, please not now."

"Just calm down. It's barely noticeable," their mother said, rolling her eyes toward Grace, indicating a small slit where the zipper had pulled away from the seam.

Their mother, to Grace's surprise, remained unruffled, stepping over to her oversized quilted purse to dump out the contents on a nearby chair. An assortment of lipsticks, orange Tic Tacs, loose change, tiny vials of perfume, and a long white envelope fell to the tiled floor.

"Mom, what's this?" Grace stooped to pick up the letter with her name scribbled on the front.

"Oh, no. In all the chaos this week, I forgot to give that to you. It came in a certified mailer. Damn! I didn't even pay attention to the return address. I was on the phone with the caterer and on hold with the florist when it arrived."

"So, you don't know who sent it?" Grace asked, afraid Rick had decided to send her a bill for the airplane ticket, the ring, and rent-a-car he'd used to retrieve her from Mistletoe.

"Uh-huh," her mom answered, a piece of thread tucked between her lips.

"Aren't you going to open it?" Betsy said, ambling behind Grace to snoop over her shoulder.

"I'm…not sure."

"Then can I read it?" Her friend's eyes sparkled with intrigue.

"No," Grace said, her own curiosity getting the best of her.

"Maybe it's a secret admirer." This came from Grace's mother who was still trying to patch the barely noticeable hole in Danielle's dress.

Grace plopped in a chair and tore open the envelope, finding a neatly folded letter with masculine handwriting.

Dear Grace,

"Oh, my God," she whispered, her fingers starting to tremble, her heart lifting to knock against her throat. She recognized the writing. The letter was from Ayden.

All three women gawked at her, Grace's mother taking the lead on the questions. "Who's it from?"

In a daze, she answered, "Ayden."

"What does it say?" Danielle and Betsy asked at the same time.

A subtle knock sounded at the door, cueing the women it was almost time for the ceremony to begin. Outside the room, the organist tapped the first chord of Mendelssohn's *Wedding March*. Spurred by a rush of hope and tidal wave of fear, Grace dropped the note, hopped up, and clapped her hands together. "We can't leave the groom waiting, can we?"

She'd made it all the way to the door when her

sister's words stopped her. "Why are you running?"

Grace halted and bent her chin toward her chest. No. She needed to keep her head high this time.

"Honey." Her mother walked over to stand in front of her and place her hands on each side of Grace's arms. "It must be important if a man wrote you a letter."

Grace conceded and stepped back to retrieve the letter from Betsy's hand. Fear of the unknown had plagued her most of her life. "But what if he wants me to come see him? We could never work. I'm not his type, we argue about the stupidest things, and he hasn't even said, not once, that he loves me."

Her mother brought her hand up to smooth the hair from her forehead. "Oh, Grace, it's the easiest thing in the world to find an excuse why not to take a chance. The hardest thing is to take that chance and accept everything, good or bad, that comes with it."

Grace let her mother's words sink in as the pianist repeated the wedding march again, this time much louder. She glanced from her mother to Danielle wondering how much she'd used them as a crutch to keep from making plans and decisions about her future. They didn't hold her back. She had held her own self back.

With more courage than she'd felt in a long time, she lifted the letter to see what Ayden thought important enough to *incriminate* himself. She read the first line to herself.

Dear Grace,

"No, out loud."

Grace made a face in Betsy's direction only to receive a more animated one from her friend in return.

"Mom, make her read the letter to us, please," Danielle interjected.

"Grace, you heard your sister."

Grace huffed out a response. "Oh, fine!" She planted her feet and prayed he didn't say something that might make her blush a thousand shades of red.

"*Dear Grace,*

I don't think I've ever written a letter in my life, even when I was deployed. You're the first I've attempted to do this with, so bear with me."

Well, that was a good start.

"Go on," the three others said in unison.

Grace brought in an impatient breath, sent them a warning glance and began reading again.

"*I love you.*"

She stopped, her heart slamming into her chest and stealing her breath. Did she somehow interpret his handwriting wrong? No. The words were very clear. *I love you.*

"That's it?" Danielle asked.

That's all Grace needed to read, but there was more.

"*I've been so wrong about so many things. Although I can't guarantee a perfect life where we'll never argue. You never listen to anything I say, and I've found I have a rather jealous streak when it comes to you. However, if you can find it in your bruised and beautiful heart to forgive me, I would like to invite you to the Christmas Eve Eve Dance.*"

"A dance?" Danielle broke in. "That's romantic…I think?"

"Shhhh," Grace scolded her sister.

"*Yes, I understand what this means, and I hope the*

legend is true. More than this, I hope you will be there. I love you. If, for some reason, you choose not to come with me, I will find a way to let you go...most likely in the Caribbean somewhere. The snow here reminds me too much of you.

Ayden"

Grace stood stunned and trembling. He loved her. *"P.S. I'd like my shirt back."*

"What legend?" Danielle asked, rattling Grace out of her fantastical stupor.

"The legend of Mistletoe's Christmas Eve *Eve* Dance!"

Grace lifted her gaze to Betsy, having heard about the dance but nothing about what it meant to go.

Her friend smiled. "Maybe Ayden should be the one to tell you."

Grace's mother ambled around to slide a comforting arm around her shoulders. "When's this dance?"

All of a sudden, Grace's euphoria deflated. "It's tonight. I'll never make it to Mistletoe in time."

"You have to try, Grace," her mother said.

"Oh, my gosh, he sent pictures."

Everyone rushed across the small room and fell behind Betsy who was holding a set of prints in one hand. Not remembering them taking any pictures together, Grace stepped around, recognizing the one Neil had taken of them in the hospital with Ayden holding Nate.

"There's more."

Grace gave a tearful laugh after Betsy placed another picture in her hand. Since she'd left Mistletoe, he'd replaced the sign in front of the bed and breakfast.

It simply read "Grace's Place at Hearth's Gate."

"He bought you a bakery?" her mother asked.

"No." Grace sniffled. "He opened a door."

Betsy grasped Grace by her shoulders and started shaking her like a ragdoll. "We have to get you to Mistletoe before it's too late."

A forceful knock sounded at the door. "Are you gals still in there?"

Suddenly remembering why they were standing in a church wearing uncomfortable mint green bridesmaids' dresses, Grace's optimism plummeted once again. "This is *your* wedding, Danielle. I have to be here—"

"Are you crazy? Betsy's right. We have to get you to the airport."

"Absolutely," Grace's mother agreed. "Betsy, bring your car around. Danielle, get on your phone and find a one-way ticket to Seattle and a train ticket to Mistletoe. You can put it on my card."

Grace watched in rare astonishment as her mother took charge, and Betsy, in all her unique grandeur, rendered a salute before tearing out through the back door in her bridesmaid's dress, white sash, and her black ankle boots.

A second later, Grace's mother grabbed her wrist and hauled her out the back door. Danielle joined after she stuck her head out of the front door and yell down the aisle. "Trevor, I love you, baby, but I owe Grace to get her to a dance. I'll be back in thirty minutes. Everyone sit tight."

Trevor yelled back, "But we're already naming our kids after her. Isn't that enough?"

Outside, Betsy honked her midnight blue Chevy.

Grace, her mom, and Danielle piled inside, the white fluff of Danielle's wedding dress drifting into the front seat. It was hard not to laugh as the adrenaline of three crazy women charioted Grace away, belting out the lyrics to Jefferson Starship's "Nothing's Gonna Stop Us Now" on the freeway.

Chapter Twenty-Five

Grace knew she'd be late when they had to fly around a storm heading into Seattle. To make matters worse, she'd misplaced her phone with everyone's numbers. She'd tried calling Betsy on a payphone at the airport, but she went straight to voicemail. With the hour growing late and too anxious to wait for the train, she decided to max out her own credit card and rent a car that would take her to Mistletoe. Only, she didn't foresee having to drive through blizzard-like conditions, slowing her further.

Knowing she'd missed the dance, she stopped by Hearth's Gate, hoping to see Ayden's truck parked in the circular driveway. No one was home. Despite believing she was too late, Grace drove to the empty Christmas Eve Eve Dance hall, the parking lot deserted except for a lone snow-covered car. She parked near the front entrance and braced for the frigid air to hit her in the face. Determined to see this through, she trudged over several inches of unplowed snow, lifted her gloved hands to the silver doorknob, and tugged. Locked.

A sob tore from her throat, her heart refusing to give up so soon. She yanked one more time and then smacked the door hard with the palm of her hand. It wasn't supposed to end this way. He was supposed to be waiting for her, and they were supposed to live happily-ever-after, with a few arguing ups and downs, of course. Now, she had no doubt he'd already booked a flight to the Caribbean. He'd never want to see her again.

She half-laughed, half-scoffed at her own romantic conclusion. At last defeated, she turned and fell against the door, watching her breath transform into white puffy clouds before her. This was the end, the last page of her and Ayden's love story. Still, she wouldn't go back and change meeting him. She found her voice and she'd come to realize that she'd used Danielle and her mother to keep from taking chances or moving forward.

"Well, look at who we have here?"

Grace pushed away to find Mr. and Mrs. Hawthorne huddled together in thick coats and mittens.

She tried to smile, but she ended up biting her lip to keep from crying. "I, um, was invited to the dance, but I think I'm a little late," she said with a tear-filled laugh.

The two people glanced at each other before Mr. Hawthorne left his wife's side to take a few keys from his coat pocket. He then moved his attention to the magnificent and twinkling sky. "As long as the moon is above us, you're not too late."

Grace shifted out of the way to let him open the door. Was it insane to want to take a peek into what might have been?

"Go on, Grace," Wilhelmina coaxed.

Grace exhaled slow and nodded. "I'll only be a moment."

The woman gave Grace a gentle pat on the shoulder before her husband scooted ahead to flip on a few lights.

Grace hesitated, noticing how strings of mistletoe

dangled from the timbered rafters. At the end of the hall stood a tall gray and white stone fireplace and a twelve-foot Christmas tree. Behind her, Mr. Hawthorne flipped on a few more switches, one of them turning on the multi-colored blinking lights wrapped around the live branches.

Mesmerized, Grace sauntered forward, drawn to three presents sticking out from the bottom of the tree. When she halted, Wilhelmina ambled to stand beside her.

"He left them for you."

"Who left—" Grace didn't have to finish her thought.

Her stuttering inhale echoed through the empty hall. "Can you give me a few minutes?" she said, the woman nodding with a sad smile.

Grace cautioned her steps, wondering if it might be a better idea to turn around and leave. Was it torture to want to know what might have been if she'd been there on time or if he'd stayed just a little while longer?

Regardless, she continued forward, lured by the magic of the tree and the mystery of the three presents Ayden had given her. Like a child, she bent and tucked her legs underneath her, stretching for the square package first. It was heavy and uneven, her hands shaking as she unwrapped the gift to reveal the snow globe she'd admired in Hawthorne's.

Grace lifted the present and shook it slightly, watching the white flecks float around the log cabin with the lit window.

"There's two more," Mr. Hawthorne said.

Grace sniffed and nodded. This time, she took less time to open the present, tearing through the long box to find the blanket she'd wrapped herself in so many times at Hearth's Gate.

"Ida made me one just like that." Wilhelmina blinked back a tear.

Mesmerized and overwhelmed, Grace wrapped the gift around her shoulders. It smelled like Hearth's Gate, woodsy and comforting.

"One more." Mr. Hawthorne's wrinkled finger pointed to the last gift.

Grace stared at the small rectangular box certain it was a bracelet or necklace of some kind, a peace offering perhaps. She reached out her hand and then withdrew it. "I can't open it," she whispered.

"You might want to try."

Grace twisted in the direction of the entryway, her eyes blinking, her heart hammering at Ayden's surprising form. "Ayden?" she said on a joyous sob.

"Did you come to return my shirt?" he asked with a smirk.

She stood, and he met her in a few determined strides, sweeping her up in a powerful and possessive embrace.

"God, it feels good to hold you again," he whispered, his grip tight, his heart thumping hard against her chest. His gaze raked over Grace's face, possessive and beguiling.

He sat her down and captured her mouth in a kiss that jolted every nerve in her body. She closed her eyes, her world tilting and spinning under his soft and slow persuasion. He cupped her head and deepened his kiss, the moment sweet, passionate and tender. It was not the end, but a glorious beginning of infinite possibilities and chapters.

He pulled away from her slightly, and she opened her eyes to find him staring at her, his dark blue eyes glinting and amorous.

"I thought I'd lost you," she said, touching his stubbled face.

"When I thought you weren't going to show, I wanted to *quit* Mistletoe and never look back. I drove around for a while, realizing I couldn't give up on us that easy." He hesitated to add, "Your timing needs some work, though."

Grace laughed and then sobered to the moment.

"What's the matter?" he asked, his warm breath brushing across her wet lips.

"That this is some wonderful dream, and soon I'm going to wake up and realize you and this place are one big figment of my imagination."

He smirked, seeming to remember what she said when they first met each other. "In case you're right, I need you to open one more gift."

He pulled away, locked her hand in his, and led her back to the Christmas tree. He lifted the last present, offering it to her. "Maggie helped me pick it out, so I hope you like it."

"You didn't have to—"

"No, I didn't have to…I wanted to, Grace."

Again, expecting a necklace or bracelet, a peace offering of sorts, she sucked in her breath when her gaze caught the glittering shimmer of a silver diamond engagement ring. She brought her hand to her mouth and felt the trickle of quiet tears on her fingers.

"It's perfect," she whispered.

He leaned over to kiss her again when the roof opened up and speakers crackled with Grace's favorite

Christmas song, "Silver Bells." He presented her a cocky grin before pulling away and offering her his hand.

"To make this official, we have to share a dance."

She sent him a curious smile. "Does this have anything to do with the Mistletoe legend?"

He nodded and grinned, making her stomach flutter in all different directions. He then pulled her against him.

"The story goes," he said, his mouth pressed to her right ear. "That the person you invite to dance under the Mistletoe moon on Christmas Eve *Eve* will be yours forever."

She drew back. "Forever? Are you sure this is what you want, McCabe?"

He thought for a moment, on purpose. Then he chuckled and kissed the top of her nose. "Of course. I don't waste wishes."

His confession astonished her. "You...wished this?"

He bobbed his head. "Not at the official tree lighting, but at Maggie's, although I wished for you to find the man who deserved you. At the time, I didn't think that man was me."

Her heart melted at his confession. "That was very sweet."

His arms tightened around her waist. "So, what was your wish?"

"Do you mean, what was my wish before you kissed me and made me forget about making one?"

His eyes narrowed. "There was a method to my madness. And since you're here with me and not Rick, I believe it worked."

She drew back. "Speaking of wasting wishes—" She smirked at him. "No…I wished…for Kyle to be able to come home for Christmas. I'd spent too may holidays without my father, I just couldn't imagine Collin and Ciara without theirs for the holidays."

Ayden stared at her for a moment before his hands cocooned her face and he kissed her for a long, glorious heartbeat. Then he pulled back and smiled. "By some miraculous reason, Kyle's unit came back early from their deployment. They arrived last night."

Grace blinked in astonishment. "Really? He's…he's home?"

Ayden brushed his lips across the tip of her nose. "And so are you."

She beamed. "I saw the pictures. Does this mean you're not selling Hearth's Gate?"

"Yes, I figured if we're planning on having eight kids, we'll need a pretty big place to raise them."

She gawked at him. "Eight?"

He nodded and grinned down at her. "Five boys and three girls."

Grace giggled inside his arms. "Oh, you're so off on the ratio of sons and daughters."

"You're right. Six boys and two girls, both with two-syllable names and beautiful hazel eyes."

She opened her mouth to argue when he silenced her with a kiss.

A word from the author…

I was born in historical Appomattox, Virginia. After graduating from high school, I joined the military and served five years in the active duty Army. After leaving, I decided to go into the Ohio Air National Guard, where I retired as a Master Sergeant in 2011. In case you were wondering, I have never flown a plane. After getting lost on my way to the recruiter's office, I was highly discouraged from navigating one.

I admit, I am an avid Jane Austen fan and try to incorporate her in my books, in one way or another. This dream of writing with Jane sometimes is an exciting adventure that may take me as far as the stars or as close as my computer.

When I'm not writing, I'm spending time with my husband and two boys, ages thirteen and ten. Without their sacrifice and understanding, I would never have been able to pursue my passion of writing or my accomplishment of becoming a published author.

No matter what I write and read, there *always* has to be a happy ending.